Skarry had never had the chance to ⟨...⟩
anything interesting. He tended the ⟨...⟩
yearned to be a hero and perform m⟨...⟩
Olluden called him simple and a dreamer, but ⟨...⟩
that one day he would surprise them all.

The wars between his tribe and the Ice Warriors had been
going on so long that peace had become a myth, spoken of
in whispers about the fire.

The world is being driven towards disaster: but what can
one young goatherd do to save it?

Caught up in the violent struggle, Skarry is drawn
through a land in turmoil. His adventures take him to cities
in chaos, over mountains of ice, and into the very Womb of
the World, and from the peoples he meets on his travels,
Skarry gathers the wisdom that may make a difference to
the fate of the world.

WINTER IN APHELION

The adventures of Skarry the Dreamer

Eleu,

Chris Dixon

many thanks — lots of love
+
Hwyl!

Chris Dixon

UNWIN
PAPERBACKS

LONDON SYDNEY WELLINGTON

First published in paperback by Unwin ® Paperbacks, an imprint of
Unwin Hyman Limited in 1989

UNWIN HYMAN LIMITED
15/17 Broadwick Street
London W1V 1FP

Allen & Unwin Australia Pty Ltd
8 Napier Street, North Sydney, NSW 2060, Australia

Allen & Unwin New Zealand Pty Ltd with Port Nicholson Press
Compusales Building, 75 Ghuznee Street, Wellington, New Zealand

British Library Cataloguing in Publication Data

Dixon, Chris
    Winter in Aphelion: the adventures of
Skarry the dreamer.
I. Title
823'.914 [F]
ISBN 0–04–440394–1

Typeset in 10 on 12 point Palatino by
Computape (Pickering) Ltd, North Yorkshire
and printed in Great Britain by
Guernsey Press Co. Ltd, Guernsey, Channel Islands

For Lyn, Sam, Molly and Janet,
amongst many others

Contents

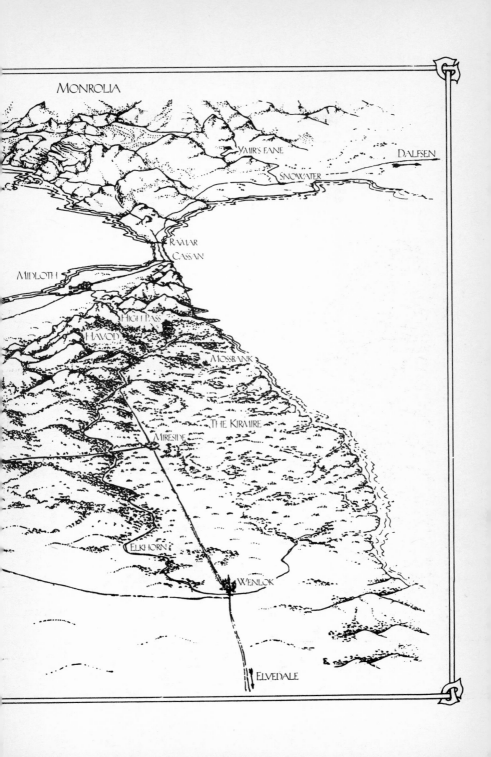

1

Skarry of the Olluden

Skarry sucked at his stone. It felt cold and hard in his mouth, as cold and hard as the markstone on which he sat, banging his heels. The Middle Mark this one was called and had been for as long as any of the Olluden could remember. Gemel the Ski, who looked as old as rock itself to Skarry, told how the Elders had thought it to be a tooth of the Stone Bear, knocked from its jaw in that first of all fights. Indeed, this markstone was not unlike a tooth, being paler than the other rocks that lay about and grooved across the top. Yet Skarry knew that by laying a cheek against the rough lichens and sighting along the groove, you could see straight to Skard, the notch of the High Pass, on the skyline far above. The track followed this flight of the eye from the markstone, across the ford, up the steepening side of the Angsoth and into the crags.

Ah, to be on high, instead of stuck low, tethered by this present task. The clunk of the wooden bells rose up from the animals at the brook. These sheep and goats were the fleece and milk of the Olluden and there were even two pigs for the meat-eaters. Hardy mountain creatures they all were with strong legs for leaping, not like the plains stock that had been bred soft for the profit of their flesh. The sheep were quiet enough if not startled and cropped at the last of the autumn flush of grass that spread like a green pool in the clearing about the markstone. The goats were more adventurous, preferring the diverse browsing where meadow met woodland and broke into tuffets with bramble and thistle and many herbs. A little further and the trunks of the oaks rose cliff-like, with many branchings, soaring tall in the shelter of the hanging valley. Here the goatlings gambolled amid the buttressed roots and the pigs snuffled for acorns.

They never wandered far and no bears or wolves or even foxes

1

would come near until the weather worsened; then Gemel would be out with his beads, chanting into the wind to keep the beasts away, for he liked not to kill them. Yet it was too early for bears, by a month at the least, and the motley flock could well enough look after itself. So Skarry's thoughts and stare were elsewhere.

From out of the woods behind him ran the path, past the stone on which he sat and down to cross the babbling Alator. The trees curved in here to make a narrow way but as the hillside steepened, so they lowered their heads, opening out into scrub and scree before meeting with the first snow of winter. The path was just a slight dip in the white as it led the gaze upward to the crags, hard and sharp with the light of the reflected sun, slick with ice and alive with blue flashings that blurred Skarry's thoughts. Here was Skard, where the track clambered near sheer before at last passing over the range. To the left of Skard rose up the grey bulk of the Angsoth and to the right that which the Olluden called simply Ice Back. Over the twin peaks ranks of cloud pressed in from the north; their advance guard had cast a white cloak about the summit the night before.

Shading his eyes against the brightness of the afternoon Skarry could make out five specks on Skard, five black dots of men moving so slowly that even a long glance made them seem still. Stare as he might the dots remained just dots at such a distance; perhaps an occasional flash as the sun caught on metal. No doubt they cursed the drifts and stumbled deep in the smother. If they had no guide with them then indeed was their passage difficult; a misplaced foot would send them tumbling down the steeps or an over loud shout loosen a slide of snow that would sweep them from the face of the mountain.

There had been many people over the Pass even at this late moon, fleeing south before the winter war. Yet who these were now, whether friend or foe, Skarry could not tell. He would have liked to have been nearer, and he could have been, for he was the son of the guide Geralt and knew the ways of the mountain. To either side of Skard were cracks and gulleys where he could have watched unseen as these five came struggling through the snow. Soldiers perhaps, Fressingfield's men flying before the Ice Warriors of the enemy. Or the horned ones themselves with their faces all covered in hair save for the red mouth, opened for an evil battle shout and rimmed with sharp teeth like the icicles of the Alator falls. In his mind's eye Skarry could see these towering figures with their short thrusting spears looking grimly downward into the valley of the Olluden, calling to their massed brothers behind them, 'See, there is smoke below, come, let us go down and take this valley for our own!'

Then, without warning, a sudden blow between the shoulders; the sky rolled up and over him, a flashing view of the woods, the flock, the grass and he was lying winded on his back at the bottom of the slope.

'Ah! Skarry, Skarry!' came a high shout and much laughter.

'Simple Skarry, suck-a-stone!'

'Simple Skarry, Skarry the dreamer!'

Skarry closed his eyes but could not banish his tormentors. Small sticks and stones began to bounce around him and a large clod burst on his head. He scrambled to his feet spitting out soil and the stone which hung from a thong around his neck.

'Lo, he rises as if from the dead!' called a mocking voice from above. This was Mullo, dressed like Skarry in thick woollen breeches and jacket. His face was twisted into a smirk and he spoke from one corner of his cavernous mouth.

'Skarry the warrior rises up, eh?' said Mullo, and he pranced about the Middle Mark waving a stick like a sword. The others shrieked with laughter, joining his capering circle. All the children were here save the very smallest and all took up Mullo's chant.

'Skinny Skarry suck-a-stone!' over and over.

Skarry clambered back up the bank, brushing the soil from his clothes and stood a little way off from the others.

'There's travellers on the Pass!' he shouted at last to divert their attention.

At that they did indeed stop their taunting and turned in sudden silence, wide eyed, to the Angsoth. The black dots had escaped the deep snows of Skard and moved out on to the track above the scree.

'Are they ours?' came the low voice of Carin the youngster.

Mullo put an evil squirm to his face and said, 'I know not. Maybe it is the enemy, maybe it is He!'

The younger children fell to shrieking, pushing at each other, dividing their gaze between the mountain and Mullo, waiting for a lead.

3

'Oh, what'll we do, Skarry?' he cried. 'Mighty Skarry, who shall save us from Him, the Misery of Ice?'

The laughter rose up as they returned to their more familiar baiting.

'What'll you do Skarry,' Mullo went on, 'for the Leveller is nigh upon us? He'll cut your father to bits and use his ribs for snowshoes!'

'If he be your father,' whined Carin.

'And what will he do to your mother?'

'He'll not touch my mother!' broke in Skarry at last. 'For I'll take my father's adze and peel Him from His backbone. I've no fear of Grimal Skoye!'

At this there was uproar; the younger ones screamed to hear the name and some rushed off for home in their panic. Mullo was taken aback and his jaw fell open. Carin the youngster waited to see what he would do but it was Lenus who thrust her dirty face up close to Skarry's.

'You've not the strength to even lift your father's adze, leave off swinging it,' she said.

The spell was broken and Mullo stormed forward, angry at his own delay.

'You skinny sapling, you'll rot for speaking His name. So you seek to steal the glory from our own heroes? Doth Auren will spit the enemy like the pig he is if Fressingfield hasn't done so already!'

He gave a great shove to Skarry and being so much the broader and heavier sent him once more heels over head down the bank. The others burst into laughter again and would have restarted their chant but Mullo looked to the Pass with one meaty hand to his brow.

'Five, warriors too; I can see their spears. And they're ours, for the banner shows the Bull of Taur.'

Immediately they fell to discussing who it might be. Many people had fled south over the Pass that autumn, coming down by way of the Middle Mark and making for Wenlock but the passage of soldiers had been the other way, to the muster at Midloth, to meet up with Fressingfield and face the Misery in battle.

'They'll have news of the fighting!' said Carin.

'Of course!' said Mullo angrily. 'Let's go meet them.' And he strode off fiercely, Carin to one side doggedly trying to keep up, Lenus clinging to his other elbow and a wake of followers to the rear.

Skarry, on his back, looking up at the sky where the van of cloud was blotting out the blue, felt even more alone. He put the green flecked stone within his mouth and sucked at it, sitting up to watch glumly as they drew away. From here Mullo's broad back looked like that of a mighty warrior and the staff he carried could easily be mistaken for a fighting spear.

Still, someone would have to tell the others, to light the fire in the Moot House and prepare food for the weary travellers. He clambered back up the bank again and set off for Havod, taking not the main track from the Middle Mark but a narrower way, no more than a faint parting of the yellowed grass and ferns such that only those who knew of it would find it. This led off between the towering oaks with their leaves all brown and gold, still waiting for the gales to bring them down; a loving tree the Olluden said, for she held on to her children long into the winter. Skarry began to run to the sound of crunching bracken, the wind in his ears, up and over a gentle rise. The trees fell back on either hand.

At first glance this clearing seemed littered with green mounds, like the old moss covered ants nests of the deep forest only so much the larger. These were the summer huts of the Olluden, lightly made from thin poles bent over and covered with birch bark and thatch, not like the winter houses in the foothills to the south; those were made with stones and turf against the cold. This was Havod, the summer haven and all that was needed to make these homes could be found in the forest. Around and about the huts were small gardens, used to grow the few plants that could not be gathered easily from the wild.

Skarry slowed as he felt the quiet in the air. There was no one to be seen. Not long ago an early evening such as this would have echoed to shouting and laughter, the madcap chasing of children and the dogs barking. Here they would share the fruits and nuts they had picked that day and drink sparkling water from the hidden springs. Perhaps Caul the song would give voice and tell of the old times when the people first came down over the High Pass and saw the hanging valley full of green and made it their home. Then would the others join in, even the youngsters, raising their voices shrill as finches and the song would rise up and rustle the crown of leaves above.

Yet at this time there was always a certain sadness as the Olluden prepared to leave for their winter home and said farewell to summer haunts, to swimming in the Alator and Elkhorn, to the climbing of the Pass, the sights from on high and the games at the High Haven. In the winter the mountain became the province of the Hagarath alone; the Olluden, the wood people, preferred lower lands.

Now Havod seemed empty of life save for a plume of pale smoke from Gemel's hut; being so old he felt the cold more. Rushing down Skarry began to call out, that travellers were on the Pass, to light the fire in the Moot House and ready food and drink, for even in the autumn the High Pass was not an easy crossing. At full pelt he swung into his own home with one hand clinging to the door pole.

'Steady, steady!' said his mother, looking up as the hut shook. 'You'll have the roof in on us.'

Irane was splitting bramble runners down the middle with a small knife. The fibres were tough and could be used to bind the teardrop frame of a snowshoe or tie the long twigs of birch on to a handle to make a broom.

'Warriors, mother!' blurted Skarry. 'Coming down the Pass!'

For a moment her body froze, the little knife poised to enter the bramble, her swinging foot held at the top of its movement.

'They're ours, mother,' Skarry went on, seeing how she chilled, 'or so Mullo says. He's gone with the others to meet up with them. They will have news of the battle!'

The excitement bit Skarry and he would rather have been with Mullo and so had first talk with the heroes. But his mother only bowed her head a little and turned it from side to side, so slowly you might have thought she had not moved.

'Don't fret, mother,' said Skarry. 'If the enemy are behind I'll not let them hurt you. Why, I have a bow and a good staff that I know how to use and there are others who can fight. We Olluden know the ways of the wood and could give Skoye himself hard reckoning in our hidden battle!'

'Ah, Skarry, Skarry don't talk so,' she said at last. 'There are few enough of us since Fressingfield called the muster. War is a

6

terrible thing even at a distance without bringing it to our homes. I pray to Ithunne there will be no fighting here.'

Skarry was shocked. 'But mother, if the evil comes to us then we must to war! We know it from the songs and stories, we must fight for what is right as did the heroes of yore!'

'Enough!' she said, suddenly sharp. 'You say the others have gone to greet these mighty warriors?'

'Aye, mother. I came straight to tell you.'

'Then who watches the animals, eh? They'll be off into the woods, chewing up the saplings and peeling bark no doubt. Go on! Tell your father or Gemel what goes on, then back to those beasts if you want supper.'

Skarry made as if to speak again then clamped shut his mouth at the sight of her stern face. To ask help of Ithunne seemed of little use he thought as he left to look for his father, for the tales told of how she was bound and helpless. No, a warrior was what was needed, Vidar the mighty with his great war mace.

His father, Geralt, he found in Gemel's hut together with that old one, both bent over a steaming bowl on the fire. The glow of the wood coals lit their faces from below such that each seam of skin was lined as if with gold. Knowing better than to interrupt this task Skarry fidgeted in the entrance. Like two sages involved in some ancient ceremony the pair leaned over the bowl, Geralt twisting and turning a length of ash within the steam. At Gemel's nod he set the steamed end between two pins of hardwood driven into a solid upright. Under Gemel's bright gaze he levered the ash just so against the pins and then, having removed it, they examined the new curve together, comparing it to that of the first. Evidently the match was not to Gemel's satisfaction for once more the ash was placed between the pins and the bend adjusted. The two heads drew together, the ski the object of their concentration and after this second close look they both appeared satisfied.

'You will learn in time,' Gemel said with a voice as creaked as two boughs rubbing in the wind. Then he turned to Skarry, his eyes a piercing blue.

'Who is watching the animals, lad?' he asked simply, yet Skarry could not answer nor hold the gaze.

'There are travellers on the Pass, Gemel,' he said after a moment. 'I came to tell you.'

7

'And who is watching the animals, eh lad?' Gemel repeated.

'No one, Gemel,' Skarry said softly. 'The others went to greet the travellers. I thought it best to come and warn you.'

The old man smiled while Skarry's father shook his head as if in disbelief.

'Well, what's done is done,' Gemel said. 'You've told us now so you had better be back to your task, eh?'

'Aye, and quick about it,' snapped Geralt. 'The wood likes not loose animals. Yain and his dogs will be up afore long to help you bring them down for the night. Get on with you!'

Skarry turned and ran at the sharp command, the stone once more within his mouth as if to stop the sob of frustration. These older ones of the Olluden seemed so simple, with not a clue as to the real importance of what went on in the world about them. He ran hard through Havod and back along the path to the mark-stone. In the distance he thought he heard the shouts of a merry company, children and deeper voices, perhaps of the warriors. Mullo would bring them to Havad by the short cut and not the Middle Mark so of all the villagers Skarry would be the last to meet them.

By the time he reached the stone his tears had stopped. The goats came back from the woods at his call and were soon roughly gathered again at the ford. Long Beard, the eldest goat, came over to Skarry and nuzzled his leg as if ready for the night. The others soon sensed her thought and began to bleat, the goatlings dancing nervously. In the gathering gloom Skarry's eyes were drawn to the High Pass. The snow clouds now filled the sky and still pressed in from the north. Skard was a shadow against their gloomy bulk and as he watched, it seemed for a moment as if the dark crags were of a sudden beclustered with the tiny spikes of spears. Then came the bark of Eka and Yain's friendly greeting. It was time to get the animals back for the night.

2

The Travellers

The goats ran madly back between the trees, leaping and twisting in their excitement to be home-going but the sheep needed the watchful eye of Eka to keep them to the path. Skarry and Yain brought up the rear and it was nearly dark by the time they reached the enclosures. Here were others of the Olluden, waiting for the evening's milking and calling out their greetings through the dusk. The pens were made up of light hurdles of interwoven hazel tied to stakes to make up sheltering walls; one was drawn aside as a gate and the animals funnelled in, the goats barging each other in their haste. Among the people there was excited talk of the arrival of the warriors and when the last of the animals was safe within, Skarry moved the hurdle across the opening and made it fast. His tasks completed he shouted his hurried goodbyes and ran off towards Havod.

Approaching the settlement he could see the flickering of torches between the trees and the sounds of many voices reached his ears as he came out into the clearing. By Gemel's hut milled a horde of chattering children, a growing crowd of women and men, the flames casting dancing shadows into the woods. Skarry's gaze was drawn to the very centre of this group, for here stood the travellers.

Their clothing and manner showed them to be foreign to the valley immediately. One was huge, like the lumbering forest bear but armoured over his chest and shoulders. His eyes under the tall helm burned with a battle fury and strength seemed to seep from his limbs. As Skarry began to push through the press to the fore the giant turned this way and that, tossing a huge sword from one great square paw to the other.

'Ready thyselves!' he called in a deep and powerful voice 'for the enemy is nigh upon you and we go in utter haste. Someone, a drink to quench our parch!'

9

Gemel handed him a ladle dipped in the rain barrel but the warrior looked very surprised and refused it. Only when Mullo came with his father's wine skin did he drink.

'My thanks, kind sir,' he said and wiped the trickle from his beard. 'Now, have you any bread? Or meat?' And the pierce of his gaze sent some hurrying off to fetch it.

'They were in the battle!' Mullo explained to the people.

'And tell us,' said Gemel softly when there was quiet once more, 'how went the battle?'

But the big warrior was tearing at a loaf and waved his mighty arm to one who stood to his side. This other was also armoured though lighter in build with a face like a bird of prey, the nose a hook. He carried a bow, not a short bow as those of the valley people but a long one, as tall as the giant beside him.

'Might there be a tavern about, to which we could retire?' he asked in a thin voice. 'No? Well, a barn or hut. At least a fire to dry our clothes.'

Then there was much shouting and jostling as the crowd began to move towards the Moot House, all trying to help lead the tired soldiers. Three others there were making them five in all, two similarly clad in breeks and breastplates emblazoned with the red Bull of Taur and the third all wrapped within a dull blue coat.

The Moot House was the largest and most permanent of the Olluden's summer buildings, big enough to take them all at a squeeze. Unlike the other huts it had a stout cleft oak frame infilled with woven hazel like the hurdles, this in turn plastered and whitened with lime. It served as their meeting house, for festivals and guests or any who came late over the mountain. Sometimes Gemel spoke of an age when even he was young and the travelling people, the Itheni, would pass through the forest and share camp with the Olluden. Then the Moot House would resound with singing and dancing and tales of distant lands and peoples, far beyond the knowledge of the foresters. Yet Skarry had never seen them, for like a dream they had long since faded from the land and few now spoke of them.

Inside the Moot House the central fire was lit already and the warmth of the flames filled the building. Soon most were within, even Gemel, sitting on a sack to one side and supping at a jar. The children pressed forward to the fire about which the warriors took their seats. The huge one drank heavily from the wine-skin and tore at his loaf but the thin bowman stood with a foot upon a keg, one hand resting on this raised knee, the other, like a bird in flight as he spoke, first hovering on the wind then diving to accent some word or phrase, the voice so soft it made the listener strain the ear to hear and hold the breath lest it should drown the words.

'At the last,' he said, 'we stood with the Lord Fressingfield and all his army, drawn up for battle in Dunan Dale and looked down upon the Isthmus, black with the hordes of the advancing enemy. Many of those in our ranks shook at the sight, their hearts quailed. So we,' and here he indicated his larger companion who gave him a nod, 'we went amongst them with strong words and at our passing they lifted up their failing spirit and stood their ground.'

'Tell them, noble Catskin,' said the bigger warrior, between mouthfuls, 'tell them well, for songs shall be writ of this great battle in the times to come.'

The light of the fire caught upon their armour and cast tall shadows upon the walls and roof that flickered as though from the rising wind without. It seemed to Skarry as though two heroes from the old tales had risen to walk the earth once more in their fierce pride.

'Bloody was the fighting,' Catskin the bowman went on. 'Many were the slain. And ever on pressed the enemy's Ice Warriors with their horned helmets dipped in blood, carving out their way. And at their head, all shrouded in ice, was He.'

There were fearful mutterings from the listeners and the parents began to pack their younger children off to bed.

'You saw Him?' Mullo asked for them all. 'You saw the Misery?'

'Saw Him?' came a bellow from the big one. 'Saw Him? Fought with Him more like, or would have, had not that Fressingfield called me back: "Glimshpill," he said, "loyal Glimshpill, we must fall back." Ah, those words stung me.' And so saying he drained the last of the wine sack.

'So you are running away?' called Gemel.

'Running? Who's running, old man?' shouted Glimshpill. 'Another drink here!' and the brightness of his eyes was fading.

'The Lord Fressingfield requires swift aid to hold the Pass,' said Catskin softly, 'and we go upon his command to Wenlok, to seek the aid of Doth Auren.'

The name was passed about the fire like a treasure.

'Did you kill many?' Mullo asked suddenly.

'Many are the slain,' said Glimshpill slowly, 'many will be the slain.' And then the Moot House was alive with voices, of fathers and mothers, wives and lovers; was Camil well? Had Mulder suffered hurt? Did Perin still live? Taraman, Artur, more.

The gathering began to break up, the people making for their own hearths, some sobbing for fear of the dead, others not knowing what to do. Mullo and Carin stayed, still pressing for answers to their questions and Lenus too; Glimshpill patted her head and pinched her grubby cheek. Skarry ignored his mother's look as she left and moved nearer the soldiers. Soon there was less than a dozen of them around the fire.

It was then that the one in blue moved over to the fire and held up his hands to be warmed. Skarry was surprised that he had not missed him before; perhaps he had been resting against the wall, near Gemel. The cloak was thrown back about his shoulders to reveal a robe of another blue beneath; no weapons were visible. His youthful head was bare, the hair very pale yellow. He stood close to the one called Catskin.

'Should we not be going?' Skarry heard him ask quietly.

'Not with him in that state,' said Catskin. 'It will pass by the morning and we will be all the faster for our rest.'

Glimshpill roused himself at the talk and hurled a crust which the one in blue avoided easily with only a slight movement that seemed to begin at his waist and rise up his body. The others laughed at the warrior's fooling.

'Come Dreamer!' Glimshpill mocked. 'Show us a trick or two before we sleep.'

The Dreamer hid his hands within the sleeves of his robe and with a smile looked about at the present company. His gaze came to rest upon Skarry who found he could not turn away from the deep blue eyes. The Dreamer held out a hand and Skarry went to him.

'You have a look about you that is not of this valley,' said the Dreamer.

'He's a dreamer too!' shouted Carin, and Mullo near choked

with laughing on the wine Glimshpill had given him. Skarry felt his face redden.

'You want not to dream, lad,' growled Glimshpill, 'the way of a warrior is yours to choose. I could show you sights, aye, sights that'd make thy heart weep with the joy of the warrior. Does thy hand not hunger to clench a sword?'

He drew his own with a rattle and it shone in the light of the fire like a freshly forged thing. Mullo's eyes were wide as he drank in the sight.

'Take my word, skinny one,' Glimshpill went on, 'and have no dealings with this blue-robed fool!'

He swung the sword whistling about his head and would have caught the Dreamer with the flat of the blade had not the other swayed back. Mullo and his partners burst out laughing and Skarry looked from one face to the next, not knowing what to do.

Swiftly, the Dreamer bent towards the fire and scooped up a handful of hot embers. Carin and Lenus both gasped and though Mullo made no sound he too was taken aback. A thin plume of smoke rose from the clenched fist. Skarry could see the flesh of the hand lit up from the red glow within. Yet the Dreamer remained silent, his face passive, the blue eyes an empty stare. Then he thrust out his hand and opened the fist right up by Skarry's face so that he started. Perhaps Glimshpill or one of the others began to say something and Skarry felt a rising shout within himself but in that instant it was as if they were frozen.

The open palm was piled with the coals, so bright that the eye was drawn in to their flicker as to the embers of a dying fire. And as he looked within, Skarry saw the shape of a bear appear, its coat so bright and shining, as if white hot. It raised up its head and gave him a look of such sorrow and pain that he felt an urge to reach out to it, to help it in some way. Then the form melted and became that of a woman, beautiful and strong with her hair like flames, yet with that same sadness. The red began to fade and a green as of the leaves in spring spread throughout the vision and in his own heart he felt a quiet settling.

The embers were out. The Dreamer held his hand over the hearth and shook the ash on to it then wiped his palm on his cloak. There was no mark. Glimshpill rose up slowly, clinging to Mullo's shoulder for support.

'Ah, foolish, foolish!' he said in a rising shout and with a stagger he thrust his sword at the Dreamer but the other easily stepped aside from the rough blow. Glimshpill knocked over the keg and would have fallen himself had not Catskin caught him with a steadying arm. The Dreamer said no more but returned to the shadows of the corner. Here he sank down and drew up his hood over his head.

'We should follow his lead in that at the least,' said Catskin, breaking the silence, 'for we have a long way before us in the morning.'

Glimshpill gave him a glazed look and sank back in his seat. His huge head went back, the eyelids drooped, the mouth fell open and he slept with a deep rumbling.

Mullo handled the fallen sword with a light in his eyes that made Skarry shiver. They were all shaken; their quiet home had not known such happenings in years.

'What did you see?' Skarry whispered to Lenus and Carin. 'What did you see in the embers?'

They frowned at each other.

'He had a handful of coals,' Carin said simply. 'It is a mean trick. I saw a pedlar do the same at the fair in Wenlok, only he put some in his mouth also.'

'I saw one who could walk through the fire in bare feet,' bragged Lenus.

'But did you not see the bear?' Skarry asked. 'Did you not feel the sadness?'

Both the others were silent for a moment but with an exchange of looks they began to laugh, quietly at first then louder. Carin shook Mullo from his daze.

'Skarry has had a vision!' he forced between his chuckles, 'Skarry the dreamer!' And Mullo soon caught the joke, joining in the mirth.

'The Dreamer saw something in you that he knew,' said Carin.

'Aye,' Mullo said, 'the same madness!'

Lenus moved close so that Skarry could see the marks of the warrior's hand on her cheek.

'He has laid a doom on you,' she said in a fierce whisper. 'He has cursed you!'

And with that they shrank away, stifling their laughter behind faces of mock fear.

14

3

The Maen-hir

Havod was alive at dawn next morning. For the first time that season, snow had fallen in the valley, a herald of that which was to come. In amongst the whitened huts the children ran shrieking, oblivious to the news that the warriors had brought. Yet the elders were not so carefree, and without any meeting or talk the Olluden had decided to leave for the winter home.

Yain had already brought their few ponies down from the hill grazing; small, strong creatures were these, short in the leg and broad backed, their quiet eyes peering out from beneath the shaggy forelocks. Now he helped to hitch them to the drags, Eka yapping about his feet, full only of excitement like the children. Others of the Olluden brought out sacks and baskets of nuts and dried fruits, nerbs and berries. Lenus struggled up from the brook with skins full of water. Here, Gemel watched over the last repairs to a drag that had cracked a shaft.

It was the activities at the Moot House that drew Skarry. Here the warriors were stirring and seemed to be preparing to leave. The huge Glimshpill emerged last looking blear eyed, his hair hanging long and wet after a dip in the rain bucket. One of the others carried his armour.

'Horses, Catskin!' he roared to the thin, hook-nosed one, 'mounts fit for Lords to speed us on our way!' He added under his breath, 'I'm damned if I'll walk any further.'

Catskin and the Dreamer went to Gemel to talk of horses and Skarry, not a little timid, made to close with Glimshpill. Then Mullo stuck his shaggy head out of the Moot House doorway.

'What do you want, simpleton?' he said with a scowl when he saw Skarry.

'I only wished to know what this Lord and his warriors are to do and offer my help,' Skarry replied.

Glimshpill laughed loud hearing this.

'This Lord,' he said, tilting his head, 'and his warriors, will ride like the wind to Wenlok and seek aid from the great Doth Auren for the hard pressed and most noble Fressingfield.'

He yawned and stretched his arms to the sky.

'Ah, a grim day yesterday. I feel better this morning, saving the head.' And he rubbed at his temples. His eyes were a deep brown, dark in the shadow of his heavy brow. The fire had gone.

'Oh, come on, Catskin! Let's get out of this place for Ymir's sake.' He began to clap his arms together and stamp his feet. 'You ready, lad?'

For an instant, with a lurch of the heart, Skarry thought Glimshpill was talking to him and a grin had already begun to break upon his face when Mullo strode up, his smile from ear to ear and a plain metal helmet upon his head.

'Aye, sir!' he said and gave a clumsy salute, right fist to the chest.

'You'll do,' Glimshpill laughed. 'You take the lead as you know the ways of the wood. I'll watch out for risk of ambush.' And he gave another great yawn.

Skarry's disappointment put a stoop to his shoulders as Mullo strutted about swinging his staff, raising a hand to feel the cold steel helm on his head. He watched Skarry sidelong and at last turned on him.

'You'll hear tales of my glory, simpleton,' he sneered, 'when you huddle about the fire, bodging your snowshoes. Glory that'll make you weep with envy and cringe in shame at the wretchedness of your self.'

Mullo drew back his lips in a grimace and suddenly made as though to strike at Skarry with the butt end of his staff. He gave an ugly laugh as Skarry flinched away.

Catskin, his bargaining finished, came over with three ponies; two thick-necked geldings and a deep-chested mare, shaggy in their winter coats with felted woollen saddle-pads, the reins and bridles of plaited rope. The Olluden could ill spare these seeing as they themselves had far to go. They bred a few of their own ponies but since the wild stock had been rounded up for use in the wars they had often been forced to barter for animals in Midloth.

Glimshpill selected the largest gelding for himself and the other for Catskin.

16

'You'd better have one,' he said resentfully to the Dreamer, offering him the lead rope of the mare.

There was a struggle to get Glimshpill on to his pony and when he was at last astride him he looked even more like a giant, perched upon this tiny steed.

'Oh, for civilisation and stirrups,' he complained loudly, settling his broad backside on the saddle-pad and taking a tight hold of the reins.

'Move on!' he roared at Mullo who pushed the weeping Lenus aside and strode off with a hard smile on his face, the staff swinging.

'You two make the best time you can,' Glimshpill said to the other soldiers and then turned his back on them. As they rode past, Skarry could no longer hold back. He ran forward and clung to the warrior's leg.

'Take me with you also, Lord,' he begged.

But Glimshpill gave him a push with his boot that sent Skarry tumbling over.

'Give it another year,' he called as Mullo led them off between the oaks towards the main track. Catskin followed, half asleep on his mount and then went the Dreamer who smiled as he passed.

'Don't seek to rush into your future,' he said. 'It is coming soon enough of its own accord.' Then he too was gone.

Last came the two soldiers on foot, making an easy pace, one lighting up a pipe. Within only a few moments, the company were out of sight leaving no trace of their passing save that Mullo had gone and Skarry's head was full of confusion.

Turning, he found the Olluden themselves near ready to move out. The huts with their light covering of snow would be left as they were, a winter haunt for the forest creatures, if the storms did not take them. The hurdles were stacked in one to await the return next summer. Yain had already begun to move out the animals with Eka and Skip, a long drive ahead through hard country. The door to the Moot House was closed though not locked; food and fuel were left within for any winter travellers who should happen to pass that way and find themselves in need.

Skarry ran to his own home to see his mother carefully wrapping the carving tools between cloth. Geralt packed blankets in birch baskets along with their few other possessions and tied them to the drag. Skitta the pony, looking hairy as a goat in his coming winter coat, stood calmly between the shafts and ate from his nose bag.

'Come, Skarry,' said his father without looking up. 'Pack what you would take, the others are near set to go.'

So ordinary did his father's voice sound that almost Skarry turned to sort his gear but in the very act he froze. He could not remain silent.

'So we are to run away,' he said slowly, bitterly.

'We leave every winter, do we not?' asked his mother.

'Not in this way!' Skarry said with a rush. 'Not all in a hurry and sweating with fear, running from an enemy we have not even seen!'

'I am neither hurried nor sweating, Skarry,' Irane said and glanced up at him.

Geralt began the methodical gartering of his leggings, wrapping the long laces around and about each calf, crossing and recrossing them at the shin.

'Soldiers have passed this way many times before,' he said quietly, 'and will come again no doubt. This is not the concern of the Olluden.'

'But Skoye is coming, the Misery of Ice!' Skarry burst out in desperation. 'He will bring his armies over the Pass and sweep across the whole of the southern lands if unopposed. There will be no safety anywhere, even in our own winter home!'

Geralt finished the lacing and stood up straight, banging his feet to settle the material.

'Will you help me tie the load?' he asked and held out the rope.

The fibrous cord swam before Skarry's eyes like a noose. Behind his father, Irane paused in her packing and though she did not turn he felt her waiting on him.

'I, I'm not coming,' he stammered at last and before the tears could start or his mind change, he spun away and began to run, to run through Havod his home, the people parting before him in the beginning blur. And as he ran he heard behind him the sounds of their departure, Gemel bidding them set out, the eager shouts to the ponies and Caul taking up the walking song, the fluid stream of notes flowing after him. He did not look back but ran on along the path towards the Middle Mark until he could hear only his own gasping breath.

At the markstone he fell to his knees and clung to it, the sucking stone within the warmth of his mouth, the thong running out at the corners. With his cheek pressed against the rosettes of rough, grey lichens he let loose his tears and cried, his body shaking with the sobs. To have been so close to such heroes yet see them just slip away from his life. And the Olluden, like frightened rabbits always ready to run and hide, never thinking that the foul marten would enter their very homes after them. The Dreamer had seen him as different from them, as worthy of greater things but it was that ox, Mullo, who had gone with the soldiers, had been asked to go with them, as guide, as warrior.

His eyes dried at last of their own and he looked out once more from his sorrow. With the rough rock against his skin his gaze was drawn to the groove on the markstone. Framed within this minute valley, far off and up in the distance, was Skard, the notch of the High Pass and his thoughts fled there like the flight of an arrow. The crags were veiled with snow, their hard outline blurred with windblown ice. Did Grimal Skoye's Ice Warriors now hold the Pass? Or was Fressingfield up there somewhere, with the tatters of his army, still awaiting aid? Why could not he, Skarry of the Olluden, at least go and see? Though the forest people left the mountains in winter, left the high routes to the Hagarath alone, still was he the son of a guide. He could go, this seemed quite clear to him.

With this decision he stood and straightened his body, stretching his limbs to ease the stiffness that comes from contact with cold stone. Taking one last look down the path, towards Havod, he saw Gemel suddenly appear, as though separating himself from a tree. The old one held up a bundle of things and looked him long in the eye. Then he placed them upon the ground and in the act of turning away, faded once more into the forest.

Skarry trotted back, somewhat surprised and looking carefully about but whether Gemel had swiftly gone or simply concealed himself to watch, Skarry could not tell; he knew the guide to be capable of either.

At the bundle he stopped and his mind emptied of thought; here were his snowshoes, his staff and cloak, the pockets lined with food. Finding another hand at work gave him still greater resolve and Skard beckoned all the more as though the placing of his possessions here blessed his choice.

So, gladly accepting the mystery, Skarry threw on his cloak, looped the snow shoes about his neck and stood up for a moment, one hand upon the markstone, the other holding his staff. Then he began the gentle walk down the dip to the ford, feeling suddenly ordinary to be on so well known a path.

The Alator bubbled and sang merrily though its banks were lined with ice. Skarry crossed by the stones above the ford and drew on his mittens against the growing cold. And, even though he had taken this way many times before, all thought was set aside as the track rapidly steepened and he felt an inner strength kindle and burn as he rose up above the world. The towering oaks of the sheltered valley gave way to shorter knarled and twisted trees, their crowns pushed low by the gales. Boulders reared up through the thin soils, the perch of the ousel in summer yet now the white-collared bird had fled south to warmer climes. Then even the scrub oak and rowan ended in jagged points between the piled screes, falling back from the weight of stone all tumbled from the flanks of the mountain. The grey gave way to white, the sharp rock seeming softened by the skin of snow, though in truth the hard outline was only concealed.

The track climbed a slight ridge with long falls to either side. Here Skarry stopped to put on his snow walking shoes and was for a moment taken back to the making of them under his father's watchful eye. How hard that had been, his fingers clumsy at the then new task as he struggled to weave the split bramble within the teardrop frame. But with Geralt's help he had finished them and what pride he had from the wearing when they were done and how light they were on the feet. The thought made him turn to look back at the world he was leaving.

The land spread below and away to the south like a map. He could see the Middle Mark and the clearing of Havod, empty and white. The track ran on through the forest though from here it could not be seen for the trees. It rose once more into view where it crested the further side of the hanging valley and here the Olluden had raised Moccus Tump long ago, a mound to guide the traveller. Some said Moccus had let his many pigs root in the woods where they had eaten all the acorns and so no oaks grew about the mound. Beyond lay the rolling hills that lowered to the Kirmire, that vast flat of wetland, and further south again

Wenlok could be seen on a clear day with its proud towers straining for the sky, home of Doth Auren, protector of the old peoples. Skarry had never been there though some of the Olluden had; they spoke of a market where wealthy lords and ladies would pay well in coin for carved work and the coin could be used to buy food from the plains, cunning tools or even flashing jewels. Yet the distant south was lost today in the banks of fog that rolled across the marshes.

There were many places to go, thought Skarry, and many things to see; then he might return in peace to his family. But now his present labour called and he turned to face the towering crags of the Angsoth.

Snow was in the air and he pulled up his hood, fastening the flap across his face so that only his eyes peeped from within. Though nearer, Skard grew less distinct as the snow came. With head down to watch his footing Skarry climbed on, placing each shoe with care so as not to tread on the rim of the other. The snow was as yet soft and he sank a little on each step; with the night's frost the surface would become hard and smooth as glass and he should need spikes on his boots.

From time to time he raised up his head to Skard and so kept to the line. The track could no longer be made out but with care he could feel when shoes or staff hit the stones piled either side to mark the way. As he approached the Pass, the wind began to howl through Skard like the breath of the giant bear, only cold as ice. Skarry stopped and tightened all the fastenings of his clothes. The cloak had straps that passed around his legs so the tail did not flap. It was not safe to allow the wind any entrance; this was the teaching of the Hagarath and as warning they told of Abdock, who had been found frozen to a rock, stripped naked by the wind for want of a toggle on his collar.

It was while Skarry was thus stooped over tying the laces about his calves that he heard the noise. He felt the coldness of his stone settle in the hollow of his throat. The sound came on the wind, beginning low and ending in a high shriek that raised the hairs on his flesh.

He crouched lower instinctively and looked ahead but even to his mountain sight Skard seemed empty of life. In the growing blast the snow hares themselves had fled to some secret retreat. But if he could travel in this then it was certain that others could

21

also. Wolves were known to cross here yet the noise had not been like any wolf he had heard before.

Where Skard cut down into the slabbed rock faces of the Angsoth the sides were sheer and clean of hold. But to the right the rise of Ice Back staggered once and in this dip there lay another way. A gully ran up, narrowing and steepening towards the summit. In summer as a child Skarry had played here with the other children many times, perhaps while the guides awaited the approach of distant travellers. They would divide themselves into bandits and guards and strive to pass in secret. Even then the Elders would grow fearful for their safety and call them down. In winter the world of the mountains was still more perilous.

It was towards the bottom of this gully that Skarry struck out, crossing the top of the snow covered scree, clinging below the crags of the ridge. The rock above was near sheer and gave some shelter from the worst of the gale yet the wind dropped its weight of snow in the slower air and he was soon floundering in the deepening drifts.

At last he came to the foot of the gully, a great crack that rose crookedly upward. Taking off his snow shoes, he looped them about his neck and began his cautious ascent.

Pressing close against the rock he tested each hold, clinging to projecting stone or putting his mittened hand within a crack. In places the stone was plastered with snow and here he dug holds awkwardly with the butt of his staff, wishing he had an axe with him. Near the top the sides of the gully closed on him until he was squeezed between the walls. The way was now vertical and he hauled himself the last bit with his feet dangling free.

At the top he tumbled forward into the relative safety of the dip and lay face up on the snow, breathing deeply. He had felt no fear while climbing, being so occupied in the present, but now he shook with the thought of a fall. He had moved too quickly for a winter climb and broken into sweat and this began to cool as he lay in the snow, so he got up to stamp his feet and flap his arms.

As he did so a second cry came on the wind, so much the sharper and not far off, a rattling howl that sent him diving to the ground in sudden terror. It was no sound he knew and he had seen and heard all the creatures of forest and mountain. Behind him, to the south, the air had closed in and he could no longer

22

see the Middle Mark. Before him, the remembered view of the descending ridge that led into Dunan Dale, down again to the sea and the far Isthmus, were invisible within the turmoil of snow. All that could be seen to the north in that blur of white was the Maen-hir, standing like an ancient wrinkled finger, pointing hugely at the sky, momentarily revealed then concealed by the swirl of white. This greater brother to the Middle Mark was similarly inscribed and showed the various ways that led off from Skard.

Skarry began to edge his way forward, keeping low to the ground, following the curve of Ice Back round and above the Maen-hir. The dark and craggy surface of the stone loomed up out of the whiteness and he could just make out other shadows around it.

Then there came a third shriek, so piercing as to pain his ears and this time he saw the flash of bright fire that came with it. For a moment the dark shapes about the Maen-hir were lit up, frozen in their gestures. A body writhed at the stone as if bound and the fire seemed to pour from about the neck. Before it stood another figure, arms upraised into the wind, the fingers bare and stretched wide. Then the light faded and the snow closed in leaving Skarry trembling.

A slight noise broke through the background of the gale, causing him to turn and his heart suddenly hammered hard in his chest. From out of the flurry of snow a huge horned figure hurtled, mace upraised in one hand, the cruel blow poised at the start of its downward sweep. And though Skarry strove to raise an arm, to make some defence, however feeble, his body heard not and simply shook.

At the last, as the towering figure bore down upon him he heard it speak. 'A lad,' it said with a laugh in a rough dialect. And it turned so sharp on its short skis that Skarry was showered with ice. The swing of the mace was slowed and became a shove that pushed Skarry in the ribs over his thundering heart and sent him toppling backwards. At that his body was freed of the grip of fear and he flailed his arms for balance but to no avail; he went tumbling backwards over the edge of the ridge and slid bumpily down towards the Maen-hir.

The snow rushed under him. He passed a figure to one side, the face as pale as the white of the sky above, the lips bright red, the eyes a little wide with surprise. Then the standing stone came at him as though it were falling, the surface sharp with detail and blotting out his vision. There was a hard crack and he seemed to be moving in a different direction though he knew not which. Then he was floating at a vast height, peering dimly down at a world grown small, peopled by ants, swarming in armies across the face of the land. Their angry chatter rose up to him, a buzzing of insects and he passed beyond the boundaries of thought.

4

Ress

Skarry awoke from a darkness within his own head to one without. At first he thought that he was blinded and in a panic tried to raise his hands before his face but he could not move his arms. The effort started up hammers in his brain like Tarvil the smith at his forge and he clenched his teeth at the sudden pain. The sensation brought memory flooding back and he froze at the image of the horned one bearing down upon him. He had been captured, that seemed certain and he began to tremble at the thought.

He wished the stone was in his mouth for its cold comfort; at least then something would be familiar in this blackness. To distract himself from the fear Skarry felt his position. He was sitting upright, his arms tied securely about a post at his back. It was dark, that was for sure, so night most likely and he felt animal skins beneath his legs. If he turned his attention from the sound of rushing blood within his ears he could hear the wind howling loud and near, coupled with the flapping of canvas. A guy rope was slack by the noise; he heard it snapping taut then loose, over and over. It needed tightening fast lest the gale would claim the tent for its own. A scream tore over on the wind, a dying scream. It made him gasp out loud.

'So you're alive then,' came a voice from the darkness and that made him start all the more. There was someone with him, close by. Unable to see or move his arms Skarry struggled to control his panic. The stone weighed heavy against his throat as he swallowed. Yet he had slept and not been harmed in his sleep, as far as he could tell.

'Who are you?' he asked tentatively, and the voice replied out of the blackness.

'I am a friend,' it said. 'I mean you no harm.'

A girl or woman by the sound, soft yet with a bitter edge that Skarry felt might easily become hard.

'Not that my friendship will be much use to you,' she said with a laugh. 'They will be coming for us soon.'

Skarry felt the fear again at this and struggled to free his arms but to no avail. His legs though were not tied.

'Where are you?' he asked, turning his head this way then that to find her voice. This darkness, he cursed, Oh for a light to see! With one foot he carefully felt about. Through his boot he could feel the wrinkled canvas and cold snow below. Then another foot.

'Is that you?' he called excitedly.

'No,' she said, 'that will be Malik. I think he may be dead.'

The sounds of the storm were suddenly increased and for a moment Skarry thought that it had taken the tent and that they were exposed to the full fury of the wind as he felt the snow blow about his face. But there came a dim light from an enclosed lantern, sputtering hardily. Skarry could make out a triangular opening filled by the frame of a huge man all swathed in furs, on his head a horned helmet and round his throat a necklace of seals teeth. The lantern lit his face from below and cast the features into a contorted grimace.

He stood to one side and held the whirling tent flap to allow another to enter. This one was lighter of build and took the lantern from the first, holding it high to illuminate the tent. In the pale light Skarry could make out the girl lying bound to his left. The one she had called Malik was just before him, an old man, very white with a blue bruise to his temple but still breathing.

Looking up to the lantern bearer Skarry started, for this one's hood was now thrown back to reveal black hair braided tightly to the head, the face all white, the lips bright red. She bent towards him, holding the lantern lower.

'A young forester, eh?' she said softly and smiled at Skarry. She seemed very beautiful to him, her eyes dark, drawing the gaze inward. With her free hand she reached down and stroked his cheek. The fingers were soft and warm to his cold skin.

'Take the old man first,' she said, turning abruptly to the horned one, 'before he dies and is no use to us.'

As swiftly she drew up her hood and another of the horned warriors entered to help the first drag Malik out. The flap was closed up and the glow of the lamp faded into the blackness. After a taste of the light Skarry felt the dark even more.

26

'I wish I could see,' he murmured. 'Oh, I wish I could see!'

'We must get away!' came the girl's voice fiercely, 'for they are sure to kill us. Stick out a leg towards me!'

Skarry did as he was ordered and was rewarded by a sudden contact.

'Ymir!' she swore. 'You near broke my shin.'

Skarry apologised immediately but she ignored him and by the sounds of shuffling and her breathing, came towards him. In the dark, what with the gale without, the panting within, the groping touch as she brushed against his leg, Skarry began to sweat with fear. The sharp cry that drove over with the wind did nothing to ease the beating of his heart. She froze at the sound.

'Malik,' she said with finality and then redoubled her activity. Skarry felt her head upon his chest as she drew near and tried to lever herself upright. Then he could feel her hair, soft against his cheek and her breathing loud in his ear.

'My hands are tied behind this pole,' he said.

'Mine also, and my feet,' she said. 'Hold now.'

By the sound she scrambled up until she was sitting beside him and he could feel her hands behind his back. That sudden comfort of warm skin came as a great relief and for a moment they gasped together, fingers intertwined. Then she began to work at his bonds.

'What's your name?' Skarry asked. 'And how did you come to be here?'

'That last needs a long answer,' she said with a sigh, 'but you can call me Ress.'

'And who are these people?'

'The woman is Malkah,' she replied. When Skarry made no reaction to the name she continued, 'It's probably just as well that you have not heard of the witch before, or her deeds. I will say Monrolians then and you will know our plight.'

Skarry heard her spit. His own worst fears were realised and he began to shake.

'Hold still now!' Ress ordered. 'They may be your enemy yet are they still human, though their present purpose is not.'

Then she gave a cry of triumph and Skarry felt his hands fall free. He stretched his arms and rubbed at his wrists for the rope had been tight and bruised the flesh.

'Come on!' Ress hissed. 'No time for that. Untie me, quickly!'

And there was such command in her voice that Skarry turned straight away and fumbled blindly at the knots. This was not an easy task in the dark and Ress cursed impatiently. At last her hands were free also and Skarry would have untied her legs but she pushed him away and in only a moment it seemed had them loose.

'Search the tent,' she said. 'Hurry!'

Skarry began to fumble about by the edge of the tent amongst a few skins and bags. Here the wind was louder in his ears but he caught the sound of returning voices.

'Ress. Ress! they're coming back!'

'All right, all right!' she said, as if annoyed at his fear and taking hold of his jerkin she hauled him towards the further side of the tent, away from the entrance flap.

The glow of the lamp reappeared through the canvas and the shadow of the horned one stooped to undo the flap.

'What are we going to do?' Skarry asked in a fearful whisper but Ress only shushed him into silence. In the dim light he saw she had a knife.

The entrance was opened with a wild flapping, the storm loud in the tent again. Ress pulled Skarry low to the ground and there came a ripping sound. Before the entering warriors could do more than look towards the noise, the fierce wind pushed in through the growing hole that Ress had made. Skarry felt the sudden pressure in his ears, then the canvas was rent asunder and they were open to the storm, high on the mountains of the Ridgeway.

The roar was near deafening and they felt the wind pushing them down. The canvas swirled wildly like a mad sail where it was still fastened and wrapped itself about the two Monrolians, sending them toppling to the ground. The light too was enclosed with them and one began to scream. Then a blast of wind caught at them and all was black once more.

Huddled in the snow Skarry started to shiver as the wind stripped him of his warmth. Ress crawled away, still pulling at his jerkin and there seemed little else to do except follow. Swiftly the freezing cold aroused him to the danger of their situation. In dealings with warriors and Monrolians he had little experience, but the wind blown ice and the mountains, at least he knew something of these. His mind began to work again.

Shelter first, this was their most urgent need. Without protection from the giant's icy breath they would freeze before even the Monrolians found them. Already his hands were without feeling and the numbness was spreading. Ress had slowed her crawling and now came back to cower against him.

'I'm freezing!' she shouted into his ear. 'What can we do?'

Skarry knew that the High Haven was their only hope, though where it lay in this blast of ice and sound he could not be certain. Gradually his eyes adjusted somewhat, the snow on which they lay whitened and he could make out a dark shadow beside him that was Ress. But where were they? He felt sure that they had not been brought far from the Maen-hir, for the screams had been close. Creasing his eyes into slits he scanned all around, striving to see the black finger of stone against the blacker sky.

Ress tightened her grip upon his arm and he too heard the distant voices blown to them on the wind. He rose and helped her to her feet. Clutching at their flapping garments and each other they began to stumble away from the shouts. A light appeared behind them, a dull glow of orange that flickered with each gust and Skarry thought he could discern the horned helmets of the warriors.

Then, like a blacker shadow, the standing stone loomed before them out of the swirl of darkness. There was no one about and Skarry ran to the stone and clung to it momentarily, his teeth chattering. With that familiar solidity beneath his freezing fingers he felt more secure, at least in the knowledge of where he was. Ress hung gasping on his arm.

Looking closely all about he noted the slight fall of ground to one side, the gentle incline here. Moving around the stone he felt for the incised marks, scraping numb fingertips over the rough stone in his effort to sense them. There! These were the three lines showing north, so moving further round he should come to the circle. Yes, this pointed the way to the Haven. Thus assured of his direction he put an arm about Ress and pushed away from the stone.

'Keep to a line!' he shouted. 'Try not to stray to the side!'

Somewhere up ahead on the crag were more signs; in lesser weather they would have been an easy guide but with sight so restricted they were trusting to luck and Skarry's feel for the mountain.

29

Almost immediately they stumbled over a body in the snow. Skarry guessed it was Malik and pulled Ress on. The last few moments stretched long and Skarry began to fear that he had led them wrong somehow. Then with relief he came upon the rough crag that ran across their path. High Haven was near he knew, but without sight of the marks to guide them he could not tell whether it lay to the right or left.

'Stay here!' he ordered Ress and she sank down into the snow. Skarry worked his way along the crag to the left, striving to feel in the snow-filled cracks for the signs of the shelter. The cold grip of panic rose from his stomach and he made to put the stone within his mouth but then held the gesture. What would Gemel have done? Surely not this blind groping. He stopped and stood away from the rock, letting the howl of the storm fill his head. Then he let the wind move him a few more paces and putting out his hand his heart leapt to find the deep crack and here the rough projection with three heavy seams cut in it. It was the High Haven, they had strayed only a little from their line.

He went back for Ress and found her near buried in the snow, but as he stooped to lift her she struggled to her feet and together they waded through the rising drifts until they reached the marks. Skarry followed the lines down with his hands. They led him to a slab of rock which with a heave pivoted inwards. He pushed Ress within then he himself entered, shutting the rock door behind. With the thud of its closing the howl of the gale was suddenly quieted and they could hear the sound of their own gasping breath as they lay exhausted in darkness on the cold stone floor.

Before long the numbness in Skarry's fingers became unbearable and he set to searching the dark chamber. It was small, only enough room for him to stand half crouching and as wide as his outspread arms. Moving back into the rock he managed six uneven paces over the rough surface before coming to the end. Here he found by touch the rock shelf on which the Olluden kept provisions for such situations.

With trembling fingers he took down a container covered in fur and from beside it on the ledge a bottle that sloshed with liquid. He sank down on to his heels, back against the stone and cradled the two objects with reverent care.

'Vidar, look kindly down upon us, O great one,' he whispered, and taking the stopper from the bottle he poured a few drops into the container, holding his face away from the invisible cloud of steam that rose up from the mixture. Carefully replacing the stopper he set the bottle down and cradled the container, his hands inside the fur of its cover. From within he saw a dull glow like a hot coal and his hands began to warm.

The radiance increased as he leaned over its heat, lighting his face and filling the cave with a soft light. After a while he gave the container to Ress and showed her how to put her hands within the fur. Then he added a few more drops from the bottle and another prayer. Ress gasped with delight at the heat and held it close.

'So you are a magician as well as a guide,' she said and Skarry flushed with the pride he felt.

'Not really', he admitted. 'I know some of the ways of the mountain, but it will be many years before I am a guide. Even my father is still a pupil in that art. But Gemel, now he is a true guide. Why, you could leave him anywhere on the mountain, naked and blind in a storm a hundred times worse than this and he would be back at Havod and supping before you could ski down.'

'Don't speak of such things,' said Ress and shivered.

'I meant no harm,' Skarry said, a little surprised. 'The fire-pot is old lore, handed down from ages past. Some say that when the Two who were One fought with the great bear, sparks flew off from their blows and the hill smiths enslaved them. Gemel says it matters not what one believes so long as it works.'

'You have yet to tell me your name,' said Ress. 'What do they call you?'

'The Olluden call me Skarry and I am the son of Irane and Geralt, who make snow walking shoes and skis.'

'Indeed!' Ress laughed and Skarry felt cheered to hear such a sound. 'And why do they call you Skarry?' she went on.

'They call me many names,' said Skarry quietly, 'though Skarry will do for now. When I return I will bring with me a bright name, a strong name that will tell of my adventures.'

Ress did not laugh at this and said only, 'Well Skarry, you saved me from the storm and made me warm and if you get me down from this mountain then you'll be hero enough for me.'

31

'And you untied me,' he returned, feeling his face colouring, 'and got me out of that tent.'

She turned to him, the glow from the fire-pot lighting up her pale cheeks but casting her eyes into shadow.

'We should sleep,' he said after a moment and busied himself preparing their bedding. There was bracken for a mattress and warm woollen blankets that he laid out. As he moved in the dim light he felt that she listened to him, turning her head this way then that to catch the sounds.

At last they lay down, Ress feeling for the blankets in the dying glow from the fire-pot. She curled up against him and they lay thus, huddled together for warmth. Skarry drifted in and out of sleep, tormented by visions of the horned warrior and a distant view of some strange city in the ice of an unknown mountain range. At times images of Irane and Geralt would rise up, their arms upraised to him. He held the sucking stone against the roof of his mouth with his tongue and as it slowly warmed he fell into a deeper sleep that silenced even the storm, still raging without.

5

Quorn

In the dim light from the fire-pot Skarry examined the stores of the Haven. There was food and spare clothing, skis and snow shoes. He laid out warm jerkins, leggings and cloaks for them both and packed a bag with some provisions; he was sparing though, for it might be that other travellers would have need of this place of safety before the winter was done.

'Do you ski?' he asked Ress finally.

She was quiet for a moment, then said, 'Skarry, there's no way that I will be able to ski out of here.'

'It's not so difficult,' he said. 'See, with these short ones you'll be safe enough. We'll go by an easy route, along Ice Back and over the Rib; the slopes are gentle, you'll see.'

'It's not that I am frightened,' Ress said. 'I'm blind.'

Skarry stopped in his packing, swinging slowly towards her. She seemed to be gazing over his left shoulder. Half expecting her to turn suddenly and catch his stare, he looked directly into her eyes. In the dim glow they were very pale, perhaps a light blue.

'Maybe you would be better off leaving me here and going for help?' she continued. 'I'll take no hurt and you'll be all the faster.'

There was nothing Skarry felt he could say. If the Monrolians did not catch him as he left the shelter, they would surely find his tracks and follow them backwards as well as forwards. Could he tell her that his people had already left for their winter home and that it might take many days to catch up with them? Or that even if by some great stroke of good fortune he should fall in with Taurians, the chances were they would not put themselves out for a blind girl trapped on the mountains.

'We'll have to go together,' he said. 'There's no other way. Do you use snow shoes?' When she shook her head it seemed another blow had been struck against them but he shrugged it off, 'No matter, you will learn soon enough. After all, you have Skarry with you, the great guide of the Angsoth!'

She gave a laugh at this and held up her left hand, the fingers open. Skarry took it and squeezed; the grip she returned was strong.

They began to prepare themselves. Skarry showed her how to wear the woollen jerkin underneath the skin tunic, how the hood flap could be fastened tight across the face or opened should she sweat with the march. Then there were the boots and leggings with the laces crossing and recrossing over the lower leg. The snow shoes were heavier than Skarry would have liked yet at least she would not forget she had them on.

When they were both ready to his satisfaction he went to the stone door and waited in silence, putting his whole being into listening. Now that the time had come to leave he felt the image of the enemy rise up and a desire to remain within the dark warmth of the Haven. Outside the sounds of the storm had died and he could hear nothing. With a silent plea to Vidar he took hold of the rock slab and opened it a little. A thin crack of light pierced the dim cavern. Ress felt it on her face and turned more towards it, raising up her head. Within the hood of her jerkin only her pale blue eyes could be seen.

Skarry allowed his sight time to adjust to the sharp light, then opened the stone further and peered out. Beyond the doorway lay a fresh white world, the crags and boulders of the mountain softened by the covering of snow. There was no one in sight, nor any tracks; their own had been obliterated along with all mark of humans save for the Maen-hir, some distance off, half white to the windward side and a long thin drift to its lee.

Directly above, a huge circle of blue had opened in the mass of cloud and the morning sun, just appearing at the eastern rim, sent down a clean light as if to greet them.

Skarry ducked back in and closed the stone, telling Ress what he had seen.

'They will have gone, their purpose was completed,' said Ress. 'Besides, the snow was as bad for them as for us.'

'They have no fear of snow,' said Skarry. 'The horned ones were Ice Warriors; their winters are to ours what ours are to the southern plains.'

34

'Let's get out in the open again,' Ress was decided. 'I need some fresh air after this hole.'

Skarry frowned at the choice of words but opened the stone wide anyway and they crawled out, sliding down the slope of drift below the crag. Ress remained lying with head back, breathing slowly and deeply. Skarry closed the entrance and brushed snow into their tracks.

Raising a hand to their shelter he called, 'Vidar! Our thanks, mighty one, for thy kindness and the loan of this safe hole.'

This last was accompanied by a look to Ress and though she could not see him she caught his tone and laughed.

'Yes, I too am grateful,' she called mocking into the sky.

'Don't sit in the snow,' was all Skarry said and pulled her to her feet. Then, taking Ress by the arm and turning east, they began their march.

She walked warily at first, placing each snow shoed foot with exaggerated care but soon, with Skarry's encouragement, her confidence grew and their pace increased. Skarry divided his attention between Ress and their surroundings, half expecting the whoop of an attacking warrior at any instant. As they progressed this fear diminished and he took more note of the wide vista of mountains and snow.

'Tell me what you see,' Ress asked, aware of his change in mood.

Not really knowing where to start Skarry said, 'This is the land of the Mountain people, the Hagarath; we Olluden are of the forests in truth. Yet we have walked these hills for many ages, since the slaying of the stone bear at the very dawn of time. See, down there – ' he broke off, embarrassed at his mistake.

'Think nothing of it,' said Ress. 'It is not the first time, nor shall it be the last.'

Skarry went on with more care, 'In the old tales the Two who were One, Vidar and Ithunne slew the great bear and the huge body fell across the face of the stone globe. The great curve of the Ridgeway and the Ulta-Zorn is its backbone. In the fight the Two were separated and mighty Vidar chose his seat from the mountains of the Ridgeway and settled on the Angsoth. That is why travellers pray to him for his aid before they attempt the High Pass.'

'It is a fair story,' said Ress. 'Where I come from Vidar is not seen as so helpful.'

'And where's that?' Skarry asked.

'Ringdove.'

'Ringdove,' Skarry repeated, savouring the name. 'Ah, that must indeed be a fair city to look upon.'

'I wouldn't know,' Ress said sharply, 'though my other senses tell me it is not so fair.'

'A place of warriors,' Skarry went on. 'We have heard the stories of its many heroes, even in our poor forest. I should like to see the great Paladin Guise, he must be like a god of old. Surely he will turn back the Monrolians and destroy them utterly!'

'Your forest is not poor!' Ress said and tightened her grip upon his arm. 'It is far richer than you yet believe. What is the matter?'

Skarry had stopped suddenly at tracks running through the snow across their path. He bent low to look the closer. There was a wide, deep furrow like that of a heavy beast moving fast from the north. At first he thought it was that of a bear, perhaps with a hurt to its leg for each step dragged into the next; yet the print, where it was more clear, seemed to have but one claw, like a talon.

'What is it Skarry?' Ress asked again.

'I thought they were tracks of a man,' he said slowly, 'but it is only a bear. We must hurry.'

Watchful he led her on. They climbed the slope of Ice Back, up from Skard across deep drifts. The crunch of snow beneath their shoes was all that broke the stillness save for the kronking of a pair of ravens, spiralling slowly, far out over the screes. As they crested the rise, the lands to the north opened out before them. The mountains of the Ridgeway lowered to the Isthmus with the sea to either side, motionless at such a distance. Beyond the narrow strip of the Isthmus the mountains rose again, so much the higher, their growing peaks soon lost in the mists. Here lay the Ulta-Zorn and the lands of Monrolia, far beyond the knowledge of the peoples of the Ridgeway.

Yet it was not the land receding into such vast distance that drew his attention. On the Isthmus was a black column, like that of the forest ants, only men, soldiers, spilling over the walls of Cassan Keep that marked the boundary of Taur. And in the middle distance, where the sea plains crumpled and folded into the lowlands and Dunan Dale began her long climb towards Skard, here the column widened into dark masses of warriors, the sharp light glinting on helms and spear points as they hurried on towards the Pass, their fluttering banners showing a grey seal on white.

'It is the enemy!' Skarry gasped and clung to Ress's arm. 'There are so many. I never thought to see such numbers!'

'Can you see any of ours?' Ress asked. 'Can you see Fressingfield?'

'No, there is none of ours. None whatsoever.'

Skarry began to back away from the sight, drawing Ress with him. He stuffed the green stone within his mouth and sucked hard at it.

'Spit it out, Skarry,' Ress said sharply to him, 'else you'll suck it to nought.'

Startled, Skarry did so and was brought back to himself. Though approaching fast the enemy were still a long way off and would take all the morning in their climb to the Pass. It might be that they had not seen them in their haste. Yet they would have advance scouts; the warriors who had captured them were proof of that. Taking Ress by the arm once more Skarry drew her back from the summit and stuck out on to a long ridge that curved off to the south-east.

'This we call the Rib,' he told Ress, 'for it is like the rib of the bear's backbone. We will not use the Pass in case Malkah's soldiers have already crossed to wait for us. We have stayed to the north of Ice Back. Now we can turn more southerly again, follow the Rib and meet up with the forest track. We are lucky the snow was so light for this way becomes dangerous with heavy falls; there are snow slides here in deep winter.'

Ress shivered and clung grimly to his arm as they hurried down the gentle slope of the Rib.

'We will be safe,' he said. 'In a moment we will – I mean I will be able to see Havod again, the summer home of the Olluden.'

And indeed, as he spoke they rounded snow-covered mounds of boulders and the view to the south was before them. Skarry looked once more upon the great forest lying within the curve of the hanging valley of the Olluden. The storm had taken the last browned leaves of the oaks and their stark branchings were black against the new white of the forest floor. Though they were further south Skarry could still make out the clearing of Havod, empty of all life. Following the line of the Alator as it splashed and tumbled along at the base of the Rib his gaze came to rest on the Falls where the hanging valley ended in sudden cliffs high above the wide, slow running Elkhorn.

With care Skarry moved out to the edge of the Rib, wary of overhanging snow that might collapse beneath their weight. The wind had blown the white into convoluted shapes, frozen waves that reared up, poised to break. Leading Ress he went on and came out from between massive drifts at the top of a sweeping drop. This was loose scree for much of the year but the early winter snow had covered it and the frost made a hard crust of the surface. Here they took off their snow shoes, Skarry wishing they had nailed boots as they began their cautious descent.

Ress slipped only once, falling past Skarry and then swinging round before him when their gripped hands held. He too went down, digging his feet in hard and managed to keep them both against the slope, hearts pounding. It was a long slide to the valley bottom and lower down the Rib's side broke into huge jumbled boulders.

Ress made as though to rise and go on but she felt Skarry's body stiffen and the sudden pressure of his arm brought her down to her knees.

'What is it?' she hissed.

'There are men below, across the river,' he said. 'It is the Ice Warriors!'

Even at this distance he could make out the horned helmets. He looked about desperately but there was no cover; they lay exposed on a vast sheet of white. Ress would have spoken but he clenched her arm the harder.

'There are more,' he went on. 'Coming out of the woods. No, wait, they are not Ice Warriors.'

In the clear air sound came swiftly and Ress was first to hear the shouts.

'They are fighting,' said Skarry. 'The Ice Warriors are four in number, they are running back to the river. Ah, one is down, an arrow. Those coming out of the trees must be ours. Yes, there are five of them hard on their heels, no, more, a sixth in blue.'

Skarry fell suddenly silent.

'What's happening?' Ress demanded fiercely. 'Do you know them?'

'Yes.' Skarry went on, his enthusiasm stilled, 'I know them. One of ours is down. They have caught them against the river. The three Ice Warriors are standing in the shallows, they will run no further. Our men are going in. Oh, there is a fierce one among the enemy, he has slain another of our heroes. Wait, ours are falling back. I see, they are going to use arrows.' After a pause he said, 'The enemy are all dead. The one in blue is coming forward. It is the Dreamer.'

Ress started at the name and leaped up.

'Let's get down there!' she ordered, and pulling him to his feet she began to call out to the soldiers below. Skarry could see them look up and two crossed the Alator, scrambling from stone to stone lower down and set out towards them. Skarry drew Ress downward, watching the others' approach with sinking heart. Long before they met, Skarry could make out the skinny frame of the warrior Catskin and with him the broad shouldered Mullo.

When Mullo recognised Skarry he stopped and came no further, choosing to wait for Skarry to come to him. Catskin paused a moment, as if aware of some rivalry between the two and then came on taking Ress by her other arm when he at last reached them. Together they slithered the last of the way down the slope to where Mullo waited.

'So, Skarry suck-a-stone,' he said and spat into the snow. 'What have you been up to, you skinny hero?'

Before Skarry could say anything Catskin spoke.

'There's nought wrong with skin and bone,' was all he said. Mullo made no reply and the other three passed him by.

Ress was silent as they made their way down to the naked trees. Skarry could see Catskin watching her from the corner of his eye. Mullo came close behind kicking at the snow and muttering under his breath.

At the river they crossed with some difficulty, passing Ress from stone to stone between them. She strode out fearlessly as if annoyed at their care. On the far bank they were met by Glimshpill looking huge in his winter cloak. In his hand he held a seal-tooth necklace that caught and reflected the white of the snow. He turned it this way then that in his great square hand and then stuffed it within his tunic.

To one side, the Dreamer bent over the dead. The Ice Warriors lay half immersed in the freezing waters of the Alator like slaughtered cattle with the horns of their helms rising at angles. The other two Taurians who had come over the Pass with Glimshpill's company shared their fate.

'The young dreamer,' Glimshpill said by way of greeting, 'and a pretty friend,' he added, reaching out a sudden arm to pull back Ress's hood so that her red hair fell about her face.

'You are indeed a mighty fighter, noble sir,' she said quickly. 'We watched your valiant battle from on high.'

Skarry was taken aback as Ress stood dwarfed before Glimshpill, her eyes seemingly staring him straight in the face. He gave a grin and tilted his head up a little, his hand poised upon the hilt of his sword.

'She's blind, Glim,' Catskin said at last and Ress turned half away, tightening her grip on Skarry's arm as Glimshpill snorted in surprise.

'I found her on the mountain,' Skarry said quickly. 'The Monrolians caught her. We escaped together.'

'You should have left her there,' Glimshpill said. 'A blind bitch will slow us down.'

'I can pay,' Ress went on. 'I have money.'

'Oh yes?' laughed the warrior. 'And where is this money? The Monrolians thought fit to leave you some, eh? No? A pity.'

Skarry was shocked by the exchange but before he could speak the low drum of hoofbeats from the forest floor signalled an approach and turning to the sound he could but marvel at the sight. Riding out of the trees upon a grey horse came a figure the likes of which he had not seen save in his dreams. The horse seemed twice the size of the forest ponies, all decked out in trappings that glittered with jewels. Along the reins hung tassels as if of gold and the brow band gleamed with silver. But the lord seated in his high pommelled saddle made even this mount look dull, for he was girt from toe to shoulder in a shining armour of interlocking plates that moved as he moved and seemed as a second skin upon his manly frame. At his side there rode another of lesser countenance and on a slighter steed, and cradled under an arm this one carried the lord's helm which was

40

graven in the image of a lion, the jaws strained wide in a frozen roar.

The Taurian soldiers all took off their helmets and bowed and Skarry would have sunk to one knee had not Ress held him up. The huge mount swept up to them champing at the bit and showing the whites of his eyes. The lord swung a leg forward over the pommel and leapt easily to the ground which seemed to tremble beneath his weight.

'My lord Quorn,' Glimshpill spoke up with a sweeping gesture of one arm, 'the advance guard of the enemy are destroyed utterly after hard battle. These two urchins,' he pointed to Skarry and Ress, 'we rescued from the very jaws of death. They were captured by our enemy and have news of his present whereabouts.'

The lord Quorn listened, his face impassive, standing easily, his hands upon his hips. The hair of his head, beard and moustache were of the colour of gold from which men gave him his name, the Lion of the South. When he spoke his voice seemed full of a quiet strength.

'It is a pity that your men could not have captured one of the enemy alive,' he said, 'as instructed.'

'My lord,' Catskin said silkily, 'we would have had them all alive but by the way they fought they had sworn the death pact with their vile god, Ymir. We had no option if we were to save these two.' He indicated Skarry and Ress who stood a little way off in awe of this bright lord. Quorn motioned Skarry closer.

'What have you to say, lad?' he asked gently. 'Tell us what you have seen.'

'The enemy, sir,' Skarry began when he had found his voice. 'Many of the enemy, sir. Some on the Isthmus and more in Dunan Dale making hard for the Pass.'

'And how many is your many?' the lord asked patiently. 'A hundred? A thousand?'

'I did not think to count, sir,' Skarry said quietly and Mullo gave a sharp laugh.

'You see?' Quorn said to Glimshpill and Catskin. 'We cannot rely on these simple peoples. You should have saved at least one of the enemy for the Dreamer to question. Now we shall have to go ourselves and have a look.'

At this Glimshpill started and Catskin spoke up hurriedly.

41

'But my lord Quorn, if this lad saw troops in Dunan, this morning, why, they will be nigh on the Pass by now and may already hold it in strength. No doubt they will be prepared and ready in ambush for the brave or foolhardy who seek to spy on them.'

'I am not a spy,' said Quorn, frowning at the choice of words. 'But your gist may well be right, Corporal. We should go carefully.'

'There is more,' came Ress's voice and they all turned to her. 'Those who took me were not simply warriors; well versed in sorcery were they and that was their intent at the Maen-hir upon the High Pass. The Witch Malkah was at their head.'

Glimshpill looked more worried than ever and cleared his throat to spit but when the lord Quorn turned to him he swallowed it down.

'The cursed flesh-eater,' he managed to mumble.

Quorn was silent for a time, his brows furrowed. The circle of blue sky passed them by, the sun slipping behind the ranks of cloud that pressed in from the north. The Dreamer left off the bodies of the dead and came over to them, looking hard upon Ress.

'We have need of your thoughts,' Quorn said. 'It seems there is a greater evil at work than soldiery.'

'When is there not?' asked the Dreamer and there was a mocking twinkle to his blue eyes. 'Come with me, girl,' he said to Ress who started at his voice. He took her a little way off; their heads bowed together as they talked.

'It is unfortunate,' said Quorn as if to himself, 'that you did not arrive sooner with your news. It seems likely that the Pass has already fallen to the enemy.'

'Noble my lord,' Catskin said softly. 'We came with all haste direct from the lord Fressingfield in his bitter plight. We could not have been faster had we been the wind itself.'

'Aye,' growled Glimshpill. 'This is so. These forest lads'll tell of our great speed.' He looked first at Mullo who nodded eagerly and then at Skarry who stared open mouthed.

'No matter,' said Quorn. 'It is done.'

The Dreamer returned to their company leading Ress on one arm.

'It is as you feared,' he said. 'The enemy are involved in some magical preparation. I must return to Ringdove with the girl. The lad too would be useful; though he does not understand, he has seen much that may prove valuable.'

Quorn said, 'I would take the lad with me as a guide upon the mountains, for I shall have to see the Pass for myself.'

Here Mullo broke in so fast that Glimshpill jumped. 'Take me, lord!' he cried eagerly. 'I am of the mountain and know the way of the fells. Take me!'

Quorn looked him in the eye then nodded his agreement.

'It is decided then,' he said. 'I will take my troop and seek out the enemy's purpose on the High Pass. This young warrior will be my guide.' Mullo grew taller at his new glory. Quorn turned to Catskin and continued, 'You, Corporal, must make all speed for Wenlock and raise the alarm. Let the Doth Auren know of the enemy upon the Pass. Take with you this forest lad who has knowledge of the land. And you, Dreamer, do as you think fit; if for Ringdove you head, then the Corporal will see you as far as Mireside, from there you will be on your own unless you choose to go on to Wenlok with them. Are we clear?'

He surveyed each face in turn and at the last when none had spoken up he gave a swirling salute that Mullo leapt to copy, Glimshpill and Catskin not so swift. Quorn motioned to the one who held his horse and hauled himself up into the saddle. With a word to his attendant he stood high in the stirrups.

'May Vidar watch over you in your peril!' he called to all and then wheeled about so sharply that Skarry thought the poor horse would go down but Quorn was away in a shower of snow. His attendant gave breath to his horn and as the echoes rolled over the woods they were answered and the ground began to drum as a score of armoured horsemen came thundering out from between the trees. Mullo waved them on, his face twisting with excitement as a small pony was brought for him. He clambered on bareback and with a grin to his lopsided face gave Skarry a last look as the troop made off for the fell track and the Pass.

Catskin watched for only a moment. 'Let us be on our way then,' he said. 'Vidar knows what that one will stir up with his heroics.'

Glimshpill spat into the snow. 'At least we're out of it,' was all he said.

There were no preparations to be made for all they had was upon them. Only two of the forest ponies were left; Glimshpill claimed one while the other was given to Ress. Catskin set off at their head followed by the Dreamer leading Ress's pony. Then came Glimshpill who pulled a wineskin from his tunic and took a heavy swig. At the rear was Skarry who stood looking back after Quorn.

On the lower slopes of the mountain the troop could be seen as bright as silver in their armour, strung like jewels along the track. They would have to dismount and lead their horses when the way steepened. Above them the towering Angsoth loomed in gathering mists. Skard seemed deserted at this distance but Skarry well knew the many places of ambush amid the snow covered crags. Sighing he turned and hastened to follow the others. Thoughts of the Olluden came into his mind, his parents and friends, for soon he would be leaving the hanging valley that had been home for so many years.

6

Crane of Mireside

For many hours they made their way through the Great Forest and the seamed trunks of mighty oaks. The sides of the track had been planted with beech years before, the smooth bark an easy guide to follow should the snows deepen. With the loss of the last browned leaves in the gale, the forest felt open and empty to Skarry. Snow had settled, in places thick across the ground, drifting about the trees and climbing the windward side of each trunk like a white shadow. Yet the path was clear where the lord Quorn's troop had pushed through from Mireside.

Catskin came back to Skarry's side after a while and talked to him. He told of leaving Havod the day before and how they had met up with Quorn late in the afternoon, not far from Mireside and been persuaded to return with him.

'He is a brave one, that Quorn,' Catskin said in his thin voice. 'But a little quick for our liking.'

Up ahead Glimshpill swigged at his wine and sang out hoarsely:

> Raise the bottle, drink it dry,
> Spit the lees in your enemy's eye.

Gradually the way began to steepen as they climbed from the shelter of the hanging valley. The trees opened out and they found themselves in a clearing at the crest of the rise. To the left of the path was a large mound.

'It is the barrow of Moccus,' Skarry explained. 'Some say that it was he who at last stopped the sheep people people grazing their herds in the wood, for they ate up all the young trees.'

'A last resting place for someone at least,' Glimshpill called out loudly. 'No such luck for us.' And he tossed the empty wineskin up on to the top of the mound.

45

As they passed, the view to the south opened before them. The path dived steeply then struck out like an arrow and far off could be seen the end of the forest and the beginnings of the Kirmire, that great flatland of marsh. The roofs of Mireside could just be made out where lowering clouds met the earth.

'We will not make Mireside before dark,' Catskin said and Glimshpill groaned at the thought of another night freezing under canvas.

'There's a shelter on the way,' called Skarry from the back. 'Little Haven it is named and has warmed many travellers caught between hearths.'

They cheered at this news and began the descent. Skarry caught up with the Dreamer who was leading Ress's pony. The sight of the south unsettled him for though he had been to Mireside once, this time he stepped out for Wenlok and tomorrow would be leaving the forest behind. He put the stone within his mouth without thinking and sucked at its coldness. Behind him the mighty Angsoth sank slowly below the mound of Moccus and Skard was soon lost to sight. He found himself thinking of the tracks he had seen upon the Rib; he felt fear that he who knew all the creatures of mountain and forest could not recognise the marks.

'Tell me of the granite bear, Skarry,' Ress said and he started from his walking dream.

Skarry turned easily to the tale for it took him back to times in the Moot House after sunset when the people of Havod gathered to hear Gemel speak of things past.

'The Olluden,' he began, 'call the stone bear Thuggundian and he was the first creature to live on this our world. The world was all rock then and Thuggundian sat alone on a granite block and the universe was quiet, as if with a held breath.

'After many ages Thuggundian looked up with his eyes of quartz and saw two giants descending from the starways. The thought of company pleased him and he eagerly waited on their coming. As they neared he saw that there were not two, but rather one, a woman and a man, joined at hip and shoulder so that the woman stood upon the left, the man on the right.

'The great bear called out and bid them welcome and for a time Vidar, who was the man, spoke easily with the beast. The woman was Ithunne and she said nothing, for her mouth was

46

frozen over. Some say that Thuggundian grew tired of their presence and that they quarrelled over who should live where. Vidar at last drew forth a sword and fought with the bear. The stone was crushed beneath the weight of their tread. Yet Vidar could do the bear no harm for the sword struck only sparks from its stony fur. Thuggundian drew himself up for a mighty blow; Ithunne strove to dodge one way, Vidar the other and so great was their strength that they tore themselves apart and were separated.

'Thuggundian was surprised and blinked his eyes amazed. Then Vidar saw that the great bear's head was joined to its body by a neck of lead. He raised up his sword and struck a mighty blow that clove the soft metal and Thuggundian's head sprang from his body and all his blood which was salt water ran out and settled into seas.

'The huge body crashed down and formed the lands of Taur and Monrolia and the great curve of his backbone became the mountains of the Ridgeway and Ulta-Zorn. Of his head, nothing is known. Many green things grew from the body of Thuggundian and where the battle had crushed the stone, there was the soil rich.

'For himself Vidar took the sun and the lands of Taur and the Olluden say that of all the mountains of the Ridgeway he favoured the Angsoth and made it his seat. To Ithunne he gave Monrolia of the north and she journeyed into the Ulta-Zorn and wrapped herself within her cloak of ice which now forever lies upon those peaks. The Olluden say that Vidar laid down his sword belt between the two lands as sign of friendship and this is the Isthmus.'

Skarry fell silent and in the coming twilight the land followed his quiet.

The Dreamer spoke first, saying, 'You tell a fine tale, Skarry.'

'It is as I have heard it, sir,' he replied. 'Thus has the story been passed down from mouth to ear through the ages. Gemel says that all people like to think that once there was a time of peace and friendship between the lands before the coming of Ymir.'

'The bear was not treated so peacefully,' Ress broke in, 'nor did Ithunne have much of a choice in her home, only the icy wastes of the north. And why was her mouth froze over?'

'From other lips,' the Dreamer said softly, 'I have heard how

Vidar in his desire for power cast out Ithunne into the lands of snow and bound her in ice upon the Ulta-Zorn.'

'But surely that cannot be!' protested Skarry. 'For was not Vidar the greatest of warriors and most noble?'

The Dreamer walked on in silence, his face towards the dark of the east where night unfurled her wings and settled them across the land. The owls took up sharp cries and called to one another in the forest.

With a start Skarry realised where they were and called for Catskin to halt as he ran to the head of the party. He took them a short distance off the path and they found a low stone shelter with a turf roof that was the Little Haven. Within was wood for fuel, dried foods and blankets. Skarry set to lighting a fire as the blackness thickened without. They did not talk much after eating of goat's cheese and wafer bread for they were all tired from the course of their day. Glimshpill fell straight asleep, curled up like a bear with his fur cloak tucked about him. He was already snoring and his nose glowed a deep red in the light from the fire. His war gear was piled in a corner and Skarry could not see how he would be ready if danger should threaten in the night.

'How do you think it goes with that fine lord Quorn?' Skarry asked Catskin before sleep.

The Corporal laughed and said, 'Who knows how it is with that madcap fool and whether he be living or dead? He would have done better to wait for Doth Auren; there is need of strong men in these times.'

Then Catskin turned on his side and was soon asleep. Skarry lay in the growing dark as the fire faded to embers and listened to the noises of the night. The cries of the owls were drowned beneath the rising howl of wind and he feared more snow.

Catskin's talk of Quorn surprised him for that lord seemed a brave warrior indeed to Skarry, yet the mention of the name of Doth Auren once more set his heart aglow. That he, Skarry of the Olluden, was on his way to Wenlok to meet and advise that great hero of Taur, surely this was a tale that would long be told around the fires of the forest people.

His dreams were troubled by a dark shape at the edge of sight. It had the sound of a hurt beast. He could not call it to come out so he might see, nor could he move towards it. He woke sweating, even in the cold of the morning.

The sky was lightening without sight of the sun. The mass of cloud continued to press in from the north and there were distant rumblings and occasional flashes from within the vapour. Yet it had not snowed again and Skarry felt they might still make Wenlok before the heavy falls.

He busied himself to clear the memory of the dream, cutting firewood with a small axe and stacking it to replace that which then had used. The rhythmic thud of axe on wood roused Ress and he turned to see her standing in the doorway of the Haven, holding to the posts and moving her head to catch the sound.

'Skarry!' She called, and again, 'Skarry!'

He went to her and gave her a morning greeting.

'Take me a little way,' she said and he led her carefully into the woods. The air was cold and in the night there had been a hard frost that gave an icy crunch to their footsteps. From within the trees a blackbird shrieked its startled cry and Ress smiled at the whirr of its wings. As they moved further from the path the woods closed in, the undergrowth piled with snow.

'It gets harder here,' said Skarry and they stopped, Ress turning to face him.

'We shall be parting soon,' she said, her pale blue eyes seeming to look over his left shoulder. The thought of her blindness awakened a sadness within him and fear for her safety.

'Can you not come to Wenlok with us, then go on to Ringdove?' he asked, but she shook her head.

'No, I cannot go to Wenlok.'

'Then I will come to Ringdove,' he said quickly, surprised at his own decision. Ress laughed and it was a bright laugh that lifted the weight of the morning.

'No,' she said, 'for the great Doth Auren has need of your counsel and knowledge of the mountains. But if after you have told him what you know, if then he has no further need of you, then you could come to Ringdove, if you so wished.'

Skarry looked into her face.

'This I would wish to do,' he said.

'Good,' she said simply. 'Take me back now. When you come to Ringdove, ask for the Dreamer, he will tell you where I am to be found.'

They walked slowly back to the Haven with their arms entwined and found the others awake and up, the Dreamer all set

49

and ready, Catskin tying on the saddle-bags and Glimshpill yawning monstrously.

'There will be evil today,' he growled between yawns. 'I can feel it in my aching bones.'

'More likely the lack of a soft bed caused that,' Catskin jibed.

'The danger is growing,' the Dreamer said seriously. 'If Quorn cannot hold the Pass then the enemy may be fast behind us, or already in front.'

'A happy thought to cheer the day,' said Glimshpill and spat into the snow.

Soon they were once more upon the road, Glimshpill at the head with a quieter song and his hand to the hilt of his sword. The Dreamer followed leading Ress on the second pony with Skarry and Catskin bringing up the rear.

For a time the path continued to fall and the trees grew even taller as the hills lowered towards the plain. Here were more ash and beech amidst the oaks, the pillars of their trunks rising upwards from the deeper soils, dividing and dividing to arch closed high above their heads. The view to the south was concealed by the web of their canopy, so black against the cloud.

In these lower lands the air was a little warmer than the mountain's blast and as the path levelled the way became wetter. The forest gave way to dense thickets of willow and alder, some fallen at awkward angles as they loosed their hold in the soft earth. At times the path was built up on a causeway that took them between dark pools. As the unseen sun strove to warm the air the snow turned first to slush and then mud that clung to each boot and hoof with a sucking grip.

'It smells dank,' said Ress.

'It is the Kirmire,' Skarry called to her.

'Not a pretty place,' Glimshpill muttered.

For Skarry this was a strange world, so damply different from the high forest of the uplands. He found himself staring out into the dark wet tangle to either side, straining to hear the slightest sound. Glimshpill's song became a soft whistling and he turned his head this way then that.

But beyond the dripping of water, the creaking of boughs and occasional birdsong there was nothing that hinted at danger. The branchings above drew apart to reveal the sky. The sun was hidden, just a pale, equal illumination. A cold drizzle began.

Ress it was who first heard more ominous sounds.

'Behind us, on the left of the path,' she called to Catskin over her shoulder. 'An animal, I think, for it sounds to have four legs.'

Catskin and Skarry stopped and peered out into the gloom but their sight could not penetrate the many thin trunks of alder and willow.

'Ah, the lass is hearing things,' said Glimshpill. 'It is understandable for one with her lack.'

Nevertheless, Catskin strung his longbow and notched an arrow, cursing the damp for it stretched the string. They went on more quietly. The birdsong had stopped and the two ponies began to blow nervously, twisting their ears about and turning their heads to look behind. Then Skarry too heard the sound of sucking mud as if feet or paws were withdrawn step by step from its clinging hold. It came from the rear, to their left as Ress had said and soon the others were aware of it also.

Glimshpill began to curse under his breath and swung down from his mount. The Dreamer moved forward to take the reins of his pony. He spoke softly to it and Ress's mount as they danced, their nostrils wide at some smell that came upon the breeze. As he talked they quieted a little and he drew them on. Up ahead the trees opened out and the stretches of dark water increased in size as they approached the Kirmire proper. The path lightened but low mists hung over the pools to either side. The noise grew louder and matched their quickened tread. They could hear clearly the splashing of mud and water as something came after them through the mire.

Glimshpill drank hastily from a bottle out of his saddle-bags, his gaze flashing between the marsh and his drink. His skin had paled and his lips were drawn out thin.

'What do you reckon?' he called to Catskin but the other did not answer. 'Not Ice Warriors surely,' he went on as if to himself. 'They would come down the track. A bear? Not in the bog. Ah, Vidar, give me an open field any day!'

As he spoke his face flushed and a vein began to beat at his temple. With a last loud curse he drew his sword with a rattle and leapt suddenly from the causeway and up to his knees in mud.

'Hurry yourselves!' he roared back at them and then, grim faced, lumbered off into the bog.

'Shouldn't we help him?' Skarry asked, as he stared after

Glimshpill. The mist swirled up about the soldier until all that could be seen was his helmeted head and arms raised clear of grasping branches, the sword a dull gleam in his hand.

'He is his own master,' said Catskin as they went on, yet he kept an eye on the spot where Glimshpill had disappeared and held his bow close to his side. Once more silence descended upon them save for their own panting and footsteps.

The silence was broken by a low howl off to their left that began as a wolf's then hardened to a thin shriek, echoing so high that Ress put up her hands to her ears.

'Hurry up there!' Catskin ordered grimly and they quickened their pace again.

From further off to their rear the call was answered. Then came loud crashings on the left that grew nearer. They started to trot down the track. The ponies snorted in fear and the Dreamer loosed Glimshpill's. It broke into a gallop and charged off ahead of them.

Catskin skipped sideways with his bow at the half-drawn, his eyes intent upon the willows whose branches began to whip about as if with a fierce wind. Skarry felt the air on his face first cold then hot and a stench that made Ress cover her nose.

Just as it seemed that the crashings could grow no louder, the low stockade of Mireside appeared up ahead through the mists. Skarry could not help but give a cry of relief as if already within this safety and as he did so the bushes and sedges at the roadside, so wildly whipping, were suddenly thrust apart. Catskin stopped instantly and swung round drawing his bow to the full. But as quickly he eased the tension without loosing the arrow for it was Glimshpill, all begrimed and panting yet his eyes bright with a sharp gleam. Catskin peered into the mists beyond him as the other heaved his soaking self back on to the track.

'Fear not, brave Catskin,' he gasped. 'For I have sent it packing with a small hurt to keep it occupied. Let us on to Mireside before it returns with its friends.'

The party hurried on the last of the way to the village though Catskin hung back with a cautious eye to the trees, his arrow still notched on the string.

Mireside was enclosed by a strong stockade of willow and alder, much of which had taken root and grown within the wall. Where the path ran up to this were two gates, one large to admit a cart and beside it a smaller human-sized entrance. Glimshpill's fleeing pony had awakened life within and amid shouts the large gates were thrown open, a dozen men rushing out with small round shields and short spears at the ready. When they saw the Bull of Taur on Glimshpill's breastplate they fell back on either hand to guard the way and so Catskin's party came to enter Mireside.

Inside the stockade the village of Mireside was revealed, a dozen timber framed buildings with mud walls and neatly thatched reed roofs save for the Moot House which was crowned with the dull red tiles from Topcliffe. To this the travellers were ushered.

'Ho there!' Glimshpill roared. 'Fresh from the fight come we, mighty warriors. A drink, a drink to quench our thirst!' And he strode off with a swagger to his step.

Skarry made to help Ress from her mount but she swung down easily and they walked together to the Moot House while the ponies were led away for feed and a rub down. At the door Skarry stopped for it was of black oak from the bog and carved in the likeness of the birds and beasts of the Kirmire.

'What is it?' Ress asked, for she heard his indrawn breath. He took her hand and pressed it against the carving and she smiled.

'The Olluden are carvers,' he said, 'yet this is the work of one from the marsh.'

Ress ran the very tips of her fingers over the feathers of heron, fur of otter, the saplings of willow entwined with honeysuckle.

'It is fine work,' she said, 'but I feel the warmth of a fire within.'

Holding her arm Skarry pulled back the door and they went inside. The walls were smooth and hung with brightly coloured mats of reed. There were benches and tables and a central fire burning in a round stone hearth.

A man welcomed them all and bid them sit on a long bench at a table where food had been set out. He was a tall creature with limbs so long and thin you would have thought them too fragile to support his body.

'I am Crane,' he said. 'Be welcome to our table.'

He spoke gently and Skarry helped Ress to her seat and showed her where to find the bread and her knife.

'It is long since we saw a brother of the blue robe,' Crane said softly to the Dreamer, and smiled. The Dreamer bowed his head in return. Catskin looked not so happy at this favour.

'We are making fast for Wenlok,' he said aburptly. 'This one,' and he nodded at the Dreamer, 'and the blind girl, will head for Ringdove.'

'They do not like the blind at Ringdove,' Crane said quietly. Skarry stopped eating.

'And here?' asked the Dreamer.

'We are a simple people,' said Crane, 'we in Mireside. In Ringdove they call us the tame Asgire to distinguish us from our wilder brethren who inhabit the Kirmire proper. But in the marshes our people put the new born blind in baskets and set them upon the waters to see if they will float.'

Skarry's mouth was an 'O' of horror at this and he looked anxiously at Ress.

'No doubt some of the ways of you Olluden would sound harsh to us, lad,' Crane went on. 'Yet the baskets are made of the bark of the birch and float as well as boats. It is an old game with us. Here in the marshes the blind are favoured, for the paths cannot be seen with the eyes. But in Ringdove they are locked up together with the dumb and the deaf and all those who are different.'

They ate in silence for a while, Skarry helping Ress to her food. Then there came the sound of a song drawing near and they turned to see Glimshpill roll through the doorway.

'You have strange visitors in your marsh,' he said to Crane and drawing his sword he threw it clattering down upon the table.

The others of the Asgire present muttered at this act but Crane made no sound or movement. The dull metal of the blade was blued as if it had been put within the heat of a furnace and there was a fresh notch towards the tip.

'We heard the call as you approached,' Crane said, 'nor was it the first.'

'Your people say they have lost two children in as many nights,' Glimshpill went on.

'That is so,' said Crane with a sad look. 'This is beyond our knowledge. There have been many tales of strange happenings on the marsh of late. There was an otter found with two heads this morning and at Mossbank four of their best fishers were taken from their boats within sight of the village.'

54

'What was following us?' Ress asked quietly.

'Not a beast that I have seen before,' said Glimshpill and sat heavily on the end of the bench.

'Was this creature like a bear?' Crane asked.

'Aye,' said Glimshpill. 'Like a bear, yet not a bear.'

'And did it burn you?'

'Not me, though I felt its heat and my blade carries the mark,' said Glimshpill and he pointed to the discoloured sword.

'Do your people know of this thing?' the Dreamer asked Crane.

'It is what took the children,' he replied grimly. 'It climbs the stockade and with its strong claws tears through the mud of our walls. It is as black as the shadow and until this day has only come with the night. Those who have felt its passage are burned but none has seen it save my boy, Lut, and now he does not speak.'

Crane's voice wavered as he spoke and he shook his head as if confused. 'These are times of great evil,' he went on softly. 'Things are not right with our world.'

'Monrolians!' Ress said vehemently. 'Their cursed magic has brought this about.'

'You must keep torches lighted,' said Catskin, 'and stand ready through the night with long spears and grapples.'

'We had hoped that you might stay,' Crane said, raising up his gaunt face to theirs. 'With two such brave warriors and a Dreamer we thought to end its ravage.'

Glimshpill looked questioningly at Catskin but the Corporal shook his head.

'Come now,' said Glimshpill. 'Surely it is but a little to ask after such hospitality. Anyway, it's cold without and shall be all the colder by night. We should at least have warm beds to sleep in.'

Catskin shook his head once more though this time it was at his own weakness rather than a refusal.

'It is to be hoped that others do not suffer through our delay,' was all he said.

'I cannot stay,' said the Dreamer, 'for my purpose relies on speed. I must get this lady to Ringdove; the knowledge she holds will further our cause.'

'Our cause?' growled Glimshpill. 'When there is fighting to be done you can bet that the blue robes will slink off. No matter, you would only get in the way.'

The Dreamer made no reply and finished his meal in silence.

'So you two will stay at the least?' Crane asked of Glimshpill and Catskin as if still not daring to hope.

'Aye!' said Glimshpill loudly. 'We will stay, marsh man, and no doubt we will kill your fearsome beast being as we are two heroes as of yore. Yet we will take three horses off you for our march tomorrow, a wage as it were.'

Crane allowed a smile upon his face and his eyes brightened as he nodded his agreement.

'You have a bargain, marsh lord,' said Ress. 'For as well as two mighty warriors you have the services of Skarry, guide and magician of the Olluden, who made fire from rock and water and knows the ways of the mountain.'

'Then indeed we are safe,' said Crane and his smile broadened. 'For many ages there has been peace between my people and the Olluden and we shall gain from having one of that race beneath our roof.' And he stood up and bowed low to Skarry like the marsh wader stooping to look within the water.

'My thanks for your kindness, sir,' Skarry managed round a mouthful of bread and returned the bow feeling the flush come to his cheeks.

The Dreamer laid his knife upon the bare plate before him and rose from the bench.

'We must leave you,' he said. 'I would be well on the way by nightfall.'

Crane led them out into the cooling air. The sky was a sea of cloud, grey and heavy with that yellow tinge to the horizon that presages imminent snow. The Dreamer sniffed at the breeze and pulled his blue robe tighter about him. The marsh people brought the two ponies out all groomed and fed and laden with saddle-bags containing food for the journey. Skarry made to help Ress mount but she sprung easily up into the saddle while the Dreamer tethered her pony to his own. It had come about so quickly that Skarry knew not what to say.

'Say nothing then,' said Ress, putting her fingers to his lips, 'save that you will see me in Ringdove.' Then she bowed her head as the Dreamer spoke softly to his pony and they started off.

'I will see you in Ringdove!' Skarry called, running a little way after them and raising his arm to wave. Then he lowered it again, feeling foolish. The two passed through the west gate, out on to the road to Ringdove. Then the Dreamer turned.

'Fear not, young Skarry,' he called back. 'I will watch over her. We will meet again, yet you must be prepared for change.'

With that they were gone from his sight and his heart felt empty and alone for it was a long and difficult road to Ringdove. Without thought his hand went to the stone about his neck and he raised it to his mouth.

'Hurry up, O stricken one!' came a sudden roar from the doorway that startled him so that he loosed the stone. 'There is much to prepare for the night's festivities,' Glimshpill went on and swigged noisily from a fresh bottle.

7

The Night Visitor

In the Moot House at Mireside the flames danced within the fire-pit and cast flickering shadows amongst the carvings and tapestries that hung upon the smooth mud walls. Most of the villagers were now inside the building and settling for uneasy sleep. The cries of the children were silenced with old songs while the menfolk strove to still their own inner disquiet by the closeness of their weapons.

Skarry sat by the fire-pit and toasted his toes; they had not been so warm in a long while. Crane sat opposite, his long legs folded beneath him, his arms cradling both his young son, Lut, and a wych elm spear. He spoke in a singing voice that carried to the furthest corners of the long house yet did not wake his sleeping child.

'In the old times, young Skarry,' he said, 'our peoples lived at peace with the world. The Olluden knew the forest as does the screech owl and bear. They knew where to find shelter should the rains be over long and which plants were good for the eating or healing. There was little need of meat save in times of hardship, for the forest gave in plenty what the Lords struggle to grow in fields. They were sufficient unto themselves and had no need to venture forth from their woods.

'And we, the Asgire, the marsh peoples of the Kirmire, we wove our boats of reeds and slipped silently through the narrow channels between the mud banks of the estuary and took fish with our spears or gathered shell creatures off the rocks at low tides. And there were nuts and berries and fruit to be collected and carefully stored for the winters. We were a proud people, a strong people who knew the ways of the marsh and might pass unharmed over swamp and bog.'

'You are dreaming, old man,' spoke up Glimshpill from his sprawling seat at the fire. 'There have always been wars; there will always be wars,' and he took up his stone and began to run it along the edge of his unsheathed sword. 'Listen to its song,' he said.

With each stroke of the stone it seemed the metal rang like a distant bell. Yet was the sound a lament, a keening.

'Can you not do that outside?' asked Crane, as the villagers stiffened to hear such a noise.

'It is cold without,' said Glimshpill simply and kept to his sharpening, working at the new notch until the edge gleamed like glass in the light of the fire.

Catskin came in at the door together with a blast of gale. He leaned his long bow against an upright and rubbed his thin arms as he neared the fire.

'It has begun to snow,' he said and crouched by the flames. 'Our journey tomorrow will be all the harder.' And here he cast a look at Glimshpill.

'You worry too much about tomorrow,' said Glimshpill, 'we probably won't even last the night out.'

'You shouldn't say things like that!' Skarry said quickly, but Glimshpill only laughed and taking a pouch from within his jerkin he nibbled at the contents. Catskin shook his head slowly.

'Give us a tale to speed the night,' he said to Skarry and settled himself at the fire.

So Skarry told of the end of the times of peace and the coming of Ymir who brought war upon the world that has not left since.

'Ymir came wandering through the starways,' he said, 'and looked longingly upon the stone globe which was now alive and green with growing things. He found Vidar in the south overstriding the Ridgeway and ordering the building of Xa Erzuran and later Ringdove. Vidar appointed lords to govern the lands and draw all peoples together as one. Yet in the north Ithunne sat in silence upon the Ulta-Zorn and watched the ice and snow, amazed at its bright beauty. The peoples of the north were wild and hunted seal, and even the Great Fish, from narrow boats made from skin and they killed any who stood in their way and ate of their flesh.

'So Ymir looked upon the lands of the north and felt a kinship with its fierce peoples and he tricked Ithunne and bound her. Some say he changed her into a great white cave bear and buried her, sealed within deep caverns below the Ulta-Zorn. He made his throne from these mountains and became ruler of the north, the god of war and treachery and deceit, and the peoples of that land came to worship him for he was strong.'

Glimshpill nodded his head throughout the telling and the moan of his sword was as a part of the story. When it was done Catskin rose up.

'It must be late,' he said.

'The moon is high,' Crane said in agrement, as though he could see her pale orb through the roof.

'It will not help us with these clouds,' Catskin continued. 'I will make a round.'

'I as well,' Glimshpill said and stood unsteadily. His eyes were shining with something other than the light of the fire.

When the two soldiers had gone Skarry looked once more at Crane, the marsh man. In the glow of the fire his tired face was sunken, the skin thin and tight over the bone. Cradled upon his crossed legs, Lut, his son, no more than three or four winters, was awake. Skarry's gaze met his and he was caught for a moment by the black pits of Lut's pupils. On a thong about the child's throat hung a pale blue stone, a perfect match in size and shape to Skarry's own.

'That is a fine stone you wear,' Skarry said quietly. Lut did not reply and though he returned the look it was as though he saw in a different way. Skarry was reminded of Ress, for Lut might have been looking over his left shoulder, gazing into an unknown distance.

'He will say nothing,' said Crane and stroked Lut's arm. Even that gentle contact brought a sudden fear to the boy's face.

'He saw something,' Crane continued, 'out in the marsh. Perhaps it was the beast your friends now stalk, perhaps another. It is ever the children who suffer.'

The frightened eyes flashed in the firelight and Lut clung the tighter to his father's legs.

'It will come all right,' said Skarry firmly, raising his open palm as if to a young pony. 'You will be safe.'

For a moment Skarry felt that there may have been a contact, that Lut almost smiled. Then his face once more took on the empty stare as though he were no longer prepared to look out upon so fearful a world. Skarry sank back exhausted by the strain. Again the blind gaze brought Ress to his mind and he felt saddened and somehow empty without her near. He thought of her on the way to Ringdove, that fair city spoken of in the old tales. Of the Olluden, only Gemel had been to Ringdove, many years back when he was a young man. The then Paladin had put out a command far over the land that craftsmen of all skills should come to undertake the restoration of the city after the Nine Winter War with Monrolia. Gemel, it was said, had carved the great Bull of Taur upon the doors to the council chamber in the Lord's Hall, though he himself never spoke of his work there. Yet he was glad to talk of the thin spires and gilt domes of the city at the end of a sack of wine when the embers of the fire glowed within the hearth.

Ringdove filled Skarry with such thoughts; it was as if the olden days had risen up in time to light the land once more. He would see that mighty warrior, the Paladin Guise, elected High Lord of all Taur and a fighter whose renown was told by all.

Yet first to Wenlok, to speak with the Lord of that place, the Doth Auren. Here was another name that kindled myths of old.

'Have you been to Wenlok?' he asked Crane. 'Have you seen Doth Auren?'

'I have seen D'Auren,' breathed Crane. 'He is a good man, for a lord. He has looked kindly upon the Kirmire and its peoples. Yet is he a troubled man for he is at the beck and call of Guise.'

The blast of cold air struck them both and turning they saw Catskin and Glimshpill return, their heads and shoulders rimmed with snow.

'You should shut the outer door before opening the inner,' Skarry said shivering. 'This is the difference between life and death on the mountains.'

Crane nodded in agreement with a smile upon his lips as the two soldiers hurried towards the fire. Skarry gave up his seat to them and taking blankets chose a place by the wall and curled himself up with his head pillowed upon a sack. Lut scrambled from his father's legs and came near to sleep though it was as if he could not look at Skarry.

Outside the noise of the storm intensified and the tiles rattled upon the roof. The light from the fire diminished and Skarry dozed fitfully, half awakening to see Crane stirring the embers and adding more wood. Catskin sat crosslegged with his head lowered, his bow cradled on his knees. Glimshpill paced about the fire with his sword unsheathed and his eyes bright as if with rage.

Skarry drifted into a dreaming sleep and found himself in a darkness like that of a cave, so black, with the thought that Ress was lost somewhere and that he must find her. Somewhere in the deeps something stirred and growled horribly. The fear wakened him again and feeling cold about his neck he hunched down within his blankets, rolling more to his side.

The wall was before his face, brought to life by the flickering glow of the fire. He became absorbed by the pattern for it conjured many images within his head. First, the forests of the Hanging Valley grew from the shadows, the tops of the trees whipping in the gale. Then all Ringdove appeared before him with its spires so bright in the morning sun. Yet the lime-washed walls blackened as with a fungus and the spires toppled. The tallest of the towers wavered and trembled and there came the noise of a distant scratching. Skarry struggled on the border of sleep but could not rouse himself. A paler shadow to one side resolved itself into the face of Lut, his eyes wide and staring. The spire seemed to melt and re-form and become a lengthening claw that forced itself through the hard mud of the wall. About the claw the mud blackened deeper than the night and Skarry felt heat upon his face.

But he could not move; he was frozen half in his sleep with this growing nightmare before him. A web of dark cracks spread about the claw and the mud began to crumble. Pieces fell pattering to the floor as the single claw enlarged the hole. Then a lump the size of Glimshpill's great fist broke loose to reveal the glow of a fire without. Skarry's heart seemed to rise up in his throat and stop his breathing with its hammering; his body began to shake with terror as the wall bulged inwards.

It was Lut who broke the silence with a sudden shrill screaming that awakened further echoes as others were roused from sleep, and with the scream Skarry was at once fully awake. He rolled away from the wall just as a large section collapsed and there came the roar of the storm, loud within the hall, together with a howl that began as a wolf's and ended as a high shriek. It was repeated and from out of the dust and snow and piled plaster, from out of the darkness, enclosed within its own fire, came that which they had waited for.

62

By the fire-pit Glimshpill was momentarily halted, one booted foot poised in mid-stride as he looked towards the noise. Then, as the creature repeated its awful shriek, a roar of his own rose up from his stomach and his eyes burned bright as torches as he over-leapt the fire and bore down upon it, his sword singing its own fearsome song as it scythed the air.

Between the two Skarry crawled away, his mind unable to think. He might have mistaken it for a giant bear had it not been for the single huge claws upon each forefoot and the terrible heat that emanated from within its body. There was a glimmer of gold at its neck.

Then Glimshpill was at it and it howled as his sword carved its chest. Yet with the blow there came a cloud of vapour and sparks and Glimshpill was thrown back with his sword once more notched and purple with the heat. His face was red with fury as he rose and the veins at his neck and temples pulsed with blood. Again he drove forward, voicing his battle cry and thrusting with the blade for where the heart might be. This time the Auf bear caught at his sword with its claw and there came the piercing shriek as of metal against metal and Glimshpill was hurled to the ground.

It stood up upon its hind legs and its broad head brushed the rafters and set sparks amongst them. The blankets upon which it stood burst into flames and it towered over the cowering Skarry. The hall was full of screams and the cold blast from without alternated with the heat of the creature's breath. It surveyed the scene then stooped its head towards him.

Once more his body listened not to his mind and he lay helpless before its growing face, the eyes like hot metal at the smith's, so bright it pained to look on them.

At the last, the left eye was suddenly eclipsed and the creature screamed and Skarry smelled its fetid breath. Then the right eye too was dimmed and Skarry saw the feathered shafts of Catskin's arrows before they burst into flame. It fell back shaking its great head from side to side and Crane came driving at it with his wych elm spear and struck it to the right of the breastbone, forcing the point home. Glimshpill was up also, lunging with his sword and pushing together they toppled the beast backwards and out of the hole it had made, once more into the darkness.

Then there was but the sound of the gale and quiet sobbing.

Someone stirred the embers of the fire to life and set up burning torches. Others looked to the fires it had started in the fight and soon put them out. Snow blew in and the air rapidly cooled.

Setting aside his bow, Catskin came over to Skarry and helped him to his trembling feet. Together they went to Glimshpill who stood with Crane at the hole it had torn in the wall, looking out. In the darkness of the night the body of the creature could be made out as a darker shadow. The snow had at first melted about it but now, as the body cooled, the drifts gathered in its lee.

'It is a Firebolg,' Crane whispered, 'a changed bear. See the collar upon it? The sign of an evil man's work.'

Glimshpill went out and removed the golden collar, cursing as the remaining heat scorched his fingers. When he was once more within they fixed blankets across the hole and so stopped the wind.

To one side sat Lut, crying silently, the tears flowing down his cheeks. As if remembering him suddenly, Crane knelt at his side and tried to comfort him but to no avail.

'It is over, my son,' he spoke urgently. 'There is nothing more to fear.'

But Skarry sank down before the child and put up his hands to Lut's shoulders.

'He weeps that you had to kill the bear,' he said, as if just realising his own sorrow. Lut looked him straight in the eyes and let loose his anguish in great wails. He rose up and fell into Skarry's arms and the other hugged him to his chest and wept also.

At the fire-pit Glimshpill took up a fresh wine-skin and drank swiftly as though to quench the fires that burned within his eyes.

8

Road to Wenlok

Skarry washed shivering at a bucket of water in one corner of the Moot House. He had not dreamed that night, as if the fight with the Firebolg had enough of the nightmare about it to satisfy his sleep. He had been awakened early by the chattering of Lut who seemed set to make up for his days of silence and followed Skarry about eagerly explaining the world and all its concerns. Crane delighted in the sounds of his son's voice and Mireside rose for the new day with the feeling of festivity high in the minds of its people.

Glimshpill had the look of one only half alive and began the day with a long pull at the wine-sack as though seeking to replenish the energy he had spent in the battle. As the villagers prepared dishes of food for a feast he eyed them sullenly and cast long glances at Catskin as though willing him to tarry a little longer. But the Corporal hurried about making ready to leave, tacking up three strong marsh ponies and filling the saddle-bags with food.

'We must take this to Ringdove,' Catskin said, coming in with the heavy gold collar from the beast in one hand, 'to show the Dreamer,' he continued. 'He will know more of these things.'

For a moment Skarry thought he meant that they would go straight to the city and found himself suddenly torn between his desire to meet the Doth Auren and one no less strong to see Ress again.

'But first to Wenlok,' Catskin went on. 'D'Auren must be told of the enemy at the High Pass.'

Glimshpill groaned loudly and struggled to his feet.

'You would have thought a hero might have a day or so to rest before his next exploits,' he said gloomily, but then brightened somewhat as the marsh people nearby gave little cheers at the sound of his voice, some coming close to clap him upon the back.

65

The three gathered together their few possessions and were soon ready to leave. Outside it had snowed much in the night yet the winds had kept it from the track and piled it against the low trees and bushes of the marshlands. The sound of cracking ice rose up from the pools to either side and a thin mist lent a haze to the distances around them, the low hills receding to the north, the wide expanse of flats to the south.

All the village gathered to see them off, some of the people beating at small hand-drums, others sounding long echoing notes upon their marsh horns. Glimshpill seemed to wake up as the younger girls of the Asgire danced about him and hugged him, striving to make their arms encompass his girth. 'Demon-slayer' they called out to him and 'Peace-bringer' and he tilted back his head and put a swagger to his stride.

At the last, as they mounted and sat ready in the saddle a hush came over the village as Crane came out. At first, Skarry almost did not recognise him for he wore the heron cloak of a marsh lord that fluttered winglike in the breeze, a richness of blues and greens with a sheen of grey to it; each feather had been found, for the Asgire would do no hurt to the heron. Upon his head rose up a cap that clung to the contours of his skull, painted in the likeness of the crane from which he took his name, with sharp eyes staring from the temples and the beak thin and pointing. On his forehead was a blue stone of the Asgire, so blue as to appear a window looking into the summer sky.

'We give thanks,' Crane said, and the song of his voice floated over the gathered company, 'to you who brought us great aid in our times of need and to Ithunne who, though bound, ever listens for those of her people who call upon her.'

The Asgire loudly shouted and once more sounded their horns, some breaking into wild dances, laughing. Crane came over to the three and thanked each in turn, first Catskin then Glimshpill.

'Young forester of the Olluden', he said quietly when he came to Skarry and Lut trotted over also, his cheeks glowing redly in the cold of the morning.

'I say my farewell to you with great joy, Skarry,' the marsh lord said and he laid his hand upon Lut's tousled head. 'And I thank you for all that you have done and that which you will do.'

Skarry bowed his head to Crane and could think of nothing

that he might say. Looking down thus, his gaze met that of Lut who laughed up at him and stretched out his short arm, clutching a fold of cloth within the little hand. Skarry reached out and received the gift opening the cloth to find within the blue stone from Lut's own neck.

Skarry undid the thong round his throat and threaded the marsh stone on to it. Holding up the ends of the thong the two stones hung together, the green of the Olluden veined with quartz, the blue of the Asgire lightly flecked with a glitter of emerald green. And then he tied them about his neck, feeling the new weight against his skin.

'My thanks, Lut of the Asgire,' he said solemnly, leaning from his saddle. 'I pray that we shall meet again.' Almost he had prayed to Ithunne yet the name would not rise from his throat. Lut laughed and jumped on the spot, caught at Skarry's hand and first kissed it then bit it so that Skarry yelped in mock hurt.

'Farewell Skarry of the Olluden,' Crane said raising his left hand, the palm open. 'I will remember you.'

The horns sounded, their deep vibration passing through the air and making the ponies prick their ears. Catskin turned his to the gate and led off, Glimshpill and Skarry following with the sounds of farewells loud in their ears. Through the gate the road to Wenlok stretched straight and empty away before them. Skarry turned once to wave to those behind, Crane and Lut framed by the main gateway; beyond them, within the stockade, already the dancing was beginning in earnest. Turning once more to the south he felt the weight of the unknown.

To the east, on their left, the early mists dissipated to reveal the huge sweep of the Kirmire stretching away to north and south. The land was broken into innumerable islands by the lace of streams and brooks. Often the division between land and water was not clear and here were the tufts of reeds and sedges of the bogs. Occasional rises like barrows thrust up from the flats and here the larger trees could grow, homes of the herons and storks.

To Skarry's eyes, it first appeared a bleak and open place with none of the shelter of the rolling hills and thick woods. Yet at the same time he felt that there was a wild and haunting beauty in that wilderness and almost he would have liked to leave the road, to go out on to the marsh, open beneath the vast expanse of sky.

All that morning they went on at an easy pace. Glimshpill soon finished his wine and resorted to songs as though to keep from thinking. Ever and again Catskin would wheel his pony about and trot back the way they had come for some hundred paces before returning.

'What do you fear?' Skarry asked.

Catskin laughed at the question. 'There is not sun enough to tell you by day all that I fear,' he said. 'But in particular, at this moment, I would not like to think that another Auf bear might be on our trail.'

This was not a pleasant thought to Skarry's mind for there had indeed been two cries when they first heard the creature, it was foolish to pretend otherwise. That there could well be more, even a pack, did nothing to ease his disquiet. Skarry pushed his pony on and she trotted forwards to draw level with Glimshpill.

'How far to Wenlok?' he asked urgently.

'Far enough!' Glimshpill gave a loud laugh. 'What? Are you afeared, mighty forester?'

'No more than any,' Catskin said quietly. 'Yet we will not have to journey alone for much longer.' And he pointed up ahead to where the sides of the causeway drew together in the distance. Sure enough, there was the black shadow of men upon the way.

'They will be going to Wenlok,' growled Glimshpill. 'Doth Auren has a nose for danger, he will be gathering his forces.'

Quickening the pace to a canter the three went on, the ponies tossing their heads to be moving faster. The shadow of men grew and became five in number with a cart drawn by two ponies. These others turned on hearing the drumming hoofs and not recognising the three, they put down their hands to their swords while some strung arrows to their bows.

'Fear not!' Glimshpill called in a voice that rolled away across the open mire. 'Fear not, for we are brothers of the summer, the Corporal Catskin and that mighty warrior Glimshpill whose name is spoken in reverent whispers at the fireside!'

The five looked at one another bemused but put up their weapons at the least. Coming closer Skarry saw that they were marsh men warmly clad in breeks and jerkins. They carried strong short bows of wych elm and light wicker shields and their cart was piled with javelins and bundles of arrows. Their leader looked hard at each of the newcomers in turn. He wore a plain metal helmet that seemed ill-fitting when compared to the softness of his features. His gaze took in the stones at Skarry's neck and it was to him that he at last spoke in a gentle voice

'Greetings to the Olluden, young forester,' he called, 'and welcome to a friend of the Asgire.'

Skarry replied in kind and asked of the marsh man his name.

'I am Hauk of Mossbank,' he said, 'and we make for Wenlok and from there to Ringdove, for the High Lord, the Paladin Guise, has called a muster to defend the land.'

Catskin and Glimshpill exchanged looks of disbelief. 'Then let us pass,' said the Corporal grimly. 'We must reach D'Auren, for Ringdove is not threatened, the enemy is behind us.'

Hauk's mouth fell open and the other marsh men stared into the distance of the north. Catskin pushed his pony on, going to one side of the cart and set off at a canter towards the south, Skarry's pony followed of its own with Glimshpill at the rear.

'You would do better to stay at home!' Glimshpill called to them as he passed. 'Grimal Skoye himself is at their head.'

They rode on leaving the marsh men in consternation. One tried to leap from the causeway as if to run off through the marsh but Hauk clung to his arm arguing. The feeling of panic rose once more in Skarry for in his desire to see Wenlok and the Doth Auren he had forgotten their purpose and the danger. He would have put his stone within his mouth had he not needed both hands on the reins.

The three rode now in silence, Catskin keeping them to a fast trot until Glimshpill's mount began to tire. At a slower pace, they came upon more of the Asgire with similar carts laden with spears and arrows that they had spent many a long evening fashioning beside the fire. Others walked alone, trailing their spears in the slush, backs bowed with an unseen burden. Some hailed them, others said nothing and more gave them only a suspicious stare.

'These are light warriors,' Glimshpill explained to Skarry. 'They would but take the flanks in any battle or perhaps the front to soften up an enemy.' He hitched his sword belt up about him and leaned form the saddle to spit.

Skarry rode with open mouth for he had never been with so many men before, even in Dunan when he had gone over the mountain with the Olluden to help with the shearing at Midloth. He counted over a hundred before he gave up. Occasional tracks drew in from the west to meet up with the causeway bringing people of the Hars lands, not the Epona proper but those who lived upon the fringes of the great plains. They had clothes of tanned leather sewn with metal plates at the shoulders and carried spears and curved swords. They had thick beards and moustaches and their skins were lined and burned with the sun though now their breath steamed about their faces.

From the growing press Skarry sensed that they neared their destination and at last he made out the points of pale spires over the horizon that rose steadily, climbing upward so delicate and faintly blue as though mixed with the stone of the Asgire. His eagerness increased as they climbed a low hill and the causeway became a track once more. And then, at last, as they reached the crest, spread there before them lay Wenlok that was also the City of Summer.

Skarry would have paused there to drink in the sight but Catskin urged them on. Yet Skarry strove to note every detail as they rode up to the city, that the Olluden might hear from his lips how the towers reached up, their walls drawing in to sharp points that seemed to scratch and tear at the clouds of winter and let forth the heavy snows. How the pale blues and greens of their stones lay so soft upon the land and blended with the distant horizons of marsh and plains and sky.

Yet he was distracted from the city by the turmoil about it for the gathering army was marshalled this way and that. The carts and waggons were ordered to one meadow, foot soldiers to another. Here were field kitchens feeding the hungry soldiers and occasional horsemen, brightly coloured cloaks fluttering, galloped from place to place. A babble of sound rolled up at them.

Towards the main gateway and its flanking towers there stood a stout captain, tall in the stirrups of a grey charger. With a short staff he ordered and directed the new arrivals. Catskin hailed him when they came within earshot and the other took a moment to look them up and down, noting the Bull of Taur upon the soldiers' breastplates.

'You are a long way from Ringdove,' he said and there was the hint of a sneer to his face.

'We have come over the Pass with news of Fressingfield and the enemy,' Catskin said simply, then added, 'and Quorn.'

70

The Captain raised his brows. 'If you have news of Quorn you had best go in,' he said. 'We have been awaiting him and his company these last two days.' Then he gave a laugh and a shake of his head. 'Yet you are a mixed trio!' he said.

'Thy ignorance as to who we are is forgotten,' growled Glimshpill. 'Thou wilt soon be enlightened on that account for within the hour these sorry soldiers,' and here he indicated the gathering army, 'will be singing songs of our fresh deeds.'

The Captain looked thoughtful and ordered a soldier at his foot to lead them within. So Skarry passed beneath the high arch of the main gate of Wenlok and entered within a city of his dreams.

Inside the walls the noise was greater still, channelled by the high-sided streets. And so too the press of people hurrying back and forth, not just soldiery but citizens and merchants who had no choice but to strive to continue their day. Up above, from tall windows and balconies pale faces looked downward to observe the rushing throng. Their guide led them deep within the city, turning this way then that through a maze of streets, past taverns and shops the like of which Skarry had never known. Here was not the squat grey rock of Midloth but rather colour and fine stonework with the carved heads of dream-like beasts at corners, dragons with spread wings and open-mouthed lions.

They came at last to a courtyard before a tower so tall that Skarry near fell off over his pony's rump with leaning back to see the top. Many roads met here and wide steps climbed from a deep pavement to a black oak door. To either side stood more soldiers, not the light infantry of marsh or plain but warriors true, to Skarry's eyes, all covered in plate armour and carrying the round shields of Wenlok emblazoned with the three ears of wheat, gold on green. Their swords were sheathed, yet behind them leaned tall shafts that marked them as the élite spearmen.

Here their guide left them after a word with these guards. Glimshpill chose to ignore them and surveyed the courtyard until they were ushered through the oaken doorway and found themselves within that great tower which some have called Forlorn Keep. With the closing of the doors there came a sudden quiet and they stood a moment as their eyes grew used to the gloom.

They were given little time to stare about, for a short fellow in bright green breeches and a blue shirt came straight to them and asked of their business, peering up at the towering Glimshpill. When he heard Quorn mentioned he was off, urging them to follow, upstairs and along corridors accompanied by the regular stamp and clank of two more guards.

The party swept suddenly into a high vaulted room whose furthermost corners were lost in shadows. The two guards with them stamped to attention and held the rigid pose. In the northern wall were three arched windows that looked out into the distant haze of cloud and billowing snow that now masked the Ridgeway. And here, framed by the centre arch such that he was but a silhouette, stood one whom Skarry knew by instinct to be that noble lord, the Doth Auren. There was the air of a sacred place in that room and for a moment none broke the stillness as though the Doth had just paused in mid-sentence. From without the noise of the army was thin and feeble.

'I cannot see the Angsoth,' came the quiet voice of the Doth and Skarry's heart eased in its furious beating at the gentleness of the tone. 'Even in summer I can see no further than my own devices.'

There was a cough from the shadows to the back of the hall and here Skarry could make out the shapes of robed figures, some seated, by a long table all bestrewn with papers and quills.

'What say you?' Doth Auren called over his shoulder. 'What answer can the sages give?'

From the darkness came a voice in reply, 'My lord, the old tales say all is as it should be; war is ever our way.'

D'Auren laughed, a sad sound. 'The answer of the armoured knight, divorced from the womb of our world.' he laughed a second time. 'Our world.'

'Is it not so?' one of his council asked but the Doth made no reply.

Then he said, 'We must wage war again, yet again. We must gird ourselves in the armour of our blindness, the weapons of our making and march out to fight others like ourselves.'

'We must to war,' one agreed, 'for the cowardly enemy will burn our homes and slay our cattle.'

Doth Auren was silent and then speaking so softly that Skarry strained to catch each word he said, 'They have burned our homes for which we laboured so long and yet our homes are in truth empty. It is not a thing which we have yet found. So must we burn their homes? And slay their cattle?'

'Aye, lord!' they cried eagerly for they missed his tone and flew beyond the mark and the fever bit within their brains as they gathered up their papers and gear. The guards gave a deep shout and raised a mailed fist each towards the ceiling. Catskin at last stepped forward as though tired of waiting.

'My lord,' he said, 'We come from Fressingfield. He has met with Skoye, the Misery of Ice.'

At this there was still greater stir and the council closed with the three but D'Auren held up his arm to stay their questions.

'You have your business to attend to,' he told the councillors and they left muttering. The guards he ordered outside and then he bid the three be seated at the long table. He himself sat opposite them, the narrow width of the table between them.

'You must tell me what you know,' he said simply.

9

Doth Auren

'Catskin, sir, Corporal of the Guard at Ringdove under the direct orders of the High Lord, the Paladin Guise.'

Skarry started at the string of titles that issued from the thin bowman's mouth and watched the Doth for his reaction. He sat easily in an oaken chair the arms of which were deeply carved with the likeness of the birds and beasts of marsh and plains. His long fingers nestled amid the forms of otters and lions and stroked at their heads.

His face was slim and pale and the skin of it seemed stretched over the close bone. His eyes were as dark as his hair and there was little difference between iris and pupil. Apart from nodding for Catskin to continue he appeared as if frozen and Skarry could read no trace of emotion in his features.

'Myself,' said Catskin, 'and my most loyal companion, were sent by the High Lord Guise to Midloth, to order Fressingfield make safe the land before winter. That lord Fressingfield thereupon set out for Cassan Keep in order to hold control over the Isthmus. Yet was he too slow, for the enemy, under the command of Grimal Skoye himself, had already taken the Keep and was within our borders.

'The most noble lord Fressingfield took it upon himself bravely to attack the enemy, coming upon him in Dunan Dale and believing him to be without horses. In the end this mattered little for the Osilo Ice Warriors slaughtered his cavalry, dragging the riders from their mounts with grapples and hooked pikes in the first snows of winter and pushed his army up the Dale towards the Pass. His line began to crumble even as he sent us hurriedly off for aid. Yet he hoped somehow to break off the battle and fall back to hold the High Pass.'

D'Auren stroked at his lank hair and asked after Quorn.

'The lord Quorn,' said Catskin, 'we met above the Elkhorn.

When he heard our news, which we laboured hard to bring him, he thought fit to take himself up the Pass and see for himself. He has not been heard of since.'

The Doth stood slowly with a shake of his head and turned once more to his high window.

'I have a letter here,' he said, taking it from his tunic and waving it in one hand, 'that came yesterday, from the High Lord himself. He does desire me strongly to go with all speed, and all my army, to a great muster at Ringdove, there to decide the battle plans of the whole land and, no doubt, march off as one to greet the Monrolian visitors.'

Glimshpill snorted loudly and turned it into a fit of coughing that spun the Doth round upon his heel. His face was as rigidly calm as before and Skarry had no clues as to the thoughts that hurtled through the mind of one so troubled, save that his eyes flickered slightly from side to side.

'He is our High Lord,' Doth Auren said, 'and your commander. No matter his faults, you should not treat him with disrespect.'

'I meant no harm, lord,' Glimshpill said with his head low and then another voice turned them as one to the doorway.

'Should you take your army to Ringdove,' she said, as she entered, 'it leaves the whole of the south undefended and Skoye will do it; he will bring his Ice Warriors over the High Pass, even in the thick of winter. They will find the land empty; they will burn this city.'

She wore a long dress against the cold, green and hanging in many folds with the train looped over her left arm. Skarry's outward gaze first fastened upon her then blurred with the ripple of light and shade as she came within the room. In his mind's eye he could see suddenly the view from Ice Back with the black hordes of Monrolia clambering eagerly upward for the Pass. At the summit they put on their short skis and hurtled headlong downward, for the south, for Wenlok.

'Don't go, sir!' he blurted without thinking, but the Doth only laughed.

'It is the High Lord who commands me,' he said softly. 'His word is the law. To refuse would be to set all Taur against me, calling me traitor, as well as leaving me to face the enemy alone.'

'What is this name, traitor?' she spoke again and they were

turned once more towards her, as the lodestone is drawn to the north. Glimshpill lowered his head as though to avoid her eyes.

'It is but a word,' she went on, 'no worse than any other. And what is so good about this High Lord, this Guise whom you would leap to serve. Here is where your heart is, not Ringdove!'

Catskin broke in suddenly, cutting off her further speech.

'There is more news,' he said urgently to the Doth. 'Simple soldiery is not all we face. The flesh eater, Malkah, has been at work upon the Pass, at the Maen-hir. This lad has seen her magic and we have felt its power.'

So saying he took his bag and drew forth the collar of the Firebolg that glowed brightly gold and seemed even now to radiate warmth. Doth Auren took the collar carefully, holding it lightly between pale fingers.

'My way is clear,' he said at last and the others started to hear the sad ring of his voice break the silence. 'Skoye was ever my foil and I must go to meet him, whatever the consequences.Perhaps Fressingfield and Quorn are still fighting somewhere in the mountains; it may be my destiny to bring them out alive from their foolish traps.'

'And who will save you from yours?' the woman hissed at the Doth, coming close by the table. 'You know that this war is wrong and yet still you seek battle. Stay here! This is your place. Let them fight it out themselves.' But as though she knew her words to fall unheard she had turned and began to leave as the Doth replied.

'I am a Soldier,' he said. 'It is not my choice, yet I am a warrior.' Then she was gone and the Doth sighed loudly and shook his head.

'I will write to Guise to explain my action. It may be that he will understand.' He did not sound hopeful to Skarry. 'Still,' he went on, 'I will need someone to deliver the letter.'

Glimshpill was on his feet immediately, snapping to attention with a clatter of armour.

'My lord!' he said. 'If I may be so bold, I am as fair and worthy a post man as will be found upon the land.'

'I will need help of a more spiritual kind also,' the Doth continued. 'Whoever takes the letter must persuade a Dreamer to come to the Pass, for we will need more than just swords to overthrow the enemy.'

'Give me thy letter,' said Glimshpill eagerly, 'and thy words and I shall deliver both and persuade not just a Dreamer, but Guise himself and all his men to march swiftly to your aid!'

D'Auren laughed. 'You have the task,' he said, 'and your Corporal with you.'

At this both Glimshpill and Catskin could barely conceal their relief.

'And I, sir?' Skarry asked, unable to contain himself and not knowing whether he wished to go on to Ringdove and Ress or back to the mountains with this brave lord, maybe to save the land.

'You have a harder doom to choose,' said D'Auren, 'for if a Dreamer will come to my aid then will he need a good and courageous guide to bring him safely to my side, one who can move swiftly on the mountains without being seen, even should he go beneath the very nose of the enemy.'

'It is where he is least likely to look, lord,' said Skarry without thinking and the Doth was forced to laugh once more.

'You are of the Olluden by the looks,' he said, 'yet you wear the stone of the Asgire also. Sometime you may tell me of your history. But now we have done with talk for we are decided. The night is yours yet tomorrow we will be on the road, I to the mountains and the enemy, you to Ringdove. The time for action draws upon us.'

As he spoke his face coloured with the rising blood and he became quick and certain in his movements. He spun upon his heel, the short cloak swirling at his shoulders and was gone from the room with the purpose of the marsh harrier that, sharp eyed, has sighted its prey.

Catskin and Glimshpill fell to congratulating themselves, clapping each other upon the shoulders that they did not have to go back to the Pass and the enemy. Skarry was left feeling not a little bemused and wondering where to go until one of the guards poked his head in at the doorway and called to lead them to their quarters. Of the woman in green nothing was said.

They were rushed once more through the vastness of the Keep, the only light coming from the narrow windows that peered out high above the gathering army, its angry chatter rising up to them like the buzzing of insects. Close beneath the spired roof, they were shown a small room each where there was a bed and a jug of water with a bowl should they choose to wash. Glimshpill and Catskin bade him farewell and set off to seek out a tavern while Skarry went into his room. He made straight for the window, opening wide the shutters and wrapping himself tighter within his jerkin against the stiff breeze.

The window looked west, the direction he would take in the morning, out over the Hars plains of the Epona that in summer was called the sea of grass. It had a soft look to it, this land, stilled in a gentle swell beneath the white snow, the low rise of hills receding into a distance of pale fire as the sun dipped at last below the cloud. To the north, Skarry's moutain was concealed by thick snow clouds that bore down upon the city. And below, the fair Wenlok with the spires falling away from his height, banners fluttering, the camps of the soldiers beyond the walls marked by many fires as night drew on them.

There came a quiet knock at the door and as he turned the lowering sun cast a last shaft of red gold that passed through the window and struck the woman in green as she entered. And in that second he thought it to be his mother, for there was a similar care in her stance as she looked within to see if he might be asleep. Yet the vision passed and he breathed again.

'I have brought you a hot drink and some supper,' she said when she saw the bed empty and him by the window. 'I am Lentua. Please forgive my hasty words before.' And she looked directly into his eyes such that he felt that she was indeed asking him forgiveness.

'I did not really understand what you were saying,' was all he could manage before that open gaze. 'Thanks for the food.'

He sat upon the bed to eat and Lentua leaned to one side of the window and looked out.

'He is not a bad man, the Doth,' she said quietly as though to herself. Skarry stopped in his eating at the words. 'He does only what he thinks to be right,' she went on. 'The other lords hate him because he is Steward of the south and has shown care towards the old races. They plot against him. His failure to go to the muster will be fatal to him. The High Lord will not stand for that. He was to marry his daughter to settle the squabbling once and for all but that will not come about now.'

'Yet you did not want him to go to the muster,' said Skarry.

'No, I do not want him to go to the muster, yet nor do I want him to go against Skoye. He is caught up in this war, he does not even see that he has no place in it. Look," she said, and drew him to the window. 'Can you still see? Down by the west gate, there is a great waterwheel, twenty paces across and each bucket as wide as a bed. It dips in the waters of the Elkhorn that run cold off your mountains. Though it may seem slow and sluggish in its ponderous turnings, such is its bound up force that should the river run dry in a night, the wheel would turn on and on. Some say that the wheel drives the river, pounding its waters into waves that echo in the distant ocean's tides.'

They were silent. Skarry stared out into the twilight and watched the huge wheel turning. Almost he could hear each slap as the buckets beat at the river and drove it on its course, but the babble of the army confused all sounds.

Lentua left soon after and Skarry settled for sleep, his food finished. Closing the shutters he lay in the darkness and listened to the thin shouts and commands rising up from below. He found that his previous excitement had dimmed and he longed for Ress to be there to talk with.

Sleep came soon and he passed the night soundly until the first light of morning roused his sleeping self to dream. Ress had been thrust into some dark cavern and he was alone at the top of a long flight of steps. He moved his feet so cautiously in the gloom and felt for the edge of each tread. She was below him somewhere, this he knew. Then he was at a doorway, an ancient door of black oak all bestudded with iron and a heavy metal ring to pull. Yet he could not bring himself even to raise a hand to the ring for fear of what might be beyond. A cold wind began to blow through the cavern carrying the smell of evil. He cried out and found suddenly that the woman in green was standing silently at his left shoulder, waiting patiently for him to ask her help.

Skarry woke sweating with fear, sitting upright in his bed. The shutters had been thrown open to admit light and the shouts of warriors, the smell of smoke.

'I did not mean to wake you,' came a quiet voice by his ear and Skarry found Lentua kneeling with a bowl of hot oats.

'I was dreaming,' Skarry said and rubbed at the remaining sleep in his eyes.

'You called out,' said Lentua. 'You called upon Ithunne in your sleep.'

Skarry turned his face away.

'You have nothing to be ashamed of,' Lentua continued. 'Ithunne is a fair goddess; she it is who will save us, if any.'

'You sound like my mother,' said Skarry.

'Then is she a wise woman also,' Lentua replied with a smile and turned to go. 'There's oats and milk to break your fast. Safe passage on your way, Skarry of the Olluden.'

'Will I then not see you again?' Skarry asked suddenly anxious. 'When we set out?'

She shook her head and said, 'I will not watch him go. I care for him too much.' And she left with her face lowered, closing the door behind her.

Skarry leapt up from the bed and in two strides was at the window with the blanket drawn about his shoulders. Outside the army had grown in the night and the land about the walls of Wenlok had been churned to mud by the comings and goings of the squadrons of foot soldiers, the troops of cavalry and the many waggons and carts all piled with gear of war. The smoke from the fires lent a veil to the sight and large flakes of snow billowed in the gusting wind. All over the field standards were raised that drew men to them like shelter in times of storm and rivalled the attraction of the fires.

'Come on, young Dreamer!' came a sudden bellow and a heavy hand that clutched his shoulder and nearly toppled him from his perch. It was the laughing Glimshpill all dressed in winter gear, a cloak as big as a small sail wrapped about him. 'Let's be off before he changes his mind and takes us with him. Things are hotting up around here.'

'There would be great glory in going with the Doth,' Skarry said.

'You eat your oats,' said Catskin. 'Glory is not something that we choose.'

While Skarry ate his breakfast then dressed, the two soldiers stood at the window, Glimshpill laughing uproariously as he spied a Captain taking a tumble in the mud. When Skarry was ready they left the room and were taken by an armed guard down through the bustling tower to the courtyard before its main doors. Coming out once more into the light made them stop and shade their eyes.

Yet to Skarry it seemed at first that it was not so much the light of the day after the dark of the tower's many stairs and passages, but rather the glory of the figure standing central in the courtyard that made them pause and bow their heads.

First there was a grey gelding of the Hars plains who looked like a stallion so thick and arched was the crest on his neck. His sleek coat was alive with the ripple of muscle and his eyes gleamed, his ears pivoting to point towards the three as they came down the steps.

Upon his broad back in a plain leather saddle sat a warrior, all girt in black armour that reflected no light and seemed as a shadow save where it was lined with white and the three ears of wheat in white upon the chest. The Doth rested easy in the saddle as though grown there, loosely holding the reins with one hand and under the other arm a helm formed in the likeness of a dragon's head so real that Skarry half expected it to breathe fire.

Doth Auren hailed them as they approached and Skarry sank to one knee, the soldiers merely saluting. Coming closer Skarry saw the breath of the horse steaming in the chill air. Yet the girth looked a little tight to him and pinched the skin of his belly.

'We must part,' the Doth said gravely. 'For we have our separate destinies to follow. This is the letter which I charge you to deliver unto the hands of the High Lord Guise of Ringdove together with your own explanations of my absence from his muster. The collar of the Auf bear you must show to his Dreamer and tell him of my need. Should he choose to come to my aid my hope is that he shall have a worthy guide to bring him safely on his way.'

This last was to Skarry who was so overcome by the weight of D'Auren's dark gaze that he bent his head and kissed the lord's armoured boot. The Doth laughed and was pleased by the gesture.

'Come,' he said, 'you will ride with me to the gates.' And with a shout he called forth three retainers each leading a fair mount; a broad chested beast like a draught horse for Glimshpill, one of lighter build for Catskin and a stocky pony for Skarry, the deep red-brown of bracken in autumn. Skarry was delighted with the pony for he seemed of a likeness to the Doth's own strong horse, only smaller. They mounted swiftly and with D'Auren at their head, surrounded at the sides and to the rear by horse warriors, they made their way through the streets of Wenlok.

Coming out of the courtyard they were greeted by the cheers of many folk who had come to see their lord depart. The sides of the streets were lined with people and every window and balcony filled, even the rooftops were precarious perches. The many shouts resounded from the tall buildings as they called out to their lord, to smite the enemy, to return victorious and safe, to look after their menfolk, husbands, fathers, sons. To Skarry there was already the air of triumph in this short journey, as if he returned from some great adventure.

The Doth turned in his saddle and motioned him forward so Skarry urged his pony on and came up at the side of the lord and together they made their way. With his eyes wide Skarry turned this way then that to take in the mass of peoples and the Doth smiled at his amazement.

When they came to the main gates their arrival was met with loud fanfares from trumpets and the tossing of banners that rose up into the sky, whirling like some great bird of legend before falling back to earth and into the arms of their bearers. Here the Doth turned his charger and stood tall in his stirrups. With a fluid movement he drew his sword and held it high over his head such that the blade seemed to penetrate the clouds above. A great stillness and quiet came over them.

'We go, my children,' he spoke into the silence and the people drank in his words. 'We go into great peril for the sake of all, of our children and our children's children. If Vidar should look kindly upon us then shall we overthrow the enemy and return victorious and once more peace shall lie upon this our land.'

The trumpets sounded again a loud fanfare and the voices of the people rose up in a mighty cheer. Doth Auren settled himself in his saddle and nodded a biref farewell to Catskin and the others. Then he turned to the north and went forth from the city and as he passed across the field, rank upon rank and company after company wheeled and joined the growing column that he led.

Skarry felt so stirred by it all that he would have dearly loved to run after the lord and follow him where ever he should choose to go, for it seemed then that this one could do no evil or harm and that those who went with him need concern themselves no more with decisions and choices, for to follow would be enough. Yet he knew that this was not to be and his hope was that after he had been to Ringdove he might see this lord again and be at his side in his time of great need.

He was roused from his reverie by Glimshpill's heavy hand, tugging him to follow and the three slowly pushed their way through the crowd that closed in after the retreating army. As they broke out of the press Catskin shouted them on and at a canter they crossed the churned mud of the fields until the torn brown earth was concealed beneath thick snow.

At the crest of the first hill they stopped and turned. From this distance the many warriors had blurred into one vast shape whose leading head was now almost out of sight, yet whose tail, swelling into rows of waggons, was only just beginning to move. All about were dotted the mass of townsfolk calling their farewells.

'He will have a job getting those carts up the mountain track,' said Glimshpill.

'It will not be he who sweats at the spokes in the icy mud,' Catskin said.

'Aye,' said Glimshpill. 'Yet he cuts a pretty figure in all that war gear. I would have thought it were a show except we did not pay to see it.'

Catskin gave a soft laugh then turned to the west.

'Let us be off also,' he said. 'Look not so sad, young Skarry, remember the one who waits for you in fair Ringdove.'

Glimshpill laughed loudly and the two soldiers wheeled their horses away and off into the snow. Skarry too turned his gaze from the city of Wenlok and its army and brought his pony about to face into the west and the land of the Epona.

10

Sulla of the Ranneye

For a moment Skarry's thoughts were balanced between the sight of D'Auren's army and an inner vision of Ress. The image of her face had fragmented and he could picture her only in isolated memories, crouching in the half dark of High Haven illuminated by the light of the fire-pot or coming through the snows of Ice Back on the very top of the world. Forcing himself to imagine her more clearly only lent greater distance to the memory such that she seemed to swim further from him and become even less distinct. Poised between the great army and her fading vision, he felt suddenly and sadly divided.

It was the cold that brought him to the present once more. Riding with the Doth he had thrown back his hood, for the excitement of their departure had warmed him from within. Yet now the inner fire was stilled and his breath clouded the air before his face and he shivered.

His pony began to stamp impatiently and Skarry stroked its neck.

'Tush, tush,' he whispered softly, 'little child of Tharlcandra, I will look after you, though I know not your name. I will call you Felder, if you will have it, for you have the look of one of the fells about you.'

The pony snorted as if in appreciation and Skarry laughed with him.

'Come then,' he said, 'we must be off.'

Felder gave a last stamp and leapt forward with Skarry bent over his neck, the thick mane flying about his face. The speed of their passage over the white drove all thought of Ress from his mind and he soon closed up with the others.

Together again the three slowed their pace. Glimshpill liked not to trot for he bounced in the saddle like a great sack of turnips, so they climbed the gentle hills at a canter and walked

84

down the further slopes. The land seemed a rolling white waste that stretched as far as could be seen in any direction and blurred with the clouds so that the horizon was lost and they appeared to be enclosed within a world of white. They crossed the occasional tracks of the snow deer and Skarry spotted the white hare of the winter standing tall on his hind legs as he watched them from a distance. The way was marked with roughly piled cairns of a reddish rock that pushed upwards through the snow on the summit of each rise.

All that morning they made their way across this undulating land until the sharp-eyed Catskin pulled up his mount and they halted at his side. Following the line of his pointing finger led their gaze to the rise ahead and even at this distance they could see where the low winter sun cast the deep prints into shadow. The tracks ran up the hillside at an angle and disappeared over the brow.

'Nomads,' said Glimshpill as they walked the horses towards the tracks. 'On their way south for the winter.'

'There is but one track,' Catskin said quietly.

'They walk in wolf file,' Glimshpill countered, 'one behind the other to conceal their numbers.'

Coming close, it was as if Skarry knew what they would find. The tracks were of an animal, a large one at that, for each print was dragged into the next as if it ran with a loping stride. The snow was slick with ice where it had first melted then frozen again.

'It is an Auf bear,' Skarry said.

Catskin dismounted and stooped over the prints, turning his head in either direction.

'It is a Firebolg,' he agreed and returning to his horse he mounted swiftly. Glimshpill looked all about with care.

'It has gone south,' Catskin went on. 'Sometime this morning I would think. We had best be on our way.'

They travelled on keeping a wary watch all around. Glimshpill grumbled over the fresh hazards of the journey and Skarry felt a cold fear over his heart at the thought of the beast somewhere in the lands off to their left.

'Do you think there are more?' he asked Catskin.

'One is enough for us to worry about, out here in the open,' said the Corporal.

'I was thinking of the Dreamer,' said Skarry, 'and Ress.'

Glimshpill gave a knowing laugh. 'You shouldn't waste your worries on that blue-skinned sage,' he said. 'He has defences of his own.'

Nevertheless, Skarry liked not to think of those two so alone and spending the night under the clouds while he had lain comfortably in a bed. He put the stone within his mouth; the blue stone of the Asgire rested against his chin.

'These are the lands of the nomads,' said Catskin, as if to distract his troubled mind. 'They are an old people, like your own, Skarry.'

'We call them the Epona,' said Skarry, spitting out the sucking stone.

'So you know of them up in your woods?' Glimshpill asked.

'We are not savages,' Skarry said, a little angrily. 'We know of the peoples of the plains and their love of horses.'

'Tell us the tale, Skarry,' said Catskin, to ease their tension. 'We have a long way to go yet.'

Skarry was silent for a moment but he could find no harm in the telling. In his mind's eye he could see Gemel light up his pipe with a brand from the fire, could hear the song of his voice as it led the Olluden through the past.

'It is said how the Two were divided,' said Skarry, 'and that their blood fell upon the rich earth. Many races sprang from that union and most noble was that of the horse, founded by Mariam, the queen of the horse and Tharlcandra, her king. Mariam led her people to dwell on these southern plains long before the humans had built even Xa Erzuran. This land they called Hars Ithiel, the place of the horse.

'Yet also from the blood of the Two came Tiu who fell upon a spark struck from the granite bear in that first of all battles. He grew to be part fire and with his fiery hands could fashion many wondrous things. He it was who set up the great workshops in the caves about the Low Pass, for the inner organs of Thuggundian were made up of many diverse metals and ores. Yet though he made many marvellous things, he could not approach the speed and grace of the horse and he looked upon them with envy.

'At last he journeyed into their lands and spoke with Mariam, their queen, and he said, "Many gifts I will give unto thee if thou would carry me when I call."

'But Mariam laughed in his face and ran up and down a mountain four times saying, "What would I want with your gifts when I have four strong legs to carry me and all that I need grows from the ground at my feet?" and she ran off laughing.

'Tiu grew angry and returned to his workshops and laboured long, fashioning a pair of wings with feathers of each of the one hundred and seventy-seven elements. Then he returned to the kingdom of the horse and showed the wings to Tharlcandra, the king of the horse, saying, "With these you will be the envy of all beasts for you will be a creature of the air and will soar higher even than the falcon."

'And Tharlcandra was tempted by the wondrous wings and said to Tiu, "Give me the wings and I will carry you once, yet I swear that I will not have even the feet of a god astride my back for more than a day."

'So Tiu fastened the wings upon the horse's back and leapt astride him and together they rose up into the sky until the earth was as a pebble below them. Then Tiu laughed horribly and tore off his boots and Tharlcandra saw that Tiu had cut off his own feet and replaced them with gold hooves, and though Tharlcandra screamed his anger Tiu slipped an iron bit between his teeth and steel reins about his head and later a bronze saddle on his broad back, and so enslaved the horse and forced him to his will. And all the horses of the cities stem from this line.

'Yet Mariam met up with more gentle peoples who watched the horse and learned her ways, and this is why the Epona talk to the horses with their voices and bodies and make no use of bits and bridles and stirrups and whips. Nor do they geld them nor let a smith near their feet for they treat the horse as a friend and equal and spit at those who enslave them.'

Skarry fell silent and bent over Felder's neck and stroked him and whispered in his ears and Felder snickered back, his ears turning to hear.

'In Ringdove,' said Glimshpill 'the city folk call the Epona thieves and tinkers and curse them when they pass by.'

Before Skarry could speak Catskin raised up his arm calling for them to halt. Looking up Skarry could plainly see the tracks, the same as those they had seen earlier.

'Is it that which we saw before?' asked Glimshpill. 'Or are there still more?'

Catskin leaned from his saddle to examine the prints. 'It is another,' he said.

Skarry shivered and looked around. The whiteness stretched away in all directions as before, yet close by there were a number of small white mounds like tuffets of grass covered in snow.

'Something is not right,' said Catskin, suddenly rising and making to string his bow. Glimshpill swung about in the saddle but before he could draw his sword a voice spoke to them loudly as if out of the ground.

'You would be well advised to remain calm,' it said.

Skarry looked hastily all about but it was in the direction from which they had come that he found the white figure. She was standing only a dozen paces from them as though they had ridden by without seeing her.

'I suggest that you step down from those creatures,' she said, motionless before them, calmly observing their slightest movements.

Glimshpill drew his thick brows together, placed his hand upon the hilt of his sword and would have spoken had not Catskin found tongue first.

'We shall do as she suggests,' he said quietly.

Glimshpill turned a sharp eye towards him yet clambered from the saddle. Skarry too dismounted and held Felder's reins loosely, taking the time to watch the woman. She wore a white cloak tightly about her body, the hood concealing her hair. Her eyes were the deepest blue that Skarry had seen. As he watched she allowed her cloak to fall open and gave the smallest gesture with her left hand. Immediately the other mounds rose up around them revealing themselves to be women and men, similarly clad in white cloaks, some with mail shirts beneath. Many carried shortbows with arrows notched upon the strings.

'Speak quickly,' said the woman. 'What is your purpose in these lands?'

'We carry a letter from the Lord of Wenlok for the Paladin Guise,' said Catskin hurriedly and took the envelope from his tunic as if in proof.

'We hold no ill for D'Auren,' she said, 'though Guise is another matter.' Turning to Skarry she continued, 'I see by your tokens that you are a friend of the marsh folk.'

Skarry touched the stones at his neck and nodded. 'I am of the

Olluden,' he said and told her his name. 'I met Crane of Mireside and it was his son who gave me the stone after we killed the Firebolg.'

At this the others in white started and looked to one another, some drawing forward as if to hear a tale.

'Then you are welcome here, Skarry of the forest peoples,' she said and gave him a sign of greeting, raising up her palm to cover her right eye. Skarry copied the gesture and the people in white stood more easily and lowered their bows.

'I am Sulla,' she went on, 'of the Ranneye, the Hars people, the Epona.' And she cast back her hood and shook out her hair which was long and thick and black.

'You have a good deal of names, Sulla,' said Glimshpill, looking her down and up while leaning casually against his patient mount.

'And you have a good deal of weight, O large one,' she returned and Catskin could not keep from laughing.

Then Sulla whistled loudly and soon they heard the drumming of hoofs upon the ground and over the further rise came a score of horses, all greys and long in the leg, their breath steaming about them.

Skarry watched with open mouth as the herd came galloping towards them, casting up showers of snow that the light broke into an aura of many colours. As they neared they parted and each sought out their own rider, and though they had no harness or bit or bridle it was the ease with which the people mounted, swinging so fluidly up on to the horses' backs, that made Skarry feel he was truly amongst the Epona.

The stallion at their head floated up to Sulla, his hoofs hardly touching the ground, tossing his head from side to side so that the mane waved on the air. Before her he halted, ears forward and as she reached up to scratch his thick neck he nibbled at her shoulder with his lips. Then he wheeled about and raising his front feet let out a short neigh as a mare came up to Sulla and bent her neck to her.

'We must make a move,' Sulla called to the three and when they were ready and she upon the mare, the stallion let out a shriek of a neigh that started them off to the west with Glimshpill, Catskin and Skarry to the middle of the group. When Glimshpill came to the side of Skarry he called over, 'You have a useful tongue, youngster, or is it merely the stones that you wear?'

Skarry said nothing but Sulla called to him to ride forward with her. His pony, Felder, squealed to be with so many fine animals and Sulla laughed and spoke to him in a tongue that Skarry did not know. Yet the tone was warm and kind and Skarry felt the pony settle in his stride and raise up his head proudly.

'You should throw away that saddle,' Sulla said to Skarry, 'then your spirits might mingle with the closeness of the blood.'

At that easy canter Sulla rode as if fused to the mare, with one hand buried in her mane and the other loose at her side. There was no movement of her body that was not the movement of the horse and in the same way Skarry could see each stride of the horse as though beginning from the rhythm of Sulla's waist.

'You ride so well!' Skarry called to her and she laughed at his surprise.

'The Epona have ridden for thousands of summers; we have learnt much,' she said. 'Yet you do well for a forester. Throw off that bridle and you will find it all the easier!'

The last felt near a command to Skarry and such was the confidence in her voice that he leaned forward to undo the throat lash. But as he did so his gaze was drawn to the snow hurtling away beneath them and the pounding of hoofs and he froze, feeling the fear and finally drew back. He half glanced at Sulla, ashamed, yet she smiled openly.

'It will come,' she said simply.

'Where do you go to?' Skarry asked quickly lest she ride away.

'We go to the muster at Ringdove,' she replied and her voice became grim.

'So you will fight for the High Lord Guise!' Skarry said.

'We have no love for Guise,' Sulla said, 'nor for the folk of the city, yet we will fight for them. We have no choice, for Guise will burn the grasslands in the summer if we do not come.'

'Surely he would not do such a thing,' Skarry said in amazement.

'He would do much worse,' she said. 'Already they have placed a ban upon the travellers, the Itheni, forcing them to pay tolls. Malbrow, the Southern Serpent, has hunted down the smaller bands on Guise's orders. His are a desperate people; their world is coming apart.'

'Guise will save us,' Skarry said, mustering his confidence. 'And there are many strong heroes to help him.'

'Like yon fine warrior?' Sulla asked, pointing her thumb back over her shoulder to where Glimshpill wobbled in the saddle. 'I have met up with such heroism before,' she went on, 'and know it by the red eyes and sore head in the morning.'

'Guise will save us,' Skarry said again after a moment. 'I am sure of it.'

Sulla made no reply though she cast him a long look. They went on in silence for some time and Skarry came to feel that they were a grim people these Epona with their lips set and only the drumming of hoofs on the frozen earth to mark their passage.

As they travelled further east the snow was less. Overhead the massed ranks of cloud broke a little and patches of blue appeared with occasional glimpses of the sun, looking coldly white and distant. The view to their right, north, grew clear as the far mists drew aside their veil. Here, where the rolling plains broke into hill and fell, there were trees, so small as to appear like a moss or lichen, thinly clinging to the rock. They were oaks, Skarry knew, the oaks of the great forest, his forest, though further east than he had ever been. And somewhere within the border of trees lay the path from Mireside to Ringdove on which Ress and the Dreamer had set out. Skarry's thoughts turned to these two and he was reminded once more of the Auf bears.

'Have you seen the Firebolg?' Skarry asked Sulla and she nodded.

'We of the Ranneye are horse breeders,' she said. 'We met up with some of the sheep people this morning who had lost animals to what they thought to be a wolf pack. We tracked the creature down and killed it. Yet there is another at least, for where we met you there were more tracks. We will come upon it soon.'

'But where are they coming from?' asked Skarry. 'And what is their purpose?'

'Perhaps they are looking for something,' said Sulla, shrugging. 'Or someone. They are beasts yet they are driven by the desire of men. The one we killed was so intent upon its task that even a dozen arrows did not make it stop to fight.'

'They will be looking for the Dreamer,' said Skarry with sudden conviction. Sulla showed no surprise.

91

'We have heard rumours,' she said, 'that a Dreamer was about. I would not choose to be with him if the pack finds him.'

'How will they find him?' Skarry asked. 'Surely he will conceal his trail?'

'Our people have heard it said that the wise of your Olluden can follow a beast even be they blind and deaf and without a nose to smell with,' said Sulla by way of an answer.

'This is true,' agreed Skarry, 'for Gemel tracked and caught a wolf while wearing a sack over his head and when the wolf licked him he let it go.'

'You have the answer to your question then,' Sulla said. 'The Auf bears find their prey by senses other than the five. They are dangerous creatures, for their power has been summoned and they will not go away empty.'

Once again they were silent and in Skarry's heart was a growing fear for Ress and the Dreamer, who seemed so alone when compared to the strong company that he now kept.

It was towards the fall of night that the outrider to their left appeared over the low rise and came hurrying down. Even before they met, Skarry could make out the black shape on the crest of the hill and needed none to tell him that it was the Firebolg.

A deeper silence settled over the Ranneye as they slowed their pace to allow their outrider to rejoin them. They strung their shortbows as they rode and put arrows to the strings.

'Can we not outrun it?' Glimshpill called.

'These are our lands,' said Sulla, 'and there are others of our people who are not so fleet as we.'

Glimshpill gave an angry growl and drew his sword. 'Must I notch thee yet again, Settler?' he asked the discoloured blade and began to whirl it about his head such that it whined through the air.

As if in answer the Firebolg gave voice and its fearful howl passed over them. Sulla split the party and a dozen of the Ranneye galloped away in a great curve that would bring them round to meet the creature's path from the side. The others halted and turned to face its approach.

For a moment as the echoes of their hoofbeats died it seemed to Skarry that there were a lot of warriors to stop a single beast. Now the other party swept down upon the creature passing both before and behind, loosing their arrows at close range. Yet though the Auf bear let out its shriek of a cry it did not falter in its stride. The shafts in its fur burst into flame and it broke into a charge towards Sulla's group.

Felder began to dance nervously as the black form approached clothed in steam and smoke.

'The Olluden say that it is unwise to face the charge of a bear,' said Skarry to Sulla.

Glimshpill grunted in agreement but Catskin was already drawing his bow for a shot.

'It will pass us by,' Sulla said. 'We will catch it from behind as we did the other.'

The sound as Catskin loosed his hold of the string was like an ancient music, the plucked string of the harp with a deeper resonance that goes beyond hearing and is felt. The long shafted arrow flew true yet at the last instant went over the Auf bear's shoulder and on into the distance as if brushed aside.

'That's one good shaft I'll not find again,' Catskin said with a surprised look to his face. He notched another arrow to the string and made to draw again.

'Leave it!' Glimshpill said angrily. 'There is the stench of Dreaming about this creature.'

'Come away!' Sulla called. 'Let it pass then we may finish it with no hurt to ourselves.'

'This has the sound of good counsel,' Glimshpill said and urged his heavy mount aside.

The Ranneye stirred uneasily and began to break, unsure as to whether to go fore or back. As they opened Skarry saw the oncoming creature with growing fear, for there was something in its determined stride as it reached out its forefeet with each leap, the back alternately bent as a drawn bow then straight as the shaft of the arrow and the hot coals of its eyes seemed to burn into him. He could hear the hiss of the melting snow and its heat grew as it neared for it was shrouded in steam and it shrieked its fighting cry.

'It will not pass!' Skarry shouted suddenly. 'It means to fight!'

It seemed he was wrong for the Firebolg passed two of the Ranneye without a glance yet as Glimshpill and Skarry began to move off it swerved at them. Skarry kicked at Felder's flanks though the pony needed no further urging and leapt into a full gallop with a whinny of fear. Over his shoulder Skarry saw the Auf bear loom suddenly large as it drew its hind legs, thick as tree trunks, beneath it and it too leapt and he knew he was not beyond its terrible reach.

The single curved claw of one foreleg carved a red passage across Felder's rump and the pony bucked and screamed with pain, yet before the claw could bite hard Glimshpill leaned from his saddle and swung Settler in a high overarm blow. The blade cut deep into the Firebolg's leg, stopping only at the bone with a shower of sparks and a bright flash that blinded Skarry's eyes.

He heard the shriek of the Auf bear harshly ringing in his head. Felder stumbled in his panic and crashed down heavily on his right side hurling Skarry forward to roll in the snow. His eyes began to clear yet he lay dazed as the creature rounded Felder and lumbered towards him, its great head swinging ponderously from side to side, the burning coals of its eyes intent upon him. Beyond, Glimshpill too was thrown from his terrified mount and even the Ranneye struggled to control their horses. There was little that Skarry could do for he had no weapon to hand. On his back he lay with his feet towards the beast and it came to him and raised itself up on its hind legs such that it towered over him.

He clutched at his throat, feeling for his old stone, the green granite with the veins of quartz that took him back to his forest home and the giant's tooth on which he would sit and watch the animals. There the bears were few and could be sent on their way with words. Yet even within this creature was there something of a bear, so Skarry spoke up to the monster, for he could think of nothing else to do.

'Ho, bear!' he called and his voice shook. 'You are a long way from home, and you wear an ugly collar that surely itches a great deal.'

The Firebolg hung motionless above him. He could feel the heat radiate from its huge body and the snow began to melt about them.

'I should have thought that you would prefer the shelter of the forest,' Skarry went on, quieter, his voice quaking. 'Have you forgotten your cubhood, running with your sisters and brothers beneath the canopy of green?'

The Auf bear's breath came in great rushes that blew across Skarry's face and singed his eyebrows. It stood there with its cruelly cut foreleg hanging forward and raised the other to its neck where the collar was tight at its throat. Skarry felt a sudden anger at its plight.

'Who has done this to you?' he hissed. 'Who has so ill-treated you, bear? I will lay odds it was the work of evil men!'

And the Firebolg raised up its mighty head to the darkening sky and let forth a howl that seemed full of sadness. It turned its gaze once more upon Skarry and the fire dimmed. Then Catskin's arrow took it in the back of the neck and the point came darkly from out of its mouth. There was a grunt from Glimshpill as his Settler bit into the beast's backbone. The coals of its eyes became embers and then died and it toppled slowly to one side and crashed to the ground. Skarry began to shake and his eyes filled with tears.

It was Sulla that shook him by the shoulder and sat him up. From a flask she gave him a drink that was sharp on his tongue yet warmed him within.

'You have a soft heart,' she said. 'Few would have taken the time to talk with such a beast while it stood over them, ready for the kill.'

'Where is Felder?' Skarry asked suddenly as if returning to himself. But the pony was alive and kicking as one of the Ranneye rubbed a salve into the long gash, speaking quietly to him.

The Auf bear lay as it had fallen, the snow still steaming about it. In death it had lost much of its appearance of terror, as though the power that had driven it had departed. Skarry squatted by the great head and put out a hand to touch the ears; they were still warm though no longer burning.

'This is yours,' said Catskin and unfastened the gold collar from about its neck, handing it to Skarry. 'You had the greater part in its slaying.'

'I am not so sure that it pleases me,' Skarry said quietly, with an eye to the still body.

'It was necessary,' Sulla said simply. 'This was the twisting of a true bear. It had no place in the world.'

Skarry took the collar, feeling its weight. There were finely tooled engravings on it, an intricate and ancient design, the intertwining forms of distorted creatures. A little further off Glimshpill spat into the snow.

'He has the air of a Dreamer about him,' he muttered in disgust, stroking the new notches on his discoloured sword.

'Come!' Sulla called and rose up. 'We can be on our way now, our lands will be safe behind us.'

They mounted swiftly, Catskin giving Glimshpill a helping heave. Skarry went to Felder carrying the heavy collar that the Corporal had given him. The pony snickered at his approach and turned to greet him. Skarry stroked his neck and ran his hands softly along his back to the gash. It was an ugly wound though not deep and the salve had stopped the bleeding.

'We must be all the quicker next time,' he whispered into Felder's ears as he mounted.

As they made ready to go on Skarry rode over to the body of the bear. There was nothing left to fear in it and the pony sniffed at its ears.

'Farewell, bear,' whispered Skarry. 'I hope you will find peace now.'

Then with a rush the Ranneye whirled their horses about and leapt into a canter that took them rapidly across the white. Shouting to one another they went, tossing their short spears high in the air and even to each other. Glimshpill brightened and began to sing a drinking song, Catskin joining in with his thin, reedy voice.

'They are glad that the beast is dead,' Sulla called to Skarry, riding up close at his side. 'We liked not the idea of leaving our lands with danger still within. It is you that we thank for our deliverance and you must wear this as a sign of our friendship.'

Sulla leaned towards him, dangling a small pouch in her outstretched hand. Skarry knew it was a stone by the weight and feel as he accepted the gift. Inside the pouch lay a stone so yellow as to appear like a golden egg yet with a sheen to it like the pottery from Elvedale. Someone had spent many hours drilling a hole through it that it might hang like a bead upon a thong.

'It is the colour of the plains at the end of high summer,' Sulla said as he tucked the pouch into his tunic pocket. 'The lowering sun turns the grasses to gold with its soft light. It is a stone not just of the Ranneye, but of all the Epona.'

Skarry thanked her for the gift.

'You have the look of the old peoples about you, Skarry,' she went on and Skarry felt a stirring of pride within him. His face began to colour with the rush of blood but when he looked at Sulla her face was open and she smiled.

The world darkened about them early with all that cloud and they rode on through a long twilight. After a time of silence they heard the drumming of other hoofs and out of the darkness came riding many more of the Epona and they hailed each other with old greetings. Skarry half dozed in his saddle to the rhythm of the horses' beat surrounded by a growing mass of the horse people.

Once he was stirred by shouts and calls and looking up saw the young moon climb into a hole in the clouds and shine down upon them, a soft and baleful light. Then the Epona sang old songs and in the gentle glow Skarry saw the hordes of riders receding far off in all directions. Later, a large group came swinging in from the south and horns sounded at the meeting. At their head came one with yellow hair blowing long and loose with the speed of his passage and many of the Epona greeted him.

Skarry began to feel the growing presence of mountains in the blackness to the north and their way began to steepen. Sensing they approached a pass, he was returned in his doze to his own Skard and the winter of high altitude, yet there was no comparison here, for the climb was neither steep nor long by his reckoning and soon they crested the rise. Shaking himself more awake he noticed Glimshpill and Catskin to either side. Felder was tiring yet Skarry sensed that the end of their journey was near.

They must have rounded the dark bulk of a ridge for of a sudden, there far below them were many lights, a myriad of lights like clustered stars, of bonfires and torches, sprawling across the land and to their centre increasing in number and intensity and faintly illuminating high towers and keeps.

'It is Ringdove,' said Catskin softly and he seemed to breathe easier.

'We will rest here!' called Sulla, riding amongst the Ranneye. She finished more grimly, 'Tomorrow we will go down to the city.'

11

Bear Baiting in Ringdove

The Epona were awake with the grey dawn that came later now each day, as the world edged into winter. Above them loomed a mass of cloud, concealing the sun and diffusing its light.

Skarry roused to the activity of the horse people as they prepared to move down from the pass. The animals were seen to first, fed and watered at small streams that cut through the hills, the mud brushed from their coats. Any who had suffered hurt on their journey were treated by the Ranneye with salves and ointments made from the herbs of the plains.

Only when the Epona were satisfied that the horses were cared for did they themselves break their fast. Some lit small fires with the little wood that lay about and cooked soups, others nibbled at oat cakes that they had brought with them. Sulla shared what she had with Skarry and he took the time to look around more carefully.

In the dark of the night he had been aware of riders joining their company but only now in the growing light did he come to appreciate their numbers. All about the track, spreading up the slopes of the flanking hills, before and behind, were horses. Horses of many colours and breeds, from the graceful greys of the Ranneye to wide-eyed ponies with blotches of black and red on their coats to the great bulk of the Pantecs from the distant south, huge and red who had been bred to haul stone when Xa Erzuran was first built; some stamped their feet as though impatient to be off while others stood calmly, their ears turning to follow each sound and they called to one another, their voices echoing from the flanks of the mountains.

The pass was as nothing when compared to the heights of the Angsoth. Here the shoulders of rock were skinned with soil and climbed gently up from a track that was more like a road, being wide enough to take two carts and having spaces where heavy loads might pause for rest. Yet as the slopes climbed they did steepen and their summits looked stonily down from on high. Beyond these peaks the greater mountains of the Ridgeway clambered off into the mists to east and west. The south gave a view out over the rolling horse plains, away into the far distance.

And to the north sprawled the city of Ringdove, a child's game of bricks with towers and buildings, bridges and roads all jumbled within its tall encircling wall. Beyond that wall the land was concealed beneath the weight of armed camps, staining the sky with the smoke from innumerable fires.

'It is a big place, eh?' said Sulla, following Skarry's gaze and he nodded in agreement. 'It will seem all the bigger when we get down to it,' she went on, not appearing pleased with the prospect.

Soon the Epona were ready and they mounted their horses. To the fore Skarry noticed the one he had seen the past night. His head was again bared, the long yellow hair floating in the breeze. His face was brown from the summer sun and seamed with the wind of the plains. When all were mounted he lifted up his arm and as one the Epona began the descent to Ringdove.

Even at a walk the noise from the massed horses echoed through the pass and a dull vibration from the hammer of hoofs passed into the ground and resounded from each stone and rock. To be amongst such numbers filled Skarry with elation and pride, for here were an old people of Taur, come to defend their land against the onslaught of a terrible enemy.

They made their way along the track which lowered gently to meet the sea plains, with many a sharp turn to avoid the steeper drops. From the growing city before them came a distant roaring as of waves upon a cobble beach. Skarry strove to fix his mind upon the thought that somewhere within these wide walls was Ress but he was soon distracted by the surging activity on the plain below.

Ringdove lay at the junction of three great roads; the one coming up out of the south that they travelled on met with two others, from north-east and north-west. Along both these roads could be made out troops marching in close order in long columns. Behind and before each body of soldiers came trains of waggons and many people in a great straggle when compared to the neatness of the warriors. To the north-east, from the direction of Dunnerdale and beyond that, Midloth, the press was even greater and many had left the crush and made their way through the fields towards Ringdove.

'There's Damon!' said Glimshpill, pointing to this mass of soldiers, near concealed within the hordes of fleeing people. 'From Dunnerdale, so the enemy cannot have come too far within the land. The other to the west will be Heighington, he brings his men from Greenport on the coast.'

Like the centre of a vast target Ringdove drew all together into a great sprawl of people and animals and waggons, churning the snow and earth to mud. The Epona viewed the sight with unease, some raising up tokens as though to ward off evil. As they came to the base of the pass they halted with the walls of Ringdove rising from out of the turmoil in the distance. Sulla came over to the three casting baleful glances at the sight.

'We must part for now,' she said simply to Skarry. 'The people will go no nearer so we will camp here.'

'Our thanks for your company, Sulla,' Skarry said. 'I should like to ride with you again.'

'It may come about,' Sulla replied and returned his smile. 'The Hars Plains are a fine place to ride in the high summer and you will be welcome there. The Epona will always know you as a friend by the stones you wear.'

She nodded to his throat where the yellow stone of the Epona had joined those of the Olluden and the Asgire.

'Yet we will meet afore that,' she went on, 'for we shall send envoys to the council and maybe you will be there also.'

Skarry nodded and they parted, Sulla wheeling about with her fine mare and not a word of command. Skarry turned less gracefully with Catskin and Glimshpill towards the smoking vision of Ringdove that dominated the view.

'I fear that it shall be a long and hard winter before that high summer,' said Catskin softly as they set out for the city.

Long before they reached the walls they came within the upheavals of the camp; row upon row of tents and improvised shelters, divided by lanes of churned mud. The soldiers huddled about the many fires and carts hauled firewood to them that they should not freeze in the night. Glimshpill began to point out the companies who had marched from the far corners of the land for the muster.

'There's Nessan's mob!' he shouted and spat in disgust. 'From the south. He it was who let the Monrolians escape us, end of last season.' He indicated a large area with more orderly lines of tents. The soldiers seemed well clothed, the officers sitting on wooden benches and arguing loudly.

'And Malbrow's lot,' Glimshpill went on more quietly, 'The Southern Serpent. Not keen on travellers is he.' The soldiers he pointed to were huddled round rows of braziers, their hands bound in strips of cloth against the cold.

The sounds of the camp beat at Skarry's ears. The carts and waggons creaked and groaned beneath the weight of sacks and barrels and the drivers, perched on high, shouted to those on foot in excited voices. The beat of a song as a company marched by rolled over the camp, the suck of mud with each withdrawn boot. There came the hammer of the smiths as weapons were wrought and the shriek of sharpening steel. Hawkers and vendors went amongst the warriors plying their trades. Here one with an armload of thick fur cloaks and a loud selling song, another with a small handcart laden with flagons of wine, another with simply water. One came carrying a small sack and pulling at a long pipe that emitted a thin plume of green smoke and a sharp odour. Glimshpill caught him by the collar and dragged him along while he arranged a bargain. Skarry saw the seal's tooth necklace exchange hands. The fight at the river when it was won seemed now so distant, in time as well as space.

All about were the countless flags and banners, many-coloured silks, marking each troop and company, kindling his memories of the old tales and the great wars of the past. Yet looking down from their proud fluttering to the soldiers all bespattered with mud and already tired with their long marches was like a dashing with cold water that extingushed the inner fire.

The pack of bodies increased steadily as they came towards the walls and soon they were struggling through a throng of people; soldiers with iron helmets carrying long spears or sacks of corn, one even a pig. Horsemen with important messages forcing their way through the crush leaving behind them wakes of insults. And townsfolk also, some just seeing the sights of this new extension to their city.

Here was one who had the look of a farmer about him and stood in a circle of space loudly cursing all for the damage to his fields. The soldiers nearby returned his insults and as Skarry rode by they began to throw mud and then stones. The farmer drew up his cloak about his head.

Here was a small cart near buried beneath a tottering pile of sacks. The skinny donkey who had pulled it was on her knees between the shafts and the carter laid into her with a thin stick, shouting all the while in a high voice, alternately cursing the animal and talking to the crowd of onlookers.

'I am a poor man,' he explained. 'How can I make a living when doomed to rely on such a pathetic creature?'

He returned to beating the donkey, raging at her weakness. Catskin put a hand on Skarry's reins and drew him past.

And here were two children, a girl and boy, sharing a sack draped around their shoulders. They crouched at the side of the way, the girl raising up an empty bowl to the soldiers and merchants who went before them. Their faces were dirty and the girl's hollow stare drew Skarry's gaze. At her throat hung a white stone upon a string.

Turning to the fore again Skarry found the dark gate of Ringdove looming over them and in this narrow way on a towering charger was a Captain in full armour with a cloak as red as blood. He stood in his stirrups and waved a small baton like a wand and shouted shrilly to all and sundry, directing them this way or that. The Captain's face was shaven as smooth as the helm on his head and he gestured most finely with his wand. To either side was his guard, lolling against the wall or leaning upon their spears.

As the three came close, the Captain turned his horse to bar their way yet continued with his directions to others. Catskin pushed his pony up to him and forced his soft voice to a thin shout.

'We have urgent news for the High Lord,' he said. 'We have ridden far and fast from Wenlok.'

The Captain in red spared the three a brief glance then returned his attention to a group of soldiers who had got a barrow load of breastplates stuck in the mud by the side of the gate. Catskin looked back at Glimshpill and gave a shrug.

Glimshpill sighed loudly then rode up beside the Captain's huge animal. Even so, their heads were level. With one fluid action he snatched the baton from the other's hand and thrust the end of it up under his chin so that the Captain's head was pushed back and the whites of his eyes showed above the pupil as he peered over his nose at the large Glimshpill, making a soft choking sound.

'We have urgent news for the High Lord,' Glimshpill pronounced carefully, 'and any delay, be it ever so slight, may cost the life of at least one noble hero.'

He accompanied the last with an upward jerk of the baton. The Captain released one white knuckled hand from its clenching of the reins and pointed towards the open gates.

'Pray proceed,' he managed in a squawk and Glimshpill left off, tossed him the baton and turned his back. Catskin and Skarry followed, the first making an elaborate bow from the saddle at the Captain who angrily eyed his guard as they concealed their mirth behind their hands. As the three entered the gate the soldiers to the side tipped the barrow in their arguing and the breastplates pealed against the wall like bells. So Skarry of the Olluden came within the walls of the city of Ringdove.

The streets were wide and had paved walks to either side bounded by rails and sheltered from above by verandahs. Here were many people, women and men draped in furs and elaborate cloaks with jewelled brocades. They leaned elegantly against the rails and surveyed those who passed before them.

The road itself was churned to mud and lined with deep wheel ruts such that it resembled a field that is ploughed when too wet, water pooling between the furrows. And its crop as such was people, moving ever back and forth, from field to city, city to field. Soldiers, merchants, shopkeepers, farmers, nobles with their ladies, some borne along in litters; the clash of colour in their clothing faded into muddy brown, softened by smoke and the vapour from their breath which hung before their faces.

'To be back in Ringdove, eh, Catskin?' Glimshpill laughed and gave the Corporal such a slap on the shoulder that he was nigh tumbled from his saddle. On the walkways and verandahs the women pointed out Glimshpill's bulk and raised small looking-glasses to their eyes to view him the better. He returned a mock salute and a large grin.

'Time enough for that!' Catskin said, catching Glimshpill's horse across the rump with his bow and sending it trotting forward with Glimshpill bouncing precariously.

103

'Where do you think Ress will be?' Skarry asked.

'You're both as bad!' Catskin said and Glimshpill roared with laughter to see Skarry blush. 'We must see the High Lord first,' Catskin continued. 'That Dreamer will no doubt be with him and he will know.'

Glimshpill led them on into the city while Skarry's thoughts were lost in the strangeness of the place. The buildings to either side towered up, their fronts lined with glazed tiles of many colours. The windows were tightly shuttered against the cold so that they appeared eyeless, blind, not that there was much to look upon, not a tree in sight, nor even a blade of grass. After some distance the muddy way was less populated, first cobbled and after that paved with grey slabs brought many miles from the quarries at Broughton. Then the buildings fell away on either hand and broke into separate houses of vast proportions to Skarry's eyes, each seeming capable of giving shelter to a small village.

They began to meet more soldiers, standing in pairs at street corners. They wore mail shirts over leather tunics and strutted back and forth with bored looks swinging long clubs idly. Like Glimshpill and Catskin they wore a bib over their chests that displayed the Bull of Taur and declared them to be warriors of the High Lord Guise. Some exchanged greetings with the Corporal.

In the distance, over the roofs could be seen a grey wall that Skarry at first took to be the further wall of the city. Yet as they neared it rose up higher and thicker and he saw that it was a vast keep. On its lofty summit were the dwarfed forms of soldiers, their spears like thin spines. The road took them up and on to a huge gatehouse with the gates open but a company of soldiers barred the way.

Sitting well back in the saddle Glimshpill hauled at his mount's reins and managed to get its front legs off the ground. He drew his sword and waved it furiously about his head.

'Make way! Make way!' he called loudly. 'For we ride in utter haste with news vital to the High Lord whom we know and love so dearly!'

The company at the gates roared with laughter and even their Captain grinned.

'Welcome back, Corporal,' he said to Catskin, coming close to hold his rein. 'I see you could not lose the loud one.'

104

'Unfortunately, no,' Catskin replied, 'though it is not for want of trying.'

'Where did you pick up the savage with the stony necklace?' one of the soldiers called but Catskin waved him into silence.

'Enough,' the Corporal said hurriedly. 'We must see Guise for Doth Auren will not make the muster.'

At this news there were groans and worried looks and the troop fell to talking amongst themselves. The Captain called grooms forth who took the horses for stabling. Skarry only released Felder when Catskin vouched for his safety and well-being. Then the Captain ushered them through the gate and directed them within.

'Have you heard anything of Fressingfield?' Glimshpill asked before they parted from him. 'We left him in a tight spot facing the Misery, oh, seven or eight days ago.'

'We have heard nothing,' the Captain said grimly. 'Not since he first gave word that the enemy had crossed the Isthmus and that he would try to contain him. Oh, we have sent messengers and scouts by the score. They do not return. All our knowledge stops after Dunnerdale.'

Inside the wall they were directed up a flight of stone steps by another soldier.

'Wait on the balcony,' he called up after them. 'He will be occupied for a while.'

At the top of the steps they came out on to the balcony that looked out over an enclosed space like a courtyard. There was a low wall at the edge of the balcony and Glimshpill leaned over. He did not stay to watch but turned and dumped helmet, sword and last his self upon the ground, sitting with back against stone, taking out pipe and the smoking mixture.

'He has seen it all before,' Catskin said to Skarry as if in explanation and together they leaned upon the parapet and looked downward.

At first, staring into the gloomy shadows, Skarry thought that someone must have caught a Firebolg, for growls and shrieks rose up to him and he could see the red open mouth and the sharp teeth. But then the flurry below resolved itself and he could see it was just a bear, an old bear with ribs close beneath the skin and a chain fastening it to the wall.

Before the bear was a stocky man, heavily muscled with thick thighs bulging under leather breeches. His back was broad and his heavy arms bare, even in this cold. He walked with a rolling gait and held his square fists away from his body as he paced about, marshalling his dogs.

'Tear him, Biter!' he commanded and a grey and sleekly muscled wolfhound leapt and tore at the bear's shoulder, falling back before the swinging nailed claw. The second, a dapple fury, sprang as the bear turned on Biter and the other shoulder flayed open as meat upon the block. Roaring in pain the bear turned but the claws sliced only air.

'Brave work, Spitter,' the dog man shouted his encouragement. 'But come Ringneck,' he called to the third. 'To work eh?'

Ringneck growled softly, low crouching, back arched, all black with banded white about the throat. Then he too sprang, straight at the bear and took hold of its nose, drawing swift blood and a cry before dancing back beyond reach.

'Har! Old Ringneck!' the dog man laughed yet he stepped back a little as the bear rose up on its hind legs.

Skarry watched in growing horror and looked to Catskin. The Corporal shook his head slowly then leaned further over the parapet.

'My Lord!' he called down. 'We have urgent news!'

The dog man stopped in his pacing and turned his face to them, the chin working as if chewing. Then he turned to the bear once more and took from the wall a long thrusting spear. Coming forward to where the bear's chain was fastened to the stone he drew forth the pin and the chain fell clanking free.

'Ho, bear!' he roared. 'Come fight a real fight and leave off this play.'

The dogs fell back growling as the bear turned this way then that and blinked its eyes. Finally, as if at last relating its torn and bleeding flesh to this man, it let out a great roar and came down on all fours into a lumbering charge.

He held his ground and aimed the point of the spear and thrust forward with all his might. With a jarring shock the spear point hit the bear between the neck and shoulder and it passed within its body, perhaps clove the heart, for the creature sank back suddenly silent and as the warrior withdrew his spear it coughed and died.

The bear-killer flexed his arms and laughed as the dogs sniffed the corpse, licking at the blood.

'Such is the way with dogs,' he said. 'And all things.'

Skarry stepped numbly back from the sight and leaned his head against the cold stone, looking up to the grey skies. From out of the silence came the sound of a heavy tread upon stone, that grew louder. Glimshpill struggled to his feet putting away his smoking kit and from out of the doorway came the dog man, the bear's blood still fresh on his face, the Paladin Guise of Ringdove.

Glimshpill and Catskin snapped to attention and hid their hearts with clenched right fist as salute. Skarry could do nothing other than stare open mouthed at his High Lord who had been spoken of so many times about the fires in the winter home of the Olluden when the nights drew in.

Guise returned the salute of the soldiers then looked askance at Skarry.

'A lad of the mountain tribes, eh?' he said.

'I am of the forest, sir,' Skarry said, cutting off Catskin's reply, 'though I know a little of the ways of the mountain.'

'It makes no difference,' Guise said dismissively and then looked on over Skarry's shoulder. 'I see you've not grown a beard yet,' he called loudly and Skarry's head was drawn around to meet the deep blue stare of the Dreamer. 'The wise have beards, all,' Guise continued. 'Where's thine? Traitorous theologian!'

'And where are your horns?' the Dreamer asked quietly and smiled. 'For the bull you be?'

The Paladin gave a shallow laugh.

'And where is your worry?' the Dreamer went on. 'For the danger to your people?'

'You do ill to remind me,' Guise muttered and some of the straightness went out of his back.

'Report!' he snapped at Catskin, suddenly brisk and officious.

'Fressingfield, ah, the Lord Fressingfield engaged substantial forces six days ago,' the Corporal began. 'Notably Osilo Ice Warriors under the command of the Misery of Ice, Grimal Skoye. Being sorely pressed he sent us for aid by way of the High Pass, a most difficult journey –'

'I know this!' Guise barked suddenly. 'Tell me of Wenlok! When will D'Auren be here?'

Catskin took the letter from his tunic pocket and handed it to Guise who tore the seal and unfolded the parchment.

'My most high and sovereign lord,' he read and then became silent, his eyes following the lines of script. As he read, his grip upon the letter tightened, the great fists clenching such that the sheet was stretched into furrows and creases. When he was finished he crushed it within his palm and hurled it out over the parapet edge.

'He will not come,' he managed between lips that were stretched thin and white. 'The mighty Doth will not come!'

His voice began to rise in volume and he gripped the stone of the parapet so tight that Skarry half expected it to break and shatter within his fists. Guise began to shake his head from side to side, his eyes bulging and he stamped heavily with one foot against the stone.

Catskin and Glimshpill moved away, staring down at their feet or looking out into the distance though keeping half an eye upon their lord. The Dreamer came forward and laid his hand on Guise's arm. The muscles were bunched into thick cords close beneath the skin. Guise started violently and turned to the Dreamer as if he had not seen him before.

'He will not come,' he said again between clenched teeth, each word forced out. 'That bastard son of a savage dares to disobey my word.'

'My Lord Guise,' the Dreamer began, speaking softly, 'I am sure that the Doth will have his own reasons for his actions and that –'

'Reason?' Guise said, then again, a bellow, 'Reason! Don't feed me dung, you shaman, he has disobeyed me!'

And he swung about, taking the Dreamer at the shoulders in his fists and throwing him up against the wall. The Dreamer made no sound of complaint and simply looked down into the other's eyes. Glimshpill and Catskin moved further along the balcony, taking Skarry with them. Yet the Dreamer's blue eyes showed no fear and he remained held hard against the stone watching Guise's purpling face.

Thus frozen in the still air the Paladin appeared to calm. The colour drained from his cheeks and his eyes ceased to bulge as though a pressure was reduced from within. He turned at last from the Dreamer and stared across at his inner keep that loomed darkly into the sky and strove to master his breathing.

'It may be,' the Dreamer said gently, 'that D'Auren is doing you the greater service, for he goes against the enemy alone and will perhaps vanquish him and so spare your warriors hurt.'

Guise said nothing though his breath quieted and he tilted his head as if listening.

'The enemy is within our lands and his easiest route is straight to Ringdove. Yet he knows that here is where we draw our might together. So perhaps he will not do it, perhaps he will cross the High Pass, aye, even in winter and take the southern lands unguarded and so come upon Ringdove from an unexpected quarter.'

'Ah, evil, evil,' Guise began to mutter under his breath.

'Aye, Lord,' said the Dreamer, 'and this is what D'Auren seeks to guard you against. For now you will be free to lead out your great army with Ringdove safe behind.'

Guise was nodding now.

'You are right,' he said. 'You are right. It is a noble sacrifice that D'Auren would make for his High Lord. I will hear none speak against him!'

Glimshpill looked relieved as the fit passed and Catskin came forward holding out the collar of the Firebolg. Skarry drew his own from within his jerkin.

'My Lord,' Catskin said, 'there is this also.'

The Paladin took the one from Catskin and handled it with a gleam in his eye, examining the workmanship and weighing the gold in his hands. The Dreamer took up Skarry's and pondered more thoughtfully.

'You did well to escape them,' he said quietly to Skarry. Turning to Guise he said, 'They are of the Auf bear, the Firebolg. D'Auren will need strong aid against the likes of this and worse.'

'It is near time for the council,' Guise said. 'I must prepare myself. There we shall decide what to do.'

Taking the gold collar from the Dreamer he stalked from the balcony, ignoring the salutes from Glimshpill and Catskin. It seemed a pressure had been removed as the early tension of a storm that is dissipated by the first crack of thunder. They breathed easier.

'Well,' said Glimshpill and yawned, 'I feel a thirst in my throat, and my belly is as empty as the heart of a rich man. The mess or a tavern?'

'The tavern, I think,' said Catskin. 'I have seen enough of this bull for many a day.' And he gestured to the head upon their tunics. 'You two have your own business to discuss, I believe,' Catskin continued to Skarry and the Dreamer. 'Yet we will meet again soon.'

'More's the pity!' Glimshpill roared and gave Skarry a shove that sent him reeling. 'Farewell for now, young savage.'

With a wave the two turned and passed within the wall, the stamp of Glimshpill's booted feet echoing after they had gone. Skarry turned at last to the Dreamer.

'Is Ress safe?' he asked immediately.

'She is,' the Dreamer replied. 'You would not recognise her.'

Skarry laughed.

'And you have changed also,' the Dreamer said.

Skarry was silent for a moment as they both turned to lean on the parapet, the vast dark wall of the keep before them. Then he said, 'I have seen more in the past few days than in all my life with the Olluden.'

'It only seems that way,' the Dreamer replied.

'I have been dreaming also.'

'That is only right,' said the Dreamer. 'You should heed them, let them seep into your action for they are your own voice.'

Without thinking Skarry made to put his stone within his mouth.

'Your necklace is growing,' the Dreamer remarked and Skarry dropped the stone. It hung with the other two upon the thong. The Dreamer reached out a hand and took up each in turn between forefinger and thumb.

'These stones will tell a story,' he said, 'the story of the old peoples.'

'I should like to hear it,' Skarry said.

'I do not know it yet,' said the Dreamer.

In the grey afternoon they stood thus joined, the Dreamer's extended hand at Skarry's neck, cradling the stones like delicate eggs within his fingers.

'You wish to see the one you know as Ress?' the elder asked at last and Skarry nodded. 'And the council?' he went on, indicating the dark bulk of the inner keep. 'You wish to be present?'

Again Skarry nodded and the Dreamer took him by the arm and led him through the doorway into the wall and together they made their way through the wide passageways of the fortress.

12

The Councils of Taur

The doors to the council chamber were of the heart of oak, the dense brown grain flecked with black. On each door had been carved the head of a bull with the horns curving outward, the eyes set with red stones that glittered in the torchlight.

To Skarry it was as if he had been transported, back to his forest home. The carving was clearly the work of the Olluden and he could feel the hand of Gemel in every contour, in each cut of the knife. Enthralled he pressed his palms against the wood and followed the incised lines with the tips of his fingers. Surrounding the bulls were a world of figures; to the centre was Thuggundian, the stone bear and behind him rose up the oak whose many branchings reached to every corner, the boughs filled with life. Above, Vidar and Ithunne descended from the starways, mightily armed.

It seemed to Skarry that a sadness had been captured in the stone bear's eyes as he sat upon his granite world. Yet the rocky globe was not devoid of life for about his feet were fashioned twining vines and many animals sheltered within the mass of leaves and amongst them, their arms resting upon the backs of a second bear and a horse, were two children, a girl and a boy.

The soldiers to either side of the door began to grow tired of Skarry's presence for he effectively blocked the entrance. Only the sight of the Dreamer, who observed Skarry closely, deterred them from moving him on. When he was done looking Skarry stood back. The Dreamer took him by the arm and with a nod to the guards swung open the doors and entered the council chamber.

At first Skarry could see little for the press of bodies, the Captains and Commanders all standing and straining forward on their toes to hear. It was quite dark, a low ceiling cut off the light. The Dreamer seemed to have no trouble in moving

112

forward, the others parting before him as though he were the wind and they tall corn. Skarry followed in his lee and found himself thrust up against a low railing looking out into a bright circle lit by racks of candles and torches.

It was the roof that caught at Skarry's gaze and he began to think that perhaps Ringdove was that fair city of his dreams. Around the circle were pillars like the trunks of trees that reared up into the vaults above to a great domed ceiling painted in frescoes of brilliant colours that depicted the archaic battles and warrior heroes of the past.

What he had first taken to be the ceiling was no more than the underside of a wide balcony that ran about the circle. This was filled with nobles and advisers, richly attired, some smoking from delicate pipes, while others drank daintily from crystal glasses. The decanters were placed upon silver trays held by servants who had the look of old peoples to Skarry. Behind these tiered seats the intricately carved panelled walls rose up to meet the frescoes above.

Yet it was to the centre of the chamber that the attention of all was directed and here was a great round table of pink marble all streaked with veins of red, as though a living thing had been flayed to expose the raw muscles and tendons.

Opposite Skarry sat the High Lord, the Paladin Guise, on a raised platform. He had washed the bear's blood from his face and sat with chin cradled on his great square palms and he seemed to stare unseeing at the marble. To his left there was a second tall chair, empty and not so finely wrought as his own. But below him, around this table, were seated more lords than Skarry would ever have thought to see at one time.

A hand fell upon his arm and looking up he found Sulla standing beside him.

'It is a long while since any of the Olluden were present at such a council, not that you have missed much,' she said, raising her voice to be heard above the babble of conversation. 'We do not usually stay for long, we have not the stomach for it,' she went on and turned to watch the circle.

'The lords of the south sit upon the left hand of the High Lord,' Sulla explained.

There were five seats here and all but one was occupied.

'The empty chair is Quorn's?' he asked and Sulla nodded.

113

'Indeed, you were the last to set eyes upon that proud one when he made for the Pass with but a score of horsemen against the full weight of the enemy.'

'And the five chairs on his right are for the lords of the north?' Skarry asked and again Sulla nodded.

'That is so,' she said. 'And the empty chair on that side is Fressingfield's who has passed beyond our human knowledge.'

The arc of the circle closest to Skarry was taken up by three seats, all filled, and it was here that he felt himself to be drawn. On the right sat one in the furs and leather jerkin of the Asgire, the marsh people. He had the beaked nose like Crane of Mireside and his limbs were as long and as thin. About his black hair was a band of willow on the front of which was set a disc of blue stone flecked with emerald.

On the left was one Skarry recognised, Sulla naming him as Hunter of the Hars plains, speaker for the Epona, whose great company they had ridden with over the low pass to Ringdove. His long yellow hair was woven into two plaits and he sat calm and straight backed in his chair.

Between these two stood one who leaned casually upon the marble and spoke easily above the chatter. He was clad in leather sewn with many plates of a dull red metal, as red as his thick curling hair that stood out from his head and covered the lower part of his face in a rough beard and moustache.

'It is Hook,' Sulla whispered as the other spoke, 'of the mountains of the Ridgeway.'

'Hear me, then,' Hook near bellowed, his voice thick with the accent of the mountain people, 'for I deem Doth Auren, Wenlok, to be in the right.' And here he gestured towards the empty seat to the Paladin's left where the Steward of the south, which was D'Auren, would usually sit.

'And we are as fools,' he went on with much hissing from those who watched. 'The Misery of Ice, Grimal Skoye, has crossed the Isthmus and is already within our lands. He has met up with our noble Fressingfield and no doubt wiped the ground with him in battle. The one they call Juss has now also come over the Isthmus to Skoye's aid and, thus reprovisioned, the Misery has made secret march and now lies camped somewhere within our own lands with his hardened Ice Warriors.

'And what have we done to hinder him? Well, the mighty and

most noble lord Quorn has gone against him, if we are to believe the reports, with all of twenty men! Perhaps he will slow him down, eh?'

Hunter of the Hars plains shook his head slowly with a quiet smile to his eyes. The marsh lord Emrod was not so silent and let out a sharp laugh.

'And Wenlok goes alone into great danger for all our sakes,' the one in red concluded, 'while we sit here and ponder.'

There was much shouting as Hook finished and one of the lords from the north side of the table rose up to answer, speaking in a hissing voice, a tall and fully armoured figure poised like a statue with one mailed hand to his sword.

'And we, gathered here with all our massed armies combined, shall go forth and find this harbinger of winter, this Misery of Ice, Grimal Skoye and hunt him out and cast him down and slay him and destroy his forces utterly.'

And the essence of power and armed might, of arrogant confidence and inevitability, flowed from him, infecting the warrior lords who sat at hand and their Captains and Commanders who waited beyond the circle, as a plague strikes down cattle, and they roared approval at this warrior plan. Some of the lords at the table threw down their swords upon the marble with a great clatter in an impulsive sign of assent.

'This is Damon, of Dunnerdale,' said Sulla as the cheering died down.

Hook remained silent, unmoved and raised his hand in a gesture of speech and the High Lord nodded to him.

'Listen then,' Hook began, 'you warriors and philosophers and lords of luxury, for I deem this necessary for you to know.

'With due regard I'll say that you mighty lords are maybe skilled at neat battles upon the plains or gentle foothills, yet are you as new-born babes before the mountains. List to what I say!' This last was directed with quiet force at Damon who had growled at the comparison.

'Skoye and his warriors are a winter people and it is in the mountains of our Ridgeway that he has made his camp. Now no doubt you have heard much by way of rumour and legend about the Ridgeway, no doubt you have traversed the few passes and were not overmuch taken aback by the danger. No doubt you have ridden across the foothills and screes, maybe even in winter, and were not largely fearful. No, I do not doubt that you have done this. But have you attempted the Low Pass in deep snow, let alone the High? Have you tried a winter march through even the lowlands or dreamed of climbing a ridge with a thousand men or ridden through the valley bottoms in the times of ice?

'No, I know that you have not done this, for you are plainsmen and city folk. But I have, and I know.

'First comes snow that rises deeper and yet deeper as the lowlands are climbed. It fills up the valleys and covers the rivers in great frozen drifts breaking into crevasses as deep as wells. Or like a carpet, clean and white, so soft as to tempt and suck down the foolish, so deep that you might not walk upon it without sinking down and smothering in its cold grip. Or up to the waist so that each step is a trial and you will succumb to exhaustion afore the cold. So lies snow, lodged in every nook and cranny, that clogs worse than mud and freezes more than just the birds.

'Second is ice, for wherever the snow will not lie for the blast of the wind, then comes the ice that coats the stone as hard and bright as glass, that bridges rivers and crawls up mountains. It lies beneath the snow to topple the unwary, or lies above, a crusted skin that'll break so easy and trap you below. And on the windward slopes you need to move and always move, for should you stop for even a moment, you'll find your boots glazed to the ice and to tarry longer will leave you as part of the mountain.

'And third is the wind that sighs so gentle at times but as oft will rise to the fury of Vidar and cut skin from bone in its might and blow the blood from your body and freeze you as you stand. Like a spear it penetrates and though you should be thickly clothed it'll work devious and enter here a cuff, there a collar and at last will burst open a pin or button and you'll find in but a moment your coat torn from your back by the icy fingers and your very soul laid bare to the blast. And the wind carries the elements of winter also, the snow to blind and cover, the rains to soak and freeze, the sharded ice to flay and pierce.

'Thus lies the Ridgeway in winter, triple cursed to those who know not the ways of the mountains.'

Hook fell silent for a moment and such was the power of his speech that no one spoke and all seemed momentarily lost in each their own thought. Skarry could not keep from nodding in

116

agreement as each point had been made, for the Olluden had learned much of their mountain knowledge from the peoples of the high places, the Hagarath.

'Too late are we to reach Skoye,' Hook went on at last, 'for he has already entered within the mountains and reached their inner vales before the deep snows of winter and no doubt built a great winter camp to survive the time of ice. And he will do it, for his men are Ice Warriors, hardened by many years of war. He'll lie hidden in the snow until the first blizzards die and then'll rise up like Ymir from the ice and with his many sleds and skied and skated warriors he'll march the inner valleys unseen and spring out from some unexpected quarter.

'So, my Lord,' Hook said and he seemed to speak only to the Paladin, 'I'll not back a march on Skoye, for we'll first have to fight the winter of the Ridgeway, then Skoye, and I deem the latter the lesser danger. I'll take no further part in this debate for I've spoken only what I believe to be the truth. But, my Lord, I'll follow your decision, whatever it may be, blindly, as a led dog, for it has always been this way.'

So saying Hook bowed low to the Paladin, turned on his heel and walked from the chamber. Hunter of the Epona and Emrod of the Asgire did follow Hook out.

Now there was much talk as the three representatives of the old peoples left and the buzz of many conversations coiled upward to the domed ceiling above. Skarry was much taken by the firmness of the speech, strengthened by the noble pledge at the last, to follow the elected High Lord whatever the consequences. Here was a fierce warrior whose loyalty was paramount and born of an inner faith indeed.

Sulla, at his side, shook her head as if with sadness.

'Poor Hook,' she said softly to Skarry. 'He is no more fortunate than ourselves. The Paladin holds many of his family as guests, so called, here in Ringdove. It is a threat as equal to the burning of the Hars plains. Nor would Emrod and the Asgire fare any better if they refused to fight, not with their protector D'Auren absent. In truth these city folk have little kindness for our ways.'

Skarry was taken aback yet he was distracted by a lord of the south who rose up from his seat and lifted a limp arm to attract the attention of the Paladin. This lord looked out through half-closed eyes and allowed no trace of emotion to escape the imprisoning bars of his lashes. His voice, light and breezy, cut suddenly through the chatter.

'My good assembled lords,' he called, in a drawl, 'I feel, perhaps as others amongst our number, that a main reason for this O so imperial diet has been, ah, overstepped? I refer, of course, to our good friend and brother lord, D'Auren. You follow, I presume?'

The Paladin Guise stopped in mid sentence with a scribe and turned slowly to this lord, his eyes narrowing. The muscles of his thick neck stood out like ropes beneath the skin and his gaze fell like a shaft upon the other.

'My lord Malbrow,' Guise the Paladin said, 'am I to understand that you wish to raise a subject which I have overpassed?'

Utter silence fell upon the chamber as a cloak and the room seemed the darker for it. But it was Damon who answered and as quickly the weight lifted, the light returned and with it the calm arrogance of Malbrow.

'I, my High Lord,' said Damon in his nasal whine, 'I and I do believe others also share this view of the Lord Malbrow,' and he indicated this one with a graceful wave of his arm, 'and, as he, we deem it a fit point for debate.'

Guise seemed frozen into that moment, unable to decide what to do. From the outer circle and the balcony came muttered ayes and at last the Paladin was forced to speak.

'I'll listen, Damon, if you have something to say.'

'Thank you, most noble Lord,' came the reply, with a trace of sarcasm at the Paladin's rebuke of title. Then Damon spoke out in defiance.

'I,' he began, 'and all gathered here, did so upon the command of our most High Lord. Is it not so?' The assent was loudly proclaimed. 'And so it is in our land. For we the electors cast our vote and so create a High Lord from amongst our numbers, one greater than ourselves, to control and unite our independencies. And we serve him in all things, to hold this mighty land as one, to further its greatness and ascend to high heights of glory and worldly power.

'And so, upon receiving a command from our most High Lord, we obey it and thus safeguard the land. But hist, for of a sudden, one of our number rebuffs the order, ignores the decree and goes against our High Lord's word.

'And I deem that by so going against our elected Lord and ruler, this one does go against us all. And for these reasons I call for a vote upon the treachery,' and he laid heavy emphasis upon this word, 'the treachery of that one, Doth Auren, of Wenlok.'

Loud were the shouts of those against D'Auren for Damon's eloquence cut like a dagger. The High Lord held up an arm for silence.

'So it seems we are to be frank, Damon,' he said. 'In which case I'll say only this. True it is that D'Auren did ignore my order and for this he must be brought before a council to put his case. Yet if he has gone alone against the Misery of Ice then it be an act more noble than any that you before me have carried through. We need D'Auren, now, more than ever and it may well be that the fate of the land hangs upon the strength of his arm. I'll put the fate of the land before your squabbles any day, for it seems to me that you Damon and you Malbrow are more concerned with D'Auren's title as Steward of the south than any supposed treachery.'

Malbrow rose and spoke without looking at the Paladin.

'I call for the siding of sides, the casting of votes, for or against Doth Auren of Wenlok. This is the right of the diet.'

Guise the Paladin hung down his head as though to blot the sight from his eyes. When he looked up once more he seemed to Skarry a troubled man.

'You have forced a siding of sides that may well break our land,' remorse and bitter anger in his voice. 'Yet the right is yours. I call upon the lords of the north to begin the vote.'

The first seat on Guise's right was empty, it being Fressing-field's but the next two lords dropped their hands to the hilts of their swords and the second spoke for both.

'As lifelong friends to the Lord of Wenlok we hold our trust. We side for him.'

'Heighington and Raven,' said Sulla, 'a loyal pair.'

Next came Damon and one called Tenora who fair flung their swords down upon the marble.

'We do side against the traitor,' Damon said and so the vote stood at two for and two against.

'Ah, that the three chose to go,' said Sulla and indeed Guise also looked sadly at the three empty chairs opposite him. Then it came to the lords of the south to make their vote known.

Malbrow was first of these and took great delight in the clatter of his sword as it hit the table top. But next to him was one who held with D'Auren, young Cirith of Topcliffe and the vote was still even.

Then there came another empty seat, this one Quorn's who would surely have sided with Wenlok, thought Skarry. Watching, he could hardly believe that this could take place, that such strength and nobility could be called traitor.

The last of the two southern lords rose slowly and with considered action drew forth their swords.

'Selham and Nessan,' Sulla whispered in Skarry's ear. 'We have lost the vote.'

Selham spoke for the two against the traitor and they laid their swords upon the marble. So the vote came to five against three and even the Paladin's own call could not redress the balance. The Captains and Commanders from without the circle gave loud shouts. Malbrow and Damon smiled at each other across the table. Guise stood up and raised both arms into the air but it was some time before there was quiet enough for him to speak.

'You have all seen the vote,' he said. 'So let it be known that Doth Auren of Wenlok is proclaimed traitor to his High Lord and country and that sentence of death is passed upon him. Let it also be known that Lord Malbrow of Malden, as senior in the south, is proclaimed Steward in the traitor's place.

'And further, let it also be known that with first light, two days hence, the assembled armies of Taur will march forth from this place and travel east to the Isthmus, there to meet up and do battle with the armies of our enemy.'

The roar of approval resounded throughout the chamber and many were the swords waved above the heads of those present. The Captains rushed forward into the circle and surrounded Damon and Malbrow, clapping them upon the shoulders and these two went from the room together with the great mass of warriors and other lords against D'Auren.

Skarry clung to the rail as if numbed, buffeted by the confusion of bodies about him. Head down he saw the blue of the Dreamer's robe at his side and grasped at it as though the contact might protect him from the madness. Slowly the flood of bodies ebbed and looking up he found that the chamber was nigh on empty.

The Dreamer led Skarry forward and they came to the side of the Paladin who still sat in his high chair. The muscles in his neck alternately bulged and relaxed and he breathed deeply. The Dreamer said nothing until the High Lord spoke of himself.

'Ah, it is a sad day,' he said softly and Skarry would have cried had he not been so fearful of the Paladin's suppressed rage.

'If Wenlok had wed my daughter then even now we might be saved. The ties of blood would have deterred those petty fools. And now, though I hold little love for thee D'Auren, I will miss thy swift mind in the thick of the fight and also those mighty spearmen of thine.'

'There is still hope, Lord,' the Dreamer said quietly and laid a soft touch on the Paladin's clenched fist. 'D'Auren is no doubt far on his way and may well reach the enemy long before he hears that he is declared traitor. Why, he may even defeat Skoye which would surely reinstate him. You have not lost his strong arm yet.'

The Paladin turned slowly to the Dreamer with a growing light in his eyes.

'And should he receive more aid,' Guise said carefully, 'then his victory would be all the more likely.' And he looked the Dreamer up and down.

'Give me the word, Lord,' this one replied, 'and I will be on my way to his side.'

'You have it,' the Paladin said simply.

'He will need a guide,' Skarry broke in. 'I know the Angsoth, the High Pass and the Maen-hir.'

Guise was silent, looking into Skarry's eyes.

'I have seen the shape of your face before,' he said after a moment's thought. 'You are of the Olluden, are you not?' and Skarry nodded. The Paladin continued, 'Then you will know the Angsoth and the High Pass but not the Ridgeway?'

Skarry's momentary elation was quashed but the High Lord caught at his shoulder.

'No, you shall go,' he said, 'for Hook of the Hagarath will do as I tell him. He will take you by the northern route to the lands you know. Then while you seek out D'Auren, Hook shall find me Skoye's winter camp. Yet I will need to send one or two others also who can return to me with the news of Skoye's whereabouts while Hook marks his position.'

121

'I know of two who will serve,' the Dreamer said. 'They are of your soldiery.'

'Choose them,' the Paladin said abruptly. 'Let Vidar bless this, our little council, for the fate of all pivots about this point. When will you leave?'

'In the morning,' the Dreamer replied and thus it was decided. Once more Skarry felt an unknown road open up before him as the Dreamer led him from the chamber. Guise made off with a new strength to his stride and a dozen armed guards fell in at his back. The Dreamer made to follow but stopped as another soldier pulled at Skarry's arm.

'The lady Recina would talk with you,' he said sharply as though annoyed that he should have to speak to one so lowly. He pointed back along the corridor to a bier or litter which rested on the floor. There were three other soldiers about it.

Skarry turned to the Dreamer with a shrug of confusion. The other put his hand to Skarry's shoulder and with a gentle push, urged him towards the litter. As if to make certain the Dreamer himself turned and with quick strides went off down the corridor. Skarry found himself alone of friends, with the soldier leading him firmly towards the litter. The sides were covered in embroidered curtains, swirls of leaves and plant forms and as he came close a white hand appeared and drew them aside a little.

Within was a lady, dressed in fine silks of green, with red hair that cascaded in bright waves about her shoulders. She smiled up at him with eyes the palest blue. Before he even realised who it was Skarry's heart began to beat loud within his chest. She seemed to be looking over his left shoulder.

'We meet again, Skarry of the Olluden,' she said simply.

It was Ress.

Skarry felt a smile break over his face, for as the coming dawn he was not sure until the very last, until the rim of the sun peeped over the far hills.

'It is you,' he said finally as his eyes pierced the mask of fine clothes and jewels. Her eyes had been lined with thin black and her lips reddened.

'It is me,' she said softly.

'Perhaps the young lady would like to return to her room,' came the voice of the Captain of her guard, thrusting his head towards them.

'Surely she will tell you if it is so?' Skarry said with some surprise for the soldier's words had the sound of a command to them rather than a question.

Ress put her hand on Skarry's arm.

'Enough!' she said sharply. 'If you will walk with me I shall return to my room. At least we shall be assured of some privacy there.'

The Captain's face took on an angry flush as Ress scrambled from the litter with Skarry's help. Holding to his arm she hurried him along the corridor with the guards struggling to keep up, the litter swinging wildly between them.

'There is a left turn ahead,' Ress said to Skarry, 'between the two columns carved with the bull's head.'

In this way she directed him and together they passed through the keep.

'I thought you might have hurt your leg,' Skarry said and Ress could not help but laugh when she caught his meaning.

'The litter is not my idea,' Ress said. 'It is my father's, for he feels that it reflects ill upon him that one of his line should be seen staggering blindly through the city feeling at the walls.'

'Yet you would not stagger,' Skarry said in surprise.

'He will not listen to argument,' Ress said with finality. 'The door with the tree carved upon it,' she added and Skarry steered them across the corridor to an oak door that brought him up sharp.

'It is the work of the Olluden,' he whispered and his hands went out to trace the design.

'It is a fair piece,' Ress agreed. 'It was to be burned when the keep was rebuilt; much of the older work was destroyed then.'

The trunk of the tree began at the foot of the door and wound its knarled way upwards, dividing and dividing, following the patterns of the wood and breaking into furls of leaves where burrs turned the grain this way and that. It had the feel of the mountain oaks in a stiff wind.

'It may have been carved by Gemel,' Skarry said. 'The great doors to the council chamber are his.'

'Let us go in,' Ress said and turned sharply on the Captain who waited with his breathless troop. 'Do you wait here,' she commanded and they entered, shutting the door behind them.

Ress put her head back against the door and sighed with relief, eyes half closed. Skarry could not help but start at the room within, for though it was plain, painted simply in white with little furniture, yet the walls were hung with relief panels and the floor filled with many sculptures and carvings of birds and beasts. Here was a stallion brought forth from a twisted piece of sycamore that gleamed whitely on the point of leaping into a gallop. There was a bear carved from the dark forest wood, the heart of oak, each hair finely tooled, the head half turned as if he had been disturbed whilst digging for honey in the trunk of the cherry.

Ress walked swiftly across the room through the sculptures, putting out her arm only as she neared the bed. She turned and sat upon the mattress, listening as Skarry circled her room, a smile to her face as he exclaimed or gasped at each new discovery.

'The stallion is the work of the Epona,' she said and Skarry agreed.

'Only they know horses so well,' he said. 'And the bear is of the Olluden,' he went on.

'Have you seen this?' she asked and handed him a small piece from a table at her bedside. It was a seal pup in a black stone that had a warm, soft feel to it and lent a sheen to the young pelt. Skarry could only shake his head in admiration for the beauty of the carving.

'It is only through living with such creatures that you grow close enough to undertake such work,' he said softly. 'Yet I know not the carvers of this piece.'

'It comes from Monrolia,' Ress said quietly.

Skarry started as though the stone became suddenly hot within his hands.

'How could they who are so evil create beauty such as this?' Skarry asked amazed.

'Evil is not the province of one people,' Ress said. 'My father killed my mother in a fit of rage when he found out that I was blind. Ever after have I been kept by nurses in half-hiding and under guard to conceal his shame.

'They say that when the doors to the council chamber were carved, my grandfather desired that his finest bull should be the pattern for the design, so he had it slaughtered and the severed head was brought bleeding to the carvers that they might copy it.

That is why it has such a hard feel when compared to the other work on that door.'

Skarry listened in silence to her words and felt the awakening of understanding within him and not a little disquiet.

'Then you are the Paladin Guise's daughter,' he said slowly. 'And you were crossing the High Pass on your way to wed Doth Auren.'

Ress turned towards the sound of his voice and nodded her head.

'And you, Skarry of the Olluden,' she said, 'are a son of the old peoples and you must help me for I shall not stay another day within this evil city and if you do not help me than shall I surely die.'

Distant through the walls came the sounds of a sonorous bell tolling. Skarry looked into her face and there were tears in the pale blue eyes that stared over his left shoulder.

'What can I do?' he asked.

13

Hook of the Hagarath

Skarry was glad to be back on Fell again and the pony seemed pleased to see him also, snickering and nibbling at his shoulder when they were first reunited. With Sulla in mind he had discarded the saddle and sat instead on a green blanket that let the heat of the horse seep through to warm his legs. After some thought he exchanged the bitted bridle for a plaited halter and Fell seemed to appreciate his greater freedom. On a rope Skarry led a second pony carrying panniers filled with provisions. Tied across the top were skis and snow shoes should the blizzards catch them.

Hook, the red king, led the party on a sturdy hill pony, all shaggy with her winter coat. His armour was of thick leather sewn with many plates, cunningly overlapped to combine a strong defence with freedom of movement. Each plate was so joined to the next that metal was cushioned from metal and he made no sound as he moved. And, like his wild beard and hair, the metal was red, the red of both copper and its alloy with tin, a dull red as of the glow of embers within the fire. He carried a two-headed axe slung over his shoulder and about his left wrist on a thong was a red stone, the red of the Ridgeway.

Behind Hook, before Skarry, came the Dreamer, similarly mounted with his blue cloak pulled tight about him. He had raised up the hood to cover his thin fair hair and seemed to sing or chant softly to himself. Then behind Skarry was Glimshpill all bundled up against the cold so that he dwarfed his mount. He pulled at his pipe, the stiff wind driving the plume of green smoke horizontally from the bowl. Catskin was about but out of sight, somewhere up ahead with his sharp eyes peeled for danger.

The road was as yet still wide enough for two large waggons to pass by with ease and the surface was smooth beneath the shallow snow, of crushed gravel upon a solid foundation.

'It must always be good, this road,' Glimshpill said when Skarry compared it to the rutted tracks he had met with. 'For this is the path of armies. The High Lords have need of this swift route in defence of the land. Mind, the enemy have found it useful in the past also.'

Behind them the walls of Ringdove receded. From the squat grey keep flew the banner of Taur, the great bull. All about the walls the camps were in turmoil as the soldiers prepared for their march. The great noise of their confusion fell away behind as the party rode on.

'I for one am glad to be out of that,' said Glimshpill. Hook turned in his saddle and looked back at each in turn.

'As are we all, by my judgement,' he said.

Up ahead the road ran straight as a spear and level, north-east across the Three Kings Basin, with the sea far off to their left and the mountains to the right. After a while Skarry rode forward with Hook and the mountain man spoke to him of the Ridgeway, pointing out each mass of snow-covered stone in turn as it rose up into the mists.

'This one is Sourfoot,' Hook said. 'Not of great height yet a plateau of tarns and bogs in summer that turn to ice with the coming of snow. The next is Sharp Shard which is gained from the fells of Sourfoot by way of Rip Edge.' And here he showed Skarry a thin ridge that led in leaps and bounds up into the cloud.

'Snow Slaughter,' Hook went on, 'the next in line, whose summit lies far above the cloud and has claimed many of the foolish. And then is Raven Tore which is all rock in a single towering crag to dwarf the castles of men. Next comes Harrow High which is also named Ice Bright and on beyond our present sight the procession continues, Stoneside and Bleak Edge, then across the Frozen Fells to the Dark Seat and by way of Illgill to Dunan and the lands you know, for from that dale rises up your own Angsoth, Vidar's Chair, from whose peaks can be seen the spires of Wenlok when the air is clear, as you so well know.'

Skarry nodded and wrapped himself tighter in his cloak as images of his homeland rose up before his inner eye.

'It is a cold wind this,' he said, 'coming off the sea.'

'It is born of the mountains of Monrolia,' Hook said and Skarry started at the name. 'We speak of this our Ridgeway as a hard teacher in winter, yet are these peaks like children to those of the

Ulta-Zorn in Monrolia. It is told how the lord of that land, the Cunerdin, and all his many men could not stand against the winter of the Ulta-Zorn.'

'You speak of the enemy,' Skarry said. 'How can you know this?'

'They are the enemies of our lords,' Hook said gravely. 'Yet are they still humans.'

'Tell me,' said Skarry. 'Tell me of their land.'

'I will tell you of the Cunerdin,' said Hook, settling in his saddle, 'and how he builded the great Winter Palace, deep in the mountains of the Ulta-Zorn. For he was a rich and powerful lord, not unlike our own Paladin and he had a fair city named Dalfsen as his seat. He loved to sit looking into the west where the hills rose up from the plains, piled one atop the other, rising ever skyward, steeper and rockier and shrouded in ice that brightly reflected the light of the sun, scattering it into many colours. These were the peaks of the Ulta-Zorn, inviolate guardians of Monrolia, where Ymir took up his seat after casting out Ithunne, so it is said in this land.

'The Cunerdin would ride out into the foothills to marvel at the beauty of the mountains and came close to death many times in snow slides and rock falls and blizzards. Then he put out the call across the land, for all the masons and carpenters and craftsmen to come to him and he laid out the design of a Winter Palace to be builded in the heart of the mountains, that he might dwell there in safety.

'His people laboured for many years, constructing a road into the hills and transporting vast weights of materials in great hazard. The Cunerdin turned away from the mountains and lost himself in other work until the time that the Winter Palace was finished. Then at last a great train of waggons was arranged and many were the people who came to Dalfsen to make that journey into the Ulta-Zorn. Guards were sent ahead together with cooks and servants, dancers and other entertainers and a great celebration was planned to mark the birth of the Palace.

'So the Cunerdin set out with his vast company, gaily singing and dancing with bands playing and they wined and dined their way to the Ultra-Zorn and entered the mountains towards the end of summer. And after many days they crested the rise of one mighty shoulder and looked down in awe upon the Palace of the

Cunerdin, built of pale marbles and rare glass and guarded by quartz figures upon the wall tops. The Cunerdin bade them all wait for he desired to make the approach alone and so they watched the speck of him and his horse as he rode down to the white gates. Yet he tarried not but rode back in utter haste and when asked he refused to speak and commanded that they return to Dalfsen, which they did.

'It is said that Rima Eskoye, forefather to the enemy's Grimal Skoye of our own time, he alone refused the command and lay in hiding until the Cunerdin and his sprawling retinue had made off hastily for Dalfsen. Then he went down to the Winter Palace and coming close he saw that the pale of the walls was not marble but snow, that the bright and beautiful flashings of the spires was not glass but ice and that the quartz figures were not carvings but the Cunerdin's own warriors, frozen where they stood.

'After, the Cunerdin looked not upon the mountains and turned his gaze upon more immediate gain. The Winter Palace lies there still, though no doubt deeply buried beneath great weight of ice and snow. The old peoples of that land say that the Cunerdin stirred up the wrath of Ithunne, even though she is bound, by building in the name of Ymir on a place once sacred to her.'

'So the winter remains unconquered still,' said Skarry but Hook gave a quiet laugh.

'There is another tale,' he said, 'which concerns the one whose name your mother doubtless used to fright you into quiet when you should have been asleep within your bed. It is of Grimal Skoye, him whom we seek.'

'Tell me!' Skarry said eagerly but Hook laughed again.

'There will be time enough for that,' he said. 'We shall need our attention now for the road. We should be safe at least to Dunnerdale yet we must move with care for there is no word of Midloth. If we find trace of the enemy then shall we leave the road and go south into the foothills of our mountains.'

'Who is that behind?' called Glimshpill and looking back they saw a small figure in the distance, black against the snow with the dark smear of Ringdove still visible beyond. Hook, the red king, exchanged looks with Skarry but said nothing.

'It will be the spies of the Paladin no doubt,' Glimshpill said and turned his back on the sight.

The weather worsened, the cold wind cutting in from across the sea, driving sleet before it. Skarry buttoned his face flap and huddled within his cloak, ever and again stealing glances behind at the distant figure. Above them the lowering cloud pressed down and the mountains to their right faded into the swirl of wind blown ice.

'Pray for a warm bed in Dunnerdale,' Glimshpill called loudly, cursing the wind for he could no longer keep his pipe lit.

'Pray that the enemy has not yet reached it,' Hook called grimly back.

'All we need, that,' Glimshpill muttered. 'A happy thought to speed the day.' And he made to spit but the flurry of wind blew it back and smeared his cloak. Angrily he took up his cursing song and the odd word reached Skarry through the growing gale.

Bitter sweet with frozen feet,
Curse the day that we did meet.

By the afternoon Ringdove had long faded into the gray gloom but a darker pall in the sky ahead slowed their pace. Catskin came galloping up suddenly and Hook had his axe unslung before he recognised the Corporal.

'We are nearing Dunnerdale,' he said. 'We must go steady, the signs are not good.'

He broke off when he caught sight of the figure in the distance behind them and froze in the action of wheeling his horse about.

'And who might that be?' he wondered, frowning with concentration and then the lines turned into those of anger. 'Have you aught to do with this?' he asked Skarry so sharply that the other could make no reply.

'Foolish, foolish,' Catskin muttered. 'We cannot wait,' he said. 'This is on your head.' And he held a finger pointed straight at Skarry before spurring his horse forward again into the snow.

Glimshpill looked baffled by the exchange and trotted on after his Corporal. But Hook turned his pony and put out a hand to Skarry's shoulder.

'Ride on,' he said. 'I will wait here and catch you up later.'

Skarry thanked him with relief. 'She told me she had a good horse,' he said, 'that knew the way by heart. Yet I will feel happier when she is with us.'

Skarry rode on after the others. There came a lull in the gale and the air cleared somewhat of its blur of ice. The wind had swept the ground clean and piled the snow in the lee of the stumps of trees. These were blackened as though from some long past fire. Innumerable, they stretched away in all directions, the sad remains of a mighty forest. Many of the huge trunks lay where they had been felled, that way and this, their hearts rotting.

'These plains were once thick with the old forest,' the Dreamer said, coming close to Skarry's side. 'Yet it interfered with the passage and formation of soldiers. It was too useful a hiding place and could conceal whole armies. So the then High lord cut it down that the Monrolians would not come upon Ringdove in secret.'

'And what of the timber?' Skarry asked, incredulous. 'How could such weight of timber be used?'

'They made a fleet of ships with some of it,' the Dreamer replied, 'and sailed it laden with men to the shores of Monrolia. But the waters of the sea froze over and bound them to the beaches. Then the Monrolians came skating over the ice and burned the ships full of soldiers. It was a mighty loss to the Taurians. But this land has often seen battles like that. Many times have the Monrolians come into this land and as many times have they been pushed back into theirs.'

'It is a tired land,' said Skarry with an eye to the stumps. 'And the trees that once gave shelter will not grow back now, for the fierce winter winds freeze the lonely saplings.'

'It is an old story,' the Dreamer said.

'Let me hear it,' Skarry asked.

'I meant,' said the Dreamer, 'that it has happened often in times past and that we suffer still from it now.'

Then they were silent and continued on the road and before them they could see the dark pall of smoke that rose up from the site of Dunnerdale. As they neared they came upon signs of a more recent wrack than the waste of stumps about them.

First there was a waggon upon its side and its load of barrels scattered about, some burst open, their contents spilled in icy sheets that made the ponies tread with care. A dead horse hung between the splintered shafts, its coat full of frozen snow. There were other snow-covered mounds of human form, some with the shafts of arrows like spines in them.

131

Catskin and Glimshpill came hurrying back with the snow flying from their horses' hoofs.

'The enemy has been here as is plain to see,' said the Corporal. 'Yet there is no sign of him being here still. We will go in together.'

Glimshpill drew his sword and let the iron blade hang at his side. As they approached they saw that the smoke rose up from dense fires within the walls. Before them the twin towers of the gatehouse had been thrown down and become jumbled piles of rubble. Further along the curve of wall were other breaches as though a giant fist had beaten at the stone and torn it up in huge lumps.

For a little distance outside the walls a clear space had been made that an attacking army should have no cover in the assault. Here, by the way the ground had been churned to mud, it looked as though the townsfolk had fled pursued by horsemen. A short run it was, to nowhere, for there was no cover, no place of safety. The snow collected in the shelter of their bodies, all sprawled in heaps with limbs twisted awkwardly.

By the shattered gates they could see where the horsemen had come together to enter, the tracks converging and digging the roadway into deep ruts. More of the dead were trampled into the earth.

Within the walls some buildings still burned, their roofs long since collapsed in showers of sparks, the fire belching forth from the piles of wreckage. Others were burned to their very foundations and smouldered dully. The reek and stench of the burning filled the air and rose up all about them.

Along the parapet of the walls the last of Dunnerdale's guard had fallen. Many were the bodies that lay where they had been cut down, between the buildings and in the roadway. Towards the centre there was like a park where there had been gardens and trees and a fountain whose water filled the breeze with its freshness and its song. Now it was a ruin and become a place for the dead.

Glimshpill began to call out, each cry louder than that before, but there was no reply. He spurred his mount on and rode desperately along each street, lined with the blackened buildings and strewn with tumbled bodies, yet there was no reply.

132

'They are all dead," the Dreamer said at last, loudly, so that all might hear.

Skarry bowed over his pony's neck, shaking his head from side to side as though to banish the sight from about him. He had not seen the likes of such destruction before.

'How can this be possible?' he said softly.

'It is the way with war,' Catskin said. 'It is no more than we did to their fair city of Snowater, two seasons ago. Save there we left not even two stones one atop the other.'

'It is the work of Juss,' Glimshpill snarled as he came back to them. 'His hand can be read in the lack of any wounded. Ah, what are we doing here? What am I doing here?' And he broke off and turned away with his hands to his temples.

'Let us leave this place,' Catskin said quickly and they wheeled the horses about and rode swiftly for the main gate.

Hook was waiting beyond the gate with Ress, well wrapped in a thick cloak so that only the top of her face and the blue of her eyes could be sen.

'Come away, come away!' Skarry cried to her as he rode up, seeking to take her rein in his hand and lead her off.

'There is no need for haste on my behalf, Skarry,' she said. 'I have not the sight to see it. Yet I have a nose and the stench will linger for some distance anyway.'

Catskin gave Ress a hard look then turned his back upon her as though to shut her from his mind.

'We cannot continue by the road,' Hook said, 'that is for sure. Midloth will most likely be the same as this.'

'Juss will be back at Midloth,' Glimshpill said, raising up his head. 'This is just a game with him, a raid. With luck there is no one about to see us.'

'We should make for the foothills,' Hook said. 'The Paladin will be coming this way tomorrow with all his armies; the enemy will not fail to see him.'

'Ah, we are flies on the wheel rim,' groaned Glimshpill, shaking his head. 'They will roll over us and crush us without even knowing that we are here.'

'There's always the sea,' Catskin mused, looking into the grey distance to the north. Glimshpill began to cough as though he had choked on something.

'A boat?' he spluttered. 'What, on water, with all that depth below? I am not that mad yet!'

'So the brave warriors make their plans,' said Ress quietly yet loud enough for all to hear. Hook turned with a broad grin but Catskin looked not so amused.

'We make for the foothills,' said Catskin. To Hook he said, 'You will have to lead us by way of the inner vales.'

'We are decided then,' said Hook and without waiting for another word he turned off towards the mountains in the south.

The wind was at their backs now, urging them on their way. The driven snow collected in the folds of their cloaks and the horses danced as gusts caught at their tails.

Once off the road they threaded their way between the blackened stumps of the old forest and soon the land began to break up as they entered the foothills that rolled away from the Three Kings Basin like huge waves before a gathering storm. Further ahead the mountains reared upward to vanish into cloud.

As they began to climb, Hook picked a path from the white ground that few would have known was there. With each step towards the towering giants before them he seemed to increase in stature himself and his voice came back to them deep and sonorous as he spoke of his mountains.

'Between us and the mountains proper is a lower range that conceals an inner valley,' he said. 'We shall have shelter there from this growing storm and wood for a fire.'

'I like the sound of that word,' Glimshpill growled and repeated it as if to savour its promise. 'A fire, a fire to warm my freezing feet.' And he stretched out his toes in the stirrups.

They wound their way upwards between great boulders all tumbled and strewn about. As they climbed, the rock changed, from the dismal grey that brought the walls of Ringdove to mind, to a warmer red as if the heart of the mountain still beat beneath the skin of winter. And gradually they came upon more and more trees, rising out of the heather and gorse. First the occasional rowan with pale bare branches, then birch and scrub oak hardily clinging amid the stone, their crowns smoothed by the wind. The tangles of black branchings writhed in the gale and creaked loudly as bough rubbed upon bough. Soon the trees thickened and sheltered them from the worst of the weather, slowing the wind and Glimshpill began to look about for a place to pitch his tent.

'We must go some way yet,' Hook called to him when he pointed out a calm hollow under some larger oaks.

So the red king led them on until the light began to fade and though they could not see the sun as it lowered, they knew that the early winter evening drew upon them. They reached at last the top of the rise and a narrow valley opened before them. Going down between the swaying trunks they came to a wall of rock where the valley side rose up suddenly steep and at the base of this crag was the dark opening of a cave.

14

Dream Haven

'Here is our home for the night,' Hook called loudly above the sigh of the wind. 'It has sheltered many of our people in the past.'

He dismounted and gave the reins of his horse to the Dreamer to hold.

'You must wait here,' he said as the others began to go forward. 'I shall see that the cave has no occupants already.' Then he turned from them and taking the axe from his back went within.

'It would be a fair trick if the Monrolians had come so far west,' said Catskin, 'and chosen this for their home also.' He drew a slim sword from its scabbard.

'He will be thinking rather of bears,' Skarry said and took Ress to one side.

Then Hook's voice came rolling like low thunder, up out of the cave mouth.

'It is safe,' he called. 'You may enter.'

Skarry went forward holding Ress's hand while the Dreamer led the horses, speaking softly to them such that they lowered their eyelids drowsily. Though narrow, the entrance was high and just within the opening the cave widened. Here a place for animals had been made, separated from the main chamber by cleft oak hurdles. There was already the smell of horses and their own mounts entered without fear. The Dreamer saw to their care while Hook prepared a fire. As with the havens of the Olluden there was dry kindling and leaving Ress within, Skarry went out in search of more fuel. In the open space before the cave mouth he found Glimshpill struggling to erect a tent.

'Surely you'll sleep inside?' Skarry asked but the other only muttered under his breath.

'He has no liking for caves,' Catskin said softly. 'But he shall

136

not be lonely for I shall stand guard with him that you may sleep easy in your hole.'

'But there is a niche for a watch within the entrance,' Skarry went on, 'and there will be a fire to warm you.'

'He has no liking for caves,' said Catskin again with an edge to his voice that sent Skarry on his way.

Out into the twilight of the woods he went, passing from trunk to trunk, the rough bark beneath his fingers. Going within the familiar creaking of the oaks, almost he was home, in the valley of the Olluden. Soon his people would reach their winter home, the Goleth, and light up the fires within the turf huts and eat of the fruits of the summer, carving and painting the long winter months out.

He began to collect timber, taking only the dead wood that had not fallen and so had dried some in the winds. The smell of the decayed fibre seemed to rise up through his nose and enter his head as images of the past: Irane, his mother showing him the lattice of tunnels left by beetles beneath the bark, Geralt hanging by his legs from a tree, the upside down face grinning wildly. And the voice of Gemel rising and lowering so gently it would turn a squabble into a dance, a game. Just across these mountains lay his own forest and the Olluden, that quiet people.

Yet he turned his back upon the vision and returned to the cave. Thoughts of the war, the lords, of Doth Auren once more held sway.

Glimshpill had put up his campaign tent, a low pyramid, carefully guyed against the wind. There was no sign of the soldier save a momentary glow through the canvas as he sucked at his pipe. Catskin, wrapped in his cloak and with sword still drawn, stamped in the cold and looked up as Skarry neared.

'I would see you safe inside,' he muttered as Skarry passed and then he turned for the tent.

A thin plume of smoke wound up out of the entrance to the cave as if from fires deep within the earth. The way had been blocked with bushes of thorn that Hook drew aside to allow Skarry entrance. Once within, the thorns were replaced and covered over with a blanket. Inside Skarry paused, for the flames of the fire awakened a red warmth in the cave walls and set the shadows dancing in the crannies and nooks. The horses stood calmly and blew loudly down their noses. By the hearth the

Dreamer sat with his cloak thrown back, his face glowing. Ress had pulled off her hood and sat beside him, the red of the walls reflecting in her hair.

'Come,' Hook said and took Skarry's arm at the elbow. 'Warm yourself.' And together they went within the cave towards the beckoning light.

Skarry laid down the firewood and sat, stretching out his feet to the flames.

'It is a fair haven,' he said. 'We should call it Hook's haven.'

'It was named long ago,' Hook said with a laugh that echoed about the cave, 'Delgen, the Dream Haven, for it is an ancient place of shelter that was used by the Hagarath long before men had laid stone on top of stone and builded Ringdove that was to be so fine a city. All the land was forest then and the peoples were travellers. Glad they were and lived well with the land. See,' and he pointed upwards to the slabbed stone of the cave roof, 'they painted of the life they found about them and rejoiced in it.'

'What is it Skarry?' Ress asked, for she heard him gasp.

'I had not noticed before,' he said in wonder. 'The roof is filled with animals! There is a deer, peering from behind a shard of rock, the grey deer that still run in the high forests. Its soft eyes are wary and ready for flight. Beyond there is a herd with the young following the does. The stags have horns like crowns and keep up a lofty watchfulness. And there's the hog with his face full of stumps, for some say this creature was once laden with antlers. There is a mighty cave bear, the shoulders like rocky peaks, the legs like tree trunks all woolly as though with mosses and lichens.

'And there are people too, some with drums and there, an old one with the skin of a bear on her back, the head over hers. She leads a child in each hand, a girl and a boy. It's like they are coming out of the rock.'

Skarry was lost in awe at the images and would have gone on but then he looked down for he heard sobbing and saw tears upon Ress's cheeks. He went to her and put his arm about her shoulder and she leaned against him.

'I'm sorry Ress,' he said softly, 'that you cannot see them.'

'It is not for that I cry,' she said. 'I have never had sight. I cry for what has been done to our world, for what is being done to our world.'

Hook grunted and put more wood on the fire. The Dreamer sat unmoving, his eyes half closed, his open hands resting lightly on his knees.

'They say in Taur,' he said, raising his lids a little, 'that Ymir, the evil one bound Ithunne and that in this way men were separated from her love of the world. Those that believe this hold that Vidar is mighty enough of himself and will overthrow the enemy and that all will be well given time. Yet I have heard from other tongues that when the Two who were One first found Thuggundian on his stone globe, Ithunne would not help Vidar slay the bear for mastery of the land, for she held all life to be precious. Then Vidar himself bound her and cast her out and killed the bear. Those that believe so hold that Vidar keeps her bound through war which is the celebration of his lonely might.'

'And what do you believe?' Skarry asked.

'The Dreamers do not weigh one belief against another,' he said. 'As all peoples believe differently, so their truths and falsehoods are different also. I try to do only that which is necessary.'

He yawned suddenly, stretching out his limbs. Pulling his cloak about him he lightly closed his eyes as though to sleep.

Hook fed the flames as Skarry and Ress wrapped themselves in blankets. The glow of the wood coals illuminated the cave roof and with each flicker of the fire the painted figures seemed to dance with a life of their own. The old one was truly transformed, the bear mask pulled low upon her forehead and she rose up, drawing the children to her as if to shelter them within her strong grasp. The crackle of the fire became her growl of warning and almost Skarry could smell the strong scent of the bear. In his half sleep it seemed that Ress was at his side, his hand in hers, and that they awaited the coming of the bear, their guardian who would see them safe through all peril. Out of the darkness at his back came the long breath of the creature and though his heart beat loudly he felt no fear. At his side was a woman in green whose red hair blazed like a fire. 'Listen,' she said, 'she is coming!' and her eyes were filled with tears of joy as she waited. Then she was gone and an agony of loneliness fell about him. Struggling in the closing darkness the bear was once more a thing to fear.

He was roused to full waking slowly, rising against the tide of his sleep. Ress was tugging at his arm.

'Skarry, Skarry,' she whispered fiercely and much as a fisher hauls in the catch, she clung to him until he broke the surface of his dreaming.

'There is something outside,' she said as he rubbed his eyes. 'I can smell it. And listen.'

Skarry stilled his breathing. At first there was nothing that he could pick from the moan of the wind. Then came the cry of a night bird, the screech owl that set his nerves on edge until he recognised the sound.

'It is only a bird,' he said, 'the night eye of the forest. It shall not harm us.'

'No, not that,' Ress hissed impatiently at him. 'Listen, and use your nose, forester.'

In his tiredness Skarry would have thrown off her arm but he saw Hook the mountain man open an eye and cast a dark look about to see who had disturbed his rest. Suddenly, Skarry caught the smell, like scorched clothing and hot iron. The fire chose to flicker into greater life that sent the shadows chasing into the far corners of the cave. A sound broke above that of the wind, the regular crunch of snow beneath a weighty tread. Hook threw back his blanket and his axe was ready in his hand. He rose up and the flames awakened the red blaze of his beard and glinted in his eye. The curve of the axe shone coldly even in the warmth of that light.

'More wood on the fire,' he whispered to Skarry then made for the entrance.

Skarry did as he was told and stirred the embers so that the sparks flew up to the ceiling. Across the fire the Dreamer stared after Hook. There came a low growl from outside that seemed to use the wind for its voice. Skarry felt the hairs upon his neck rising and his heart began to hammer in his chest. The growl continued, a grating sound that seemed to enter his mind directly through the skull rather than by way of the ears. The growl rose into a shriek that had Ress holding her head and then they heard the noise of confused shouts.

'There are others outside who may need our aid,' the Dreamer said softly from the fire.

'Just leave me room to swing my axe,' Hook replied and pulled aside the thorn bushes.

The cave mouth opened blackly into the night. In the light

from the fire Glimshpill's tent could be seen, shaking violently as though someone struggled to get out. Then a darker shadow moved in front of the sight and filled the opening to the cave. The heat from the beast blew over them as it lowered its great head to peer within. The burning eyes looked down upon Hook who stood suddenly still, as if frozen by the very size of the creature, his axe hanging loosely in his right hand.

Skarry saw the Dreamer thrust both hands into the blaze of the fire, then turn, each outstretched fist glowing redly from the coals clenched within as he advanced upon the Auf bear.

'Begone,' he said in a voice so quietly strong that the wind was stilled and a silence fell over them. Framed within the cave mouth he raised up his arms to the Firebolg and opened his fists. The coals lit up the face of the creature as it stood poised over him.

'You who work through this being, begone,' he said again, 'for thou shalt be brought down and shalt speak out of the ground. Thy speech shall be low out of the dust and thy voice will be but a whisper.'

The fires within his hands blazed brightly like torches and sparks showered forth from the flames and crackled as they fell upon the fur of the beast. Then smoke began to issue from out its nostrils
and mouth and it rose up to its full height and moaned horribly.

There came a sharp crack and the collar sprang from about its neck and flew into pieces. The Firebolg sank down on to its four feet, seeming to shrink in size and it looked about as though confused. Then it backed slowly away, turning at last to lumber off into the darkness.

The flames died on the Dreamer's palms and he dusted his hands upon his cloak. Glimshpill at last burst from his tent with Settler bared in his hand.

'Where is it?' he called fiercely. 'Come, brave Catskin, stand at my back and we shall not let it pass!'

He waved the sword about in the air and set it whistling in the night. Catskin came out slowly.

'I must ask for your pardon,' the Dreamer said to Glimshpill, 'for I have stolen the night's honour and your strong arm is not needed.'

'Ah, but you let it go,' Glimshpill said. 'I would not have been so gentle.'

141

'Aye,' said the Dreamer. 'Yet it will not return. Will you not join us in the cave?'

'All the more reason to keep to our tent now,' Glimshpill said. 'Most likely the cave is its home and it has gone to fetch its brothers.'

So saying he ducked within his tent and the Dreamer replaced the thorn bushes in the entrance to the cave.

'So this is the creature that you spoke of,' Hook said as if rousing at last from a trance.

The Dreamer nodded.

'They are the witch Malkah's changelings,' he said, stooping to gather up the shards of the collar. 'A life is required for their making and the collar binds them to the will of the sorceress; her purpose is written in these designs.'

'Can you read it?' Skarry asked.

With his fingertips the Dreamer traced the swirling images graven on the collar.

'In times gone by,' he said slowly, 'the name of the enemy would be set here and the Firebolg would hunt him down. Yet these are more subtle; they look within both past and future and so seek out those whose simple actions might turn the fate of the world.'

'And are there more of the beasts?' Hook asked.

'There will be five or seven in the pack,' the Dreamer replied. 'There's a liking amongst sorcerers for such numbers.'

'The Ranneye killed one,' Skarry said, going on more slowly, 'and I had my part in the killing of two. And you have set one free,' he finished softly.

'It is not a choice you had, Skarry,' the Dreamer said simply.

'So there are one or three left,' Hook said as though to himself.

'Aye,' said the Dreamer, 'and she knows now that we are here, for she will feel my breaking of her spell.'

'The poor creatures,' Ress said softly.

'It is what is happening to all things,' the Dreamer said. 'It is the might of Vidar without the grace of Ithunne.'

15

A Dividing of Ways

Skarry was awakened by the sound of Glimshpill's morning cough from outside.

'Ah, Ymir, it's cold,' came his voice. 'My piss crackles in the snow as it turns to ice.'

'It will be colder yet,' said Hook as he cleared the entrance to the cave. 'When it freezes before it reaches the ground, then will it be cold.'

'A happy thought to begin the day,' Glimshpill sighed and poked his head within the cave to take a hasty look around.

'How did you fare in your tent?' Hook asked.

'Better than I would have done in here and that's for sure,' Glimshpill replied. 'I may be a hero as of old but these shadowy places make my skin creep. Ah, there are paintings too; I would bet they make a ghostly dance in the firelight, eh?'

He gave a shiver to his shoulders and went out hurriedly. They packed their belongings in silence, dressing warmly in thick winter tunics and cloaks. When they were ready the six stood together in the clearing before the cave mouth. The Dreamer tucked his hands within the sleeves of his robe and stared at the snow between his feet.

'Well,' said Glimshpill at last when no one spoke. 'What are you going to do, eh?'

'Surely we go on to find the lord D'Auren,' Skarry said, confused by the question.

'Then just as surely we're not coming,' said Glimshpill and slumped down on to his rolled up tent. 'We've had enough of this, eh Corporal?'

Catskin nodded though he turned his face away. Hook smiled and showed no surprise.

'The loyal warriors!' Ress laughed.

'Your presence has not helped,' Catskin said quickly, turning to her. 'You are not unknown this time.'

'Aye,' growled Glimshpill. 'Kidnapping the High Lord's daughter is not a crime I should like to be charged with. No, we'll stay here, set up a decent camp somewhere with our fine tent and wait till Guise goes by with his mighty army. I would give it up also if I were you. We could say we got lost in the snow, saved his daughter, whatever.'

Glimshpill laughed loudly but this speech was at last too much for Skarry.

'And what of our noble purpose?' he began slowly, incredulous, going towards the soldier. 'Surely the fate of many is balanced upon our choice of action? What of the lord D'Auren who is counting on our aid and the Paladin who put his trust in us?'

Glimshpill's laugh died.

'Can you not conceive the folly of your own words?' he said. 'Have you not used your eyes on your journey? This Paladin of yours cares not a toss whether we live or die so long as his purpose is achieved. The same can be said of D'Auren, they are all lords after all is done. Ask of her!'

Glimshpill pointed to Ress who turned her blue eyes towards Skarry and for once he felt that she looked directly at him and could feel his confusion. He waited upon her word.

'I care not for my father or for Ringdove,' she said, 'I make no secret of that. To be honest I think it matters little what course we choose for I cannot see that the likes of us shall turn the fate of the world. You'll just have to decide what it is you really want, Skarry.'

Glimshpill nodded at this. Skarry rose, looking this way then that as if suddenly lost, each face returning an empty look.

'Then what are we to do?' he asked despairingly. 'What am I to do?'

'Well, I'm going on,' said Ress firmly. 'For my own reasons. Whether any travel with me or not, I'm going. I am decided.'

'I will come with you,' said Hook, 'I have no choice in the matter if my family are to live.'

'And D'Auren is still human,' came the Dreamer's quiet voice. 'He may yet have need of my help. I will go on also.'

'Well the lad will go with the girl at a blind guess,' Catskin said coldly. 'He would do anything for her, that is plain to see.'

144

'And you?' Skarry said with anger. 'You will desert your lord and leave good people to die!'

'I thought we had done with all this talk of lords,' the Corporal said with a shrug.

'I was a fool to take on this job,' Glimshpill muttered. 'Rather I should have taken a hammer to my own sword hand.' He spat into the snow and turned away, breathing heavily as if holding himself in.

'You think only of yourself, hard man.' Skarry said, taking a step forward. Hook took him by the elbow but Skarry threw his hand off saying, 'And you call yourself a warrior!'

'You!' Glimshpill roared, turning so fast that the snow flew from his shoulders. His right arm came up and the square fist loomed hugely in Skarry's face yet the blow was not finished.

'You have much to learn, young Dreamer,' the soldier said, suddenly quiet.

'And you, iron man.' Skarry could not help but add.

Glimshpill looked him full in the eyes for a moment then spun around and walked off a dozen paces.

'Away with you!' he cried without turning. 'Away with you, for you shall be the death of me if I come with you!'

Hook looked at Catskin but the Corporal shook his head.

'I cannot leave him,' he said softly.

'Then we will take your horses,' the mountain man said, 'for we shall have the greater need. You can walk down to Dunnerdale road when the Paladin Guise passes with his army and spin him what yarns you like.'

Hook unslung his axe and hefted it in his hands but Catskin put up his palms.

'Take them,' he said. 'We are sore enough from the saddle as it is.'

The Dreamer helped Ress to her horse and she mounted quickly while Hook kept a watchful eye on the two soldiers. Skarry tied the extra horses in a string behind Felder then jumped across the pony's back and swung his leg over. The Dreamer started off and led the way out of the hollow and along the narrow valley with Ress behind him. Skarry cast a last defiant look back at Glimshpill but the other smoked his pipe and did not see. Then Hook leaned from his saddle and pulled at Skarry's reins, turning Felder away from the soldiers and into the east.

145

As they passed from sight, ducking their heads beneath the branching oaks, Catskin half made to run at them then stopped and swept his arm about as if to wipe them from his sight.

'You are fools,' he cried. 'You are fools!'

The sound of his shouting carried far in the cold air, echoing about them and on into the vale ahead. The words beat in Skarry's head, matching the rhythmic pulse in his temples, yet he pushed back the anger. Before him, Hook, the red king laughed and shook his shoulders as though freed of some burden.

The four rode forward into a deeper stillness, the breeze shushing into silence. In the valley bottom even the river was quiet, the water flowing soundlessly below the ice. The mountains to their right rose ever more steeply until the slopes broke into the tumbled rock and crags of Raven Tore, climbing swiftly into the lowering cloud.

'The further one is Ice Bright,' Hook said, gesturing up towards the mountains as though to draw Skarry from himself. 'The snow never leaves its summit, even in the hottest of summers.'

'Then is the winter never conquered?' Skarry asked.

'The winter is not something to conquer, lad,' Hook said seriously. 'It is to be lived with. Though it is said that one did make a fight of it and win, a tale you would no doubt like to hear,' Hook went on before Skarry could ask.

'It is a tale of Grimal Skoye,' the mountain man said loudly and Ress started at the name and dropped back that she might hear also.

'Darlak is his home,' Hook began, 'or rather his castle, for it is said that the Osilo ice plains are his home proper. Darlak sits upon the western seaboard of Monrolia, a mighty fortress, darkly guarding its sheltered bay. I was outside its walls many years ago when the then High Lord, Nimmer, had pushed far into the enemy's lands during the summer campaign. That was a sorry tale; starving, cut off and unable to break the fortress. But I was to tell you of Grimal Skoye.

'One winter the snows fell for five months without pause and even Grimal's Ice Warriors could not fight. It became ever colder and the great ice seas began to flow over the northern mountains of Monrolia. The western ocean froze and the Osilo peoples could not break through the depth of ice to fish. The snow deer fled to more southerly lands yet the people could not for by then they were tied to their cities and possessions. They began to die.

'Grimal Skoye put on his war gear and called for his charger, Ashnomadai, who was harnessed as for battle with iron studs in the leather and a guard about his head formed into the likeness of a screaming bat. Then Grimal Skoye mounted Ashnomadai and taking his stoutest lance he threw the gates wide and rode off into the blizzard shouting his war cry and was lost to sight.

'For five weeks his people kept a look-out for him and many froze as they sat within the watchtower peering from the window slits. Then the clouds broke and they saw the sun for the first time in seven months and they rejoiced. And in the midst of their celebrations Grimal Skoye returned, looking weary and hungry with his lance broken off in splinters and Ashnomadai hardly able to put one hoof before the other. The ice seas to the north fell back, the ocean melted and Grimal Skoye was hailed by his people as saviour and conqueror of the winter.'

Skarry was silent, unable to decide how to take this story of the enemy. Ress too said nothing though she smiled and raised up her face as though seeking the touch of the sun in the clouds above.

'How do you come to know these things?' Skarry asked at last. 'Things of people who are supposed to be our enemy?'

'They were not always our enemies, Skarry,' Hook said. 'Before the cities we did not think of this as our Taur, that as their Monrolia. We lived in our own fields and forests, our own marsh and mountain. We knew of others through the travelling peoples who brought news and carvings and cloth from far off places and took ours in return. Ah, I don't know,' he broke off. 'It is the cursed cities!'

He kicked at the flanks of his horse and rode on ahead to make safe the way. All about them the mist closed in, snow alternating with a fine drizzle that settled on their cloaks giving them a soft sheen.

Ress called to Skarry and he rode up beside her thinking that perhaps she was tired. When he came to her she spoke softly as though others might be listening.

'There is a sound,' she said, 'that I do not know. It comes now and then on the wind. Like stone on stone with a beat to it.'

'It will be the stone chat,' Skarry said quickly, 'warning the birds of our approach.'

Ress turned to him. She used no gestures when she spoke yet her open stare felt weighty to Skarry.

'It is there again,' she said. 'If you knew how to listen you would hear it, forester.'

Straining his ears Skarry thought he might have caught an echo of distant hammering.

'Do not fight to hear,' Ress said. 'Still yourself and it will come to you.'

So Skarry halted Felder and relaxed his seat into the warmth of the pony's back. He let his mind empty of fears and hopes and as he did so the sound came to him and grew louder so that he was surprised that he had not heard it before.

'It's louder,' Ress said.

Before them, the Dreamer halted as Hook came back, grim faced, out of the swirl of mist.

'It is the enemy,' he said, drawing close. 'They are above us somewhere, signalling to one another.'

'It may be that they have not seen us,' the Dreamer said.

'Maybe,' Hook agreed. 'They are a fair bit higher and in the thick of the mist. Yet we must be careful. I will ride ahead. Will you drop behind?' he asked the Dreamer, looking askance at him. He continued by way of explanation, 'It may be of help if you can conceal our trail. The youngster can bring the girl and the spare horses in between us.'

After a moment the Dreamer agreed.

'Have you a weapon?' Hook asked Skarry. 'Take this then.' He handed over a long dagger in its sheath and said, 'Think carefully before you use it. If you hear anything then get under the trees, as far from our path as you can.'

He finished and, whirling his pony about, made off down the valley and into the mist.

'Well then, Skarry,' the Dreamer said. 'Mind you keep an eye on this one and seek not to rush into your future, it will come soon enough of its own accord.'

He waved them on and Skarry started off, leading Ress's pony with the string of horses behind. Within moments the Dreamer was lost from his sight and the mists closed in until they were isolated within their own grey world. Skarry could see no more than twenty paces in any direction yet he could follow Hook's trail easily enough, for the marks of his passage were clear in the snow and going over rock he had scratched at stones by his wayside with the point of his axe.

'Are you frightened Skarry?' Ress asked.

'No,' he replied, 'for I have been in hotter pans than this. Once on the Angsoth I tried to cross under Steepside in the spring and found the snow I walked on sliding downward in the beginnings of an avalanche. My father was angry when I told him I rode the slide all the way to the bottom. He thought I had done it on purpose.'

'But there were no Monrolians awaiting your descent,' Ress said.

'That is true,' said Skarry and was silent for a moment. 'But I've been in a tighter spot still, at the Maen-hir, captive of Ice Warriors and a witch, yet I came out unharmed, and far richer,' he went on.

'That is true, also,' Ress said and laughed.

They moved on, the echoes of the stone talk coming occasionally from on high, the mist confusing and concealing direction. Skarry strained his eyes with staring at the white wall yet nothing was revealed to him beyond the circle of ground centred around them. And the white seemed to close in about him alone, for what difference did it make to Ress whether it be dull or clear?

'We are in strong company,' he said by way of reassuring both of them.

'Not so,' she answered. 'We are on our own. It will always be so.'

As if to prove her wrong there came the sudden drumming of hoofs and before Skarry could even think of the dagger he carried, Hook came riding out of the mist and up to them.

'Monrolians,' Hook said grimly as he came close. 'They hold the way. We will have to climb.'

Skarry stared fearfully into the mists from which Hook had come, but could make nothing out. Hook cut the string of ponies loose and hurriedly drove them off into the woods on their left, then taking the reins of Ress's pony he cantered across the valley bottom towards the mountains. Skarry followed, looking all about, the echoes of the stone talk coming in short bursts.

'What of the Dreamer?' he called to Hook.

'He will find us,' Hook replied and went on, drawing Ress behind him.

As they began to climb the valley side their pace slowed. Here the screes had swept down, spilling into the trees and brushing them aside. Their way grew steadily more difficult as they circled piled boulders, long since fallen from the high crags above. Ress was thrown about in her saddle and at last Hook brought them to a halt beside a shattered rock.

'We must leave the horses here,' he said firmly. 'The enemy will find our trail any moment and be on to us.'

'I can hear no sounds of pursuit,' said Ress thoughtfully. 'Though the stone talk seems louder.'

Skarry watched the slope below them and held tightly to the dagger Hook had given him as the mountain man helped Ress from her mount. With some sorrow he clambered down from Felder and swiftly took off his halter and blanket. He would have stayed a little to say his farewells but Hook pulled at him, dragging him upwards. The pony whinnied plaintively.

With Ress between them they climbed a rocky outcrop rearing from the loose screes, their breath coming in gasps and soon they were sweating even in that bitter chill.

'We climb too fast!' Skarry gasped at last as they rested for a moment against a grey boulder.

'There is no one behind us that I can hear,' said Ress.

'We must hurry,' was all Hook would say and once more pulled them upwards.

As Ress and Skarry tired, the mountain man appeared to grow in strength, the grip of his hands upon their arms like a vice, dragging them on so that when Ress slipped, Hook pulled her roughly over the stone. Above them in the mists the sound of the stone talk came suddenly loud and clear as if only just beyond the wall of white. Ress stopped immediately and Skarry looked to Hook.

'It is the enemy,' he said in surprise. 'Have you led us right to them?'

'It is not the enemy,' said Hook slowly. 'It is my people, the Hagarath.' And he raised his wrist and pointed to the red stone of his armlet.

Skarry and Ress allowed themselves to be helped upwards a few more paces and they came to a place where the hillside had been cut back a little to make a level space. The edge was protected by a low wall and to the back there was a simple shelter of canvas on poles and logs to sit upon. Though still beyond sight the stone talk was almost on them. Hook walked out into the space and called a greeting into the mist, still holding to their arms. There came a distant reply and Hook sighed with relief.

'I would have you understand,' he said slowly to them both, 'that I bear you no ill will. I am driven by things beyond my control. Your father, the High Lord, he holds my family as hostage. Now that I have you he may strike a bargain with me.'

Skarry stepped away from Hook, shaking free his arm. Ress could not keep from laughing bitterly.

'Ah, Hook,' she said, 'most noble of the old peoples, that you should be forced to this.'

'I am sorry lady Recina,' he said and would not look her in the face. He kept the tight grip upon her arm.

Skarry sat slowly on the edge of the level and shook his head in disbelief, the whole teetering world of warriors and heroes tumbling now in his mind. Small stones rolled out of the fog above them as the unseen others scrambled down the screes. They caught the occasional sound of voices, no words were clear. Hook waited in the centre of the level place, his shoulders relaxed, his breathing easy and it was only at the last that he realised something was amiss.

As the first shadow loomed down on them Skarry recognised the hornet helmet and let out a shout of warning. Hook was already freeing his axe as the Ice Warrior stepped out of the fog and grinned at them, idly banging two stones together.

'We were surprised you fell for it so easily, mountain man,' the Monrolian said and laughed, 'yet we have no fight with you. Be off into your hills and you shall not be harmed.'

As he spoke he was joined by two more Ice Warriors carrying short thrusting spears and round shields. Their cheeks and foreheads were tattooed with thin blue spirals that moved as they moved, confusing the eye. Hook, who had seemed so huge and full of power turned slowly to Skarry and Ress and appeared now as an old man, the rusty red of his beard and drooping moustache going to grey. With slumped shoulders he came to them.

'I am sorry, lad,' he said slowly and his voice was broken. 'I have made things hard for you, yet I will strive to make all well again. You must take the stone of my people that they shall not have it.'

So saying Hook pulled the red stone from its thong about his wrist and gave it to Skarry. Their gaze met and as the red king breathed deeply a grin came to his face and the weather marked cheeks flushed red with blood. The grin became lopsided as Hook called up his rage.

'Fly!' he whispered fiercely to them both and then he turned about, the axe scything the air and a roar burst from his mouth, rising from deep within him and he fell upon the enemy.

Ress dragged Skarry away and once over the edge of the level place they slipped and rolled down the scree a dozen paces. Skarry struggled to his knees, pulling against Ress who tried to drag him down.

'I must help him!' he gasped as from above came the clang of metal upon metal and the hoarse shouts of the men as they fought.

'No!' Ress ordered. 'Don't leave me here alone, we may yet escape.'

'But he needs my help,' said Skarry urgently. 'I cannot leave him to fight alone. If there are only a few of them we could all come out of this trap!'

'You don't know what you are saying,' Ress said quietly with a fierce undertone to her voice. She began to lower herself blindly down the scree.

'Wait!' Skarry yelled at her, turning his head from her to the sounds of the fighting and back again, not knowing what to do.

Looking up he saw the shadow of Hook come to the edge of the level, the axe cutting a swift rhythm in the air. The red king took a hasty look behind him and as he turned, Skarry saw that there were arrows stuck into his chest and legs, the shafts broken and hanging down from his armour. When he saw Skarry still lying there his face dropped and he turned back to the fight with renewed vigour.

'Run!' he cried. 'Run!'

And suddenly he stopped, the axe poised on high for a final blow that was not to be made. The panting of the Ice Warriors came out of the stillness and then the sound of their bows, twice more and Hook jerked with each impact. Slowly he toppled backwards and then with a great clanking the armoured body came hurtling passed Skarry and disappeared into the mists below, narrowly missing Ress who clung against the stone sobbing. Above them the first Ice Warrior came to the edge of the drop.

'Where are you off to, my children?' he called. 'You have nowhere to run.'

Ress began to slide down the scree and with a great leap the Ice Warrior came down at her, the stones flying beneath his feet. In three bounds he passed Skarry and had Ress by the arm, hauling her back up the slope. When she struggled he cuffed her hard about the head and tossed her up on to his shoulder.

Skarry felt the red stone clenched within his hand and with the other he drew Hook's dagger and waved it at the warrior.

'Put her down,' he said firmly, then his voice began to quake. 'You shall not harm her.'

The Ice Warrior laughed when he looked up and with one flick of his forearm he swung his spear, the butt end catching Skarry first across the wrist then on the return striking his forehead and awakening bright lights that seemed to spin about him. Other voices laughed loudly as Skarry staggered to his knees and he was roughly grasped by his arms and pulled back up the hillside.

The laughter broke off as below them there appeared the glow as of a fire within the mist. It sent out rays of coloured light that curved and coiled towards them. Suddenly grim and silent the Monrolians hurriedly pulled their two captives up on to the level ground of the shelter. Skarry made as though to shout and was given another blow on the head. In the mist the fire grew still brighter and nearer. The Ice Warriors set off across the scree, Ress slung like a sack over the shoulder of one, Skarry dragged between the other two. Slowly the fire receded and was finally gone. The only sound was the panting of the Ice Warriors as they strongly carried their captives off into the mountains.

153

16

Malkah

Imprisoned within the grey circle of mist the Ice Warriors made their way rapidly across the screes sending stones tumbling down below them. Ress was carried in turns, tossed between them as though she were a small child. Skarry they directed forcefully with the butts of their spears and though used to mountain marches he was pushed to match their pace. Looking back into the mists he could see no sign of the fiery glow and every step seemed to increase his feeling of helplessness.

The screes met at last with a gorge running up into the mountains and here the Monrolians stopped and fastened spiked frames to the soles of their boots.

'You'll have to be careful now, lad,' one of the Ice Warriors said. 'I'll keep a tight hold though, don't you worry.' He laughed and placed a rope noose about Skarry's neck.

'Get a move on,' their leader commanded and they began to climb upwards along the edge of the gorge.

Soon they were on old snow that had thawed and frozen again. It was a steep slope and the Ice Warriors kicked foot and handholds through the crust of ice, drawing the tethered Skarry behind them. Rising above the mist he gained a clearer view; the grey sea to the north and the mountains stretching off on either hand, their boulder strewn slopes snow covered, concealed. As far as he could tell this was the flank of Ice Bright that they crossed. Above them the cloud layer cut off any sight of the summit.

The warriors were silent as they climbed, saving their energy for each and every step. They inhaled deeply through their long noses and breathed out of their mouths in great clouds of steam. Skarry gasped for breath and the jerking at his lead came all the more frequent. His head ached from the blow he had been given yet he was relieved to see Ress stir and hear her moan.

154

'She wakes, Mord,' the one carrying her said to the leader.

'About time,' he replied. 'I thought you'd killed her. That would not go down so well with the Father, or our mistress.'

The climb steepened and above them loomed a great crag that spilled occasional snowfalls. Boulders were precariously piled at the foot of the cliff and from behind these stepped two more Ice Warriors with arrows notched upon the strings of their short-bows. They wore thick woollen breeches with leather skirts over and the white fur coat of the snow fox about their shoulders. Their faces also were decorated with spiralling lines and one had filed his front teeth into points.

'Hurry, Mord!' this one called. 'We saw the fire light of a Dreamer behind you.'

'Ah, you worry over much, Atli,' another said with a laugh as they came together. He will not follow us across the open, not with your sharp eye watching out for him.'

'Or my sharper arrow,' Atli replied and they all laughed.

'He has no fear of arrows,' Mord said more seriously. 'Yet our mistress will handle him, now that we have the bait.'

Then he called for them to move on and they started along the base of the crag leaving Atli to watch the rear. Now the red of the rock where it rose up out of the snow lent a warm glow to the air, yet the stone was limned with ice and its flashings confused the eye and distorted distance. They fell to scrambling over boulders that had cracked from the cliff long ago through the slow weathering of the seasons. Some had crashed down and continued the fall to the valley below, taking trails of scree with them, others had embedded themselves within the top of the slope as if grown there to form the obstacles of their present way.

After a while they came to a place where the crag opened in a wide gully that ran upwards, a crack in the side of the mountain, filled with scree and narrowing as it entered the mists above. The gully opened out into a more gentle slope surrounded by huge stones that they clambered over and within they found two tents, white as piles of snow. As they approached the larger of the two a coldness began to form in the pit of Skarry's stomach. As though sensing his fear the Ice Warriors closed about him, leaving no chance of escape.

From the tent came forth one who was well wrapped in furs. Through a narrow slit in the hood could be seen hard dark eyes

155

that set shivers rippling in Skarry's body, even before he recognised her.

'Be welcome,' said Malkah, extending her arms towards them, her voice soft as the sighing wind in trees.

She came forward to meet them, unbuttoning the face flap and pulling back her hood. Skarry was drawn around as she circled them, turning to keep her in sight. Black as the raven's wing was her tightly braided hair and skin as white as snow. Her lips, as though she had bit her tongue, were red as blood.

Stopping by the warrior who carried Ress she looked closely at her face, nodding the while and then turning to Skarry.

'We meet again, young forester,' she said quietly and her red lips formed a precise smile. Skarry could read nothing within the dark eyes.

'Set the girl on her feet,' she commanded and the one carrying Ress put her down and shook her by the shoulders until she cried out. She put out her hands and swayed yet she did not fall.

'Are you there Skarry?' she whispered, turning her head about to catch the sound.

'I'm here, Ress,' he said and made to go to her but Malkah stepped between them.

'That is a pretty necklace that you wear, forester,' she said. 'It has grown since last we met, at the Maen-hir, on the High Pass. And it may be that you have also.'

She took the thick glove from her left hand, reaching up to the stones about his neck, taking each one in turn. Her fingers were warm on Skarry's throat.

'Beware, Skarry,' Ress began quietly. 'Her warmth is deceptive, for her heart is cold as ice.'

'Not true, you blind bitch!' Malkah turned vehemently on Ress and the blood showed redly in her flushed cheeks.

'Don't harm her!' Skarry could not help but shout.

'So she has ensnared you also?' Malkah asked disgustedly. 'Or is it merely pity for the ill-formed?'

'She's the daughter of the High Lord Guise,' Skarry said desperately. 'He will surely pay a good ransom for her safe return.'

Malkah burst into laughter that pealed up the gully above them, the echoes dying slowly.

'I know of her lineage,' she said, 'and I know her father better

156

than you. He will be glad to be rid of her; the blind bitch embarrassed him. Surely you know these Taurians, young forester, they have no liking for the different.'

'I am a Taurian,' Skarry said stubbornly. 'And proud of it, as are my people.'

This time Malkah did not laugh but shook her head slowly.

'You are a fool for a start,' she said. 'Yet a pretty one and that is in your favour at the least. Though why you should waste your looks upon her is another matter.'

'My Lady,' Mord broke in. 'We slew a mountain man who was with them but there was another also, following at their rear. A Dreamer we would suppose by the fire we glimpsed within the mists.'

Malkah nodded.

'It is he,' she said. 'He shall not escape me this time for we will be all the more ready.' And she reached out a hand to either side, the left to Skarry's cheek the right she buried within Ress's hair and tugged at it so that her head was shaken from side to side.

'Well,' she went on, 'you two will be well out of the way when your supposed saviour comes looking. Mord, you will take them across the Isthmus where there will be no purpose in their trying to escape. We will fall back to the Stones to await the Dreamer.'

Skarry's heart quailed and he began to tremble at the very thought of Monrolia.

'Take me to Grimal!' Ress said suddenly and Malkah laughed.

'You are impatient, lady Recina,' she said. 'But my orders are to send you on to Darlak where you will be secure.' Malkah observed their fear and then stooped and picked a handful of snow from the ground.

'This is where you are going,' she whispered fiercely to Skarry, opening her fist before his face.

Her eyes assumed a greater depth like two wells that drew him within. On her palm the snow crystals flashed and shimmered and took on the proportions of vast mountains whose peaks scratched at the clouds, whose inner valleys harboured ponderous glaciers, the ice floes breaking into huge crevasses.

'It is the land of eternal snow,' Malkah's voice came to him distantly, 'the home of ice.' And it seemed that a cold hand squeezed at Skarry's heart and he began to shake. The vision of such towering mountains bore down upon him and he was reduced to the size of an insect, dominated by their awesome weight of ice and stone, for the vast bulk dwarfed the purposes of men, looming over the puny armies that crawled hopelessly within their shadow. Bright little sparks sprang up about them as the cities that once seemed so brave and powerful were laid waste before their indifferent gaze.

Yet as it seemed that the very thought would crush him he became aware of his own stones about his neck and Hook's within his tunic pocket, the red stone of the mountain people, and it warmed him. Within the vision of the mountains he found a glow like a fire in winter and then he was himself again, looking into Malkah's eyes.

'You have indeed grown,' she said quietly and dashing the snow aside she ran her wet fingers over her hair. 'We shall meet again, young forester.

'As for you,' she said, turning to Ress, 'I am burdened with your safe keeping else I would kill you now, but should you try to escape me again, then shall you suffer.'

As she spoke Atli came suddenly scrambling over the rocks below and up to them.

'He's coming,' he gasped hurriedly. There was both excitement and fear in his face. Behind him the mists began to take on the colours as of a fire and a low humming vibration filled the air about them.

'Take them away, Mord,' Malkah said quickly. 'I must prepare for our guest.' Her red lips formed a thin smile and she stared into the colouring mist, breathing deeply. She raised up her arms towards the sight, her hands opening, though whether to give or receive Skarry could not tell.

Mord gave him a shove in the back that suggested the direction they were to take.

'You are lucky she took a fancy to you,' he said with a smile as they moved away. 'She can be rough with those she does not like.'

Then Mord took up the lead once more, another Ice Warrior carrying Ress over his shoulder and they made their way around the boulders and out of the gully, heading east along the flank of the mountain. And it seemed to Skarry now that their position grew more and more hopeless for every step took them further from the firelight of the Dreamer and nearer to Monrolia, the land of the enemy, the place of snow.

All the rest of that morning and on into the afternoon they crossed Stoneside below the Frozen Fells and the Dark Seat until by way of Illgill they came to a gentler slope that Skarry recognised as Dunan. Turning to the south his eyes blurred with tears yet his mountain, the Angsoth, was veiled in snow. Now it seemed that all hope left him, as though he turned his back forever upon the place of his birth.

In Dunan Dale were long columns of Monrolian soldiers marching south. Here field kitchens and tents had been set up and the men rested awhile and ate, standing around fires that sent up thin plumes of smoke. They were warmly garbed in sealskins with leather boots and full hoods. On their feet they wore snow shoes and they carried short skis amongst the equipment on their backs. The army stretched beyond sight in either direction and war songs rolled confidently across the vale of Dunan.

'Your Fressingfield made a foolish stand here,' said Mord. 'He could not hope to hold his own against the Father, Grimal Skoye, and his own Ice Warriors, not with the first snow of winter in the air. See, those mounds in the snow, here is Fressingfield's gallant soldiery piled ten deep to keep each other company in this their last resting place. And higher up, you will not see from here, is his head upon a spear where Grimal laid him down with his own hand. How can you hope to stand against such might, eh?'

As they neared the troops, the soldiers began to call out to one another, asking for news. When they heard that Mord had prisoners they shouted and jeered at Ress and Skarry.

'Ah, but he is a pretty one!' they called, 'with a weighty necklace about his throat, though a little on the skinny side.'

The catcalls followed them down the valley until Mord called them to a halt beside a gathering of tents. Here there were horses tethered and a number of sleds. Mord spoke to those who stood idly by and one mention of Malkah's name was enough to procure a sled and team for their journey. Mord returned to them with a grin on his face.

'We shall travel in comfort now,' he said, 'and not a little style.'

So saying he swung Ress up into the back of the sled where she sat crushed between two of the Ice Warriors. Mord mounted at the front, beckoning for Skarry to join him, while the fourth warrior sat on Skarry's left and took up the reins. Clicking at the ponies he set them trotting down the slope with the snow rushing beneath the runners and the wind in their faces.

Below them the road levelled as they came down on to the flats by the sea that was the easternmost point of that land called the Three Kings Basin, for the cities of Midloth, Dunnerdale and Ringdove were strung one after the other along the great east–west road. The Jewels of the North they were once called though they were not so bright to look upon now. Skarry could see the walls of Midloth away to his left but the banner that flew from the keep was not Fressingfield's hawk but a crude hammer, like a club that Mord said was that of the lord Juss.

'Brother to our mistress is Juss of Snowater,' he went on, 'and great is his renown in Monrolia, some say to rival even that of the Father. Yet we of the Osilo call him the Wolf.'

Turning east the road was near filled with other sleds bringing forth provisions from Monrolia to fuel the mighty invading army. Here were the cooks and smiths, the shepherds driving before them huge flocks who would not see the coming of summer. And further off from the road were herds of reindeer who meekly followed their leader, a beast with antlers like the branchings of a tree, in turn led from a halter by a small figure well wrapped in sealskin.

Mord raised up a small triangular pennant that was embroidered with the image of the grey seal as it dives through the water.

'It is the sign of Skoye,' he said to Skarry, but those of the soldiers they now passed who saw it, though they parted before the sled, turned aside their faces and muttered to one another.

'These are Juss's men,' Mord explained. 'Juss and the Father were raised as brothers in Darlak and together came of age to take up the Chieftain's Bowl. To decide between them, they were set the task of gaining the horns of the white musk ox that lives hardily in the far north. Juss failed, though he took many men with him. Grimal Skoye went alone and lived with the wolves and when they came at last upon the herd, he led the hunt. Yet while the wolves singled out a lame calf, Grimal Skoye charged alone through the herd and took the white bull itself by the horns and threw it down and killed it.

'There is envy here,' he gestured to the marching warriors, 'for they follow wolves whereas we follow the Father.' And the blue spirals on his cheeks wrinkled as a broad grin came to his face.

With a stiff breeze off the sea the last of the mists cleared and Skarry found himself looking out over the Isthmus and his heart quailed.

'What is it Skarry?' Ress asked, hearing his indrawn breath.

'It's the Isthmus,' he said. 'Black with the soldiers of Monrolia. Cassan Keep it taken, the seal of the Misery flies above it, and another, a book and a sword.'

'It is the Cunerdin's,' Mord said dismissively, 'the supposed leader of Monrolia.'

'Fear not,' Skarry said, turning in his seat so he could see Ress squeezed between the bulk of the two Ice Warriors. 'I shall see you safe, Ress, I promise you.'

Ress allowed a smile to touch her face and held out a hand but before Skarry could take it one of the warriors beside her struck it away. Mord began to laugh quietly.

'Ah lad, you do not know what you are saying,' he said. 'We are to take you to Darlak, across the Isthmus, past cordons of guards and hordes of soldiers. Far shall we travel into that land and you will be beyond all hope of looking upon your own mountains once more. The game is ended for you, young hero; you will finish your days as a guest of our city.'

'That may be so,' Skarry said. 'Yet I bring my own mountains with me.' And so saying he took from his tunic pocket the red stone of the Ridgeway and placed it with the others on the thong around his neck.

Out of the silence that followed came Ress's voice like a thin song on the wind.

'He cannot foretell the future, Skarry,' she said. 'Hold to your hope, for both our sakes.'

Mord laughed again and shrugged his shoulders, indifferent.

The towers of Cassan Keep loomed above them as they slowed to make their way through the many people. The bastion of the northern way it had been called, for it sat central on the Isthmus and to either side its walls ran down into the sea. Amongst the battlements masons and artisans worked at a new parapet that would protect them from the south. In the distance beyond the Keep, across the narrow Isthmus, as though a reflection of Cassan, Skarry could make out the grey walls and towers of the

Monrolian fortress that guarded their own lands. Beyond that the mountains rose up swiftly and towered into the cloud.

Mord's eyes burned at the sight and a grin came to his weatherbeaten face. Yet Skarry's eyes filled with tears and a great weight seemed to press down upon him. The gateway to Cassan was suddenly about them and they passed within its shadow then out into the light once more through the northern gate. With despair in his heart Skarry knew himself to be beyond the fields of Taur.

The Isthmus stretched north before them, so narrow that with a strong bow and a true arrow you might shoot from the beach on one hand into the water on the other. The rock lay bare in slabs; not a tree to be seen nor even a blade of grass. All had been cleared to make the killing ground where, in the songs of the past, a myriad warriors had fallen in defence or attack, on one side or the other.

Into this bleak waste the sled ran and the runners took up a harsh squealing where the snow had been blown thin. The Monrolian wall grew large before them, the gates of the fortress darkly beckoning as the mouth of some huge beast, the arrow slits of its many eyes filled with armed guards who called down as they approached. Then the shadow fell upon them and they entered within the land of Monrolia.

17

The Land of Eternal Snow

The sled halted within the darkness of the Monrolian Keep. Mord looked about them carefully. They were in an enclosed space where the road ran through the tower; behind lay the gate to the Isthmus and Taur, before them the black oak of the doorway into Monrolia, studded with knobs of iron and much scarred from the blows of weapons. Yet these high doors were closed.

'Ho!' Mord shouted impatiently and his voice echoed hollowly, rising above them. 'Open the gates! We have not the time to sit about.'

There was no one in sight and no answer came to his request. In the slight warmth of the Keep the dark stone dripped wetly. Steps climbed within the walls and there were catwalks and balconies above from which to defend the way but these were empty; the tower seemed suddenly deserted.

'Then must we open them ourselves,' Mord muttered angrily. 'Go on, Bork!' he said to the soldier on Ress's left. 'Get these gates open and let's be moving.'

Bork clambered from the sled and stamped his way to the doors. Skarry realised that Ress had laid her hand upon his shoulder and reaching up his own he clasped it. She felt cold.

'They are not even fastened,' Bork called back to them. 'I will soon have them open.'

Pulling at the iron ring he leaned away with all his weight and the huge door began to swing ponderously open. Light flooded through the widening gap and Skarry could make out the foothills of the Ulta-Zorn rearing into the cloud. Beside him he heard Mord sigh with the sight and the Ice Warrior's body relaxed.

'Greetings,' they heard Bork say to someone without and then he seemed to leap suddenly backwards. In that frozen instant Skarry saw that Bork had been stuck in the stomach with a thrusting spear, the point projecting from his back. He began to cough dark blood, his hands about the shaft as though to draw it forth from his body. Then he sat down, a look of surprise to his face.

Mord had his sword out in the space of a heartbeat but he made no move to leave the sled. The warrior to Skarry's left tensed himself as if on the point of leaping into battle. The doors were swung wide to reveal a dozen heavily armoured troops waiting without, their beaked helmets cocked to one side as they sighted along their arrows.

'Let's not be hasty,' Mord said quickly, allowing his sword arm to fall. 'I can see that you have orders and don't want to hinder you in any way. If you tell me what you want, then perhaps I can help?'

Sitting so close, Skarry could see the sweat start on Mord's brow and run in thin trickles down his face and neck. The warrior who had been driving still made no move save for a slight clenching and unclenching of his fists at the reins.

Quickly the soldiers at the gateway encircled the sled as others appeared on the catwalks above with arrows and spears directed downwards. They wore dark tabards that concealed the emblems on their chests. Skarry squeezed Ress's hand all the tighter as these grim-faced ones stared at them.

'Come,' Mord said, making much of returning his sword to its scabbard. 'Where is your commander? Surely something can be arranged; we are all Monrolians after all is said and done.'

He spoke confidently yet Skarry could detect a quaver in his voice.

'Get out of the sled, Mord!' came a command from above. 'Carefully now.'

Looking towards the sound, Skarry saw one descending the steps. He was thin and bent and his eyes were creased into slits.

Mord's face paled further and very carefully he climbed down from the sled. Skarry turned to the warrior beside him but still this one made no move save for his gripping at the reins. For a moment Skarry thought that the soldier had a small bird perched upon his shoulder, for there was a flutter of feathers at his neck. Then he noticed the dark stain spreading across his chest where the arrow head pushed out. The man began to tremble and his eyes opened suddenly wide as he stared through the gateway into the mountains beyond. He raised up one arm as if reaching for the distant peaks, the fingers straining open and then he lurched forward and fell between the shafts. The horses stirred uneasily in the traces and kicked back at the body.

Turning slowly Skarry looked into the sled. The soldier there was already dead, leaning back as though asleep save that his eyes were open and staring blankly upwards into the shadows of the roof far above. Ress sat silent and still, her left hand still raised and tight upon Skarry's shoulder.

'Well met, Zimler,' Mord said quietly by way of a greeting to the one who staggered down the steps. Mord's look flitted about like a bird afraid to settle and he trembled.

'Take him!' the small man ordered and the troops jumped at his bidding. Gripping Mord by the arms they stripped him of his sword and dagger.

'You are right about one thing,' he said to Ress as they led him away. 'That I cannot foretell the future is clear now to all.' And then he was taken off through a small door leading into the depths of the fortress.

The bodies of the dead were dragged clear of the sled and piled against the walls. The one Mord had called Zimler limped over and climbed awkwardly into the sleigh. One of the soldiers joined him on the other side of Skarry and took up the reins. Skarry heard the sounds of more taking their seats behind.

'Clear up here!' Zimler said thinly to one of the soldiers. 'Send your report on to me at Snowater.'

The soldier he spoke to gave a salute, raising his right fist to his ear and then stepping back as the driver slapped at the horses' backs with the reins. They leapt forward and with a crack the runners broke free from the ice. From out of the darkness of the Keep they came once more beneath the sky, a sky so full of cloud and each cloud so full of snow that Skarry wondered it had not yet begun. Zimler too looked upwards with a smile to his face.

'Winter is upon us, eh?' he said and Skarry gave a nod in case he was talking to him.

'Be welcome,' Zimler went on, as though making an announcement, 'be welcome to Monrolia,' he chuckled, 'and be silent now.'

In confusion Skarry turned to watching as the sled entered into Monrolia. The Isthmus widened rapidly, the coasts receding to east and west, the land scattered with marching camps and many groups upon the road, of troops and laden sleds. Zimler ignored all those they met and the sled drove on. Before them the mountains clambered upwards in ragged screes and ridges.

Looking into these mountains, Skarry found himself wishing he could see their summits. The Ridgeway that he knew was more rolling fells with sudden crags rising from the slopes, screes spilling like fans across the heather as though the earth had thrust fists of rock up through the soil. Yet here in the Ulta-Zorn the writhings of the land beneath the weight of that first of all fights had been all the more violent. Almost the rock began from the sea plains, a sudden uprising of stone that climbed sheerly, a mass of grey lined with dark cracks. The vast weight of rock thrust skyward sharply into the cloud.

At the foothills the road divided and taking the less congested fork to the north-east they were soon more protected from the winds. A wide stretch of land lay here between mountains and sea, a land of pools and bogs, frozen now into sheets of ice. These were bounded by hardy pines and birch, their northern sides coated with windblown ice.

The way before them was marked only by upright stones to their right, at distances of an easy arrow shot, for the snow swept over the surface of the road and it could not be told from the plains about them. Looking far ahead Skarry could make out other sleighs coming their way. Zimler exchanged the seal pennant that Mord had raised for one bearing the book and sword of the Cunerdin and the soldiers removed the dark tabards to display their own similar colours.

'Let us look at you,' Zimler said at last and turned in his seat, pushing Skarry to one side.

Ress sat silently between her new guards and her face began to colour as though she felt the weight of his stare upon her.

'So this is the daughter of Guise of Ringdove,' Zimler said and the corners of his mouth twitched upward a little more. 'Not much to look upon, though perhaps pretty beneath the dirt.'

He put out his hand to her hair. Ress flinched at the touch and he in turn drew back his reach. The smile faded from his face and a frown came to his brow.

'You are lucky that I am only to deliver you.' he said coldly. 'Had you been mine you would not be so fortunate.'

166

'And whose are we then?' Ress spoke up defiantly and Skarry almost laughed to hear her voice so strong.

'Your ignorance is excused,' Zimler said, 'for soon all Taur will know him whom I serve. I am the principal adviser to the Cunerdin Perry, lord of all that you now survey.'

He took from his tunic a small disc of gold on which was graven the open book and sword of the Cunerdin. Zimler thrust it proudly before Ress's face, holding it there for a moment before realising his mistake.

'Clearly I am wasting my time on you,' he said angrily and returned the disc to his tunic.

'Then what of our previous captor?' Ress asked. 'The lady Malkah had first claim to us and ordered us taken to Darlak for Skoye.'

'The lady Malkah,' Zimler said with unconcealed sarcasm, 'while perhaps wisely expelling you from your own country, is a little too individual for the Cunerdin's liking. As for Grimal Skoye, he is a primitive and shortly will concern us no more, if you follow my meaning,' Zimler chuckled.

'What is that you are saying?' Ress asked coldly and Skarry was struck by the change in her mood. If Zimler noticed he gave no clue.

'Oh, he can fight well enough,' Zimler admitted grudgingly, 'for a barbarian; and in that sense he is useful to the Cunerdin, as any tool is useful to a craftsman. Yet it does not last; the tool becomes blunted or misshapen with use and will not cut true. Then is it cast aside and a new one taken up.'

'My father never cast aside a blunted tool,' Skarry said without thinking, 'for he would labour with it and grind and hone its edge until it was all the keener.'

'Be silent!' Zimler turned on Skarry with his face raised in purple blotches and struck him a weak blow about the face. 'How dare you speak so to me, you peasant! What do you know of the ways of civilised peoples?'

He fell silent as another sled approached, raising one hand slightly as greeting. Like the others coming from the north-east this was laden not with soldiery but rather with commanders or lords in bright armours of bronze and rich cloaks. They carried flagons of wine and sang loudly such that in the growing darkness Skarry could hear them long before they met. Zimler

167

stared down his nose at them and they returned courteous salutes, momentarily interrupting their festivities. After they had gone from sight they might hear a burst of laughter before the singing began again.

Occasionally they passed buildings like small walled farms and at one of these they changed horses before hurrying on into the coming night. The woman who received them there carried out Zimler's sharp commands fearfully. Later the adviser nibbled daintily at peices of dead animal on a plate held by one of his men, though the prisoners were given nothing.

Skarry fell into a half sleep with the rocking of the sled, the sighing of the wind. Although no moon could be seen through the thick cloud, he felt that it was near full; its light seemed gently to illuminate the whole sky and a pale, even glow filtered through to wash across the land. Zimler made no move to stop for the night and only wrapped himself tighter in his cloak.

The bulk of the mountains to their left became dark and Skarry's closing eyes were drawn towards their shadow. All through that long, cold night he hovered between sleeping and a jolting wakefulness without seeming to rest. After a time the darkness of the Ulta-Zorn took on shapes that he thought he recognised and almost he was convinced that he was home in Taur, perhaps taking the road from Midloth and that there was the vale of Dunan leading up to his own mountain of the Angsoth. At these times his heart was filled with such a yearning that he near cried in his loss. Then the face of Gemel appeared in the shadow of a crag and the old man looked kindly down upon him as if indeed this was but a dream and he would wake soon to the sounds of his forest and the Olluden singing, and there was no war and no suffering. At these times he felt filled with a joy that strove to break out and his heart beat strongly.

He found himself wondering whether the old man was alive still or if he had at last chosen to end his time and lain down in the snows of the Angsoth as his father had before him. In the mountains the wizened face of Gemel melted before Skarry and in its place, forming from the features of the old man, he saw the dark head of a bear, its eyes bright with quiet intelligence.

'Ah, bear,' he said softly, 'you of all creatures have always looked kindly upon me and caused me no harm. Would that you could help me now in my time of greatest need.'

At first he had seen the image as that of the brown bears of the forest but as if the moon shone suddenly through a break in the cloud, the bear became as white as the fresh snow of winter and its eye burned like a warm fire, deep within the folds of the Ulta-Zorn.

Then Zimler was shaking him roughly and he awoke to the half light between winter's night and morning.

'Shut your noise will you!' came the angry voice. 'You make as much chatter asleep as awake.'

Looking around, Skarry saw lights ahead, those of a town glimmering through the dawn.

'Snowater,' Zimler announced. 'And about time too. I am ready for a hot bath after this freezing travelling.'

As they approached, Skarry saw that it was walled with stone yet the work had been hastily done, in places piled roughly between timber shorings. Within the walls were few large buildings, much of the space being taken up by rows of tents.

'Ah, it is not the same place since your cursed armies burned it,' said Zimler and clouted Skarry over the ear. 'It was once a fine, rich place where a man could enjoy himself. We've not had the time to rebuild it yet, what with the war to consider. But that will come.'

At the gates Zimler let out an impatient yell and the doors swung open. But instead of driving in as Skarry expected, Zimler clambered stiffly down and made to enter alone.

'You know where to go,' he said to the soldier who held the reins, 'and you know where to find me.' With that he turned on his heel and hobbled within the walls. The driver turned the horses to the left and pushed them into a trot. Skarry saw that they followed another way, marked this time by larger, rougher stones to either side, each inscribed with figures which, though he could not read them, felt akin to the old stone script of the Olluden and the Hagarath. Before them the road led into the foothills of the mountains and here a distant crag loomed hugely like the head of a great cave bear and the rock was lined whitely as if with quartz. Skarry's heart lifted somewhat for he was at least glad to have missed the Monrolian town.

'Is our journey to end with a knife between the ribs?' Ress asked from the back of the sled. 'And our bodies left for the white fox to pick at?'

The driver gave a short laugh and replied not unkindly.

'We are not murderers,' he said. 'You are to be taken to the Fane, Ymir's Seat, in the mountains where you will be safe.'

'Safe from whom?' Skarry asked.

'From yourselves,' the soldier replied more sternly. 'Believe it, for should you try to escape, then shall I kill you.'

The others in the back laughed and took out parcels of food that they unwrapped and shared with their prisoners. They ate hungrily as the road began to wind its way between the hills. The snow thickened on the ground yet though the horses had harder work the way remained largely clear where other sleds had travelled since the last snow fall. The land rose steeper as they moved on into the mountains following the narrow valley upwards. Ahead the great bear's crag leaned out and seemed to hang over them as they neared.

Rounding a last bend at the head of the valley brought them to a wide plateau below the crag and here lay the Fane, Ymir's Seat. With its walls whitened by snow it seemed to have grown from the very winter, a sprawling citadel, its inner towers circled with bands of copper. From its tall chimneys pale smoke writhed up through the stilled air before the crag.

The driver urged the horses on and as they came down the road towards the Fane the gates opened as though in greeting. But another sled drew forth from here and as they passed, Skarry could see that all their number wore badges of rank and jewels. These ones laughed at some joke and took no notice of the other sleigh once they had seen the garb of the soldiers.

Before they reached the walls a company of guards came running out with spears ready, some to cover the entrance, two more coming close to the sled. They wore winter gear with high fur-lined boots and thick cloaks. When the cloaks parted as they ran, Skarry could make out the book and sword of the Cunerdin.

The soldiers in the sled handed over passes before they were allowed through, the guard parting before them. Inside they found an open courtyard with heavy doors leading off from it, the walls topped by watchtowers. A Captain with an embroidered edge to his cloak swept up to them accompanied by four soldiers. He carried a slate which he examined carefully.

'The lady Recina,' the driver stated, 'and a Taurian peasant.'

'The lady to the Holding Rooms,' the Captain said efficiently.

170

'The peasant can go in with the servants.' And he wrote with a marker upon his slate, frowning with concentration.

'Hold to your hope, Skarry,' was all Ress had time to say as they were taken from the sled. Looking back over his shoulder Skarry watched as she was led through one of the doors while he was drawn towards another by two of the soldiers. The door closed upon his sight of her and he was left feeling hopelessly alone. They went along a plain corridor, its smooth walls washed white, the booted footsteps of the guards making a hollow ringing. They passed more doors of thick pine, the solid timbers joined with square black nails, the points driven through and clenched over. On each side were iron fittings to take a bar that kept closed the door.

At the end of the corridor they went down four steps and the leading soldier drew aside the bar and opened the door. Inside were five people in plain tunics huddled about a hearth.

'You will take your orders from the prefect,' the guard said to Skarry and indicated one of those within who had risen as they entered.

This one was broad shouldered and sported a disc on his tunic, over his heart, embroidered with the sign of the Cunerdin. He grinned lopsidedly at the new arrival.

'Well Skarry, you skinny hero!' said Mullo. 'What have you been up to?'

18

Ymir's Fane

Mullo steered Skarry firmly towards a long table and pushed him into the seat at one end. Then, with sharp words of command, he directed the five other servants in the preparation of a meal. They hurried to do his bidding and made no show of protest when he laughed at their clumsiness. They were young, their faces pale except for around the eyes where the sun and wind had burned the exposed skin.

The meal was laid upon the table and they all sat, Mullo taking the chair at the head and he it was who gave the order to begin. Skarry's hunger overcame his suspicion and he ate of sprouted grains and nuts, savouring each mouthful. Mullo observed him throughout with a grin to his face, stuffing the food into his own mouth almost as though he did not notice he was eating. They ate in silence, the others keeping their eyes to their food.

When they were done, Mullo had the youngest servant pour him a glass of wine that he first sipped daintily then downed in one gulp and helped himself to another.

'Well, Skarry,' he said at last, 'how do you like your new home – better than a hut in the forest, eh?' and he pushed his chair back to lean against the wall. 'More wood on the fire!' he barked suddenly and laughed as the youngster jumped to carry out his command.

'What are you doing here, Mullo?' Skarry asked at last while the other poured himself more wine.

'I came the same way as you,' he replied. 'The Ice Warriors had set a trap for Quorn on the High Pass. He wanted to be a hero but they shot him down before he could even show them his sword.' He began to snigger and spluttered on his wine.

'Quorn's troops weren't so foolish, nor me. I was brought here as a prisoner.' He shrugged his shoulders, 'Things are not bad, the food's good, wine, shelter. They are straight, these Monro-

172

lians and they know what they want from servants. I am quick to learn so they made me prefect.' And he pushed out his chest, pointing to the badge.

'So now you serve the enemy,' Skarry said slowly.

The other servants doubled the pace of their eating as Mullo came suddenly upright, slamming the chair legs to the floor.

'Well, skinny Skarry,' he said grinning, 'I know and care little for this word right, or the other, wrong. Here they have different stories. They say that Ymir is good and came down from the starways with Ithunne and that the evil Vidar carried her off and holds her forever captive on the Ridgeway. To me it does not matter which way you tell it. I am here and with care I can make something of myself. If I work well for them, then they will have me as an aid to the soldiers, or perhaps one of the visiting commanders will need a guide on the Angsoth.'

'You cannot mean it,' Skarry said. 'Surely you would not lead the enemy into our mountains. It is the act of a traitor!'

The others stopped their eating but did not look up. Mullo rose slowly, shaking his shoulders and walked around the table towards Skarry. From within his tunic he took a short, fat stick which he began to crack sharply into the palm of his hand.

'You should be careful, skinny Skarry,' he said in a low voice. 'For I am master here, and you must do my bidding. One word from me will get you a beating off the guards. And if that does not settle you,' he went on, 'then perhaps I shall give you one of my own.'

There came the sounds of footsteps drawing towards the door and Mullo hastily pocketed his stick, giving Skarry a fierce look with his mouth twisted into a snarl. He straightened his tunic just in time for the soldier who stuck his head within the room.

'Two for temple duties, Prefect,' this one commanded of Mullo.

'Aye, sir!' Mullo said crisply and snapped to attention. 'I'll take the newcomer myself.'

'As you wish,' the soldier said and held the door for them to leave before barring it behind.

Skarry had expected the soldier to stay with them but he hurried off down the corridor.

'I am all the guard you need, skinny Skarry,' Mullo said and grinned lopsidedly.

He swung Skarry about and by way of another door they entered a wider corridor that ran along one side of the courtyard through which Skarry had entered the Fane. From the bare white of the servants' areas they were plunged into a sudden richness, the floor carpeted with thick rugs of interweaving designs that quieted their footsteps. In the patterns Skarry could make out the oak, its branches winding over and under each other. The walls were hung with tapestries that depicted rank upon rank of Monrolian soldiery, their banners flapping in a stiff gale that blew from the mountains. On these lofty peaks sat a giant figure who gazed serenely down upon the battle, a sword in one hand, an open book in the other.

Halfway along the corridor they came to the main doors which led out into the courtyard. Two guards leaned casually against the doorposts, raising their heads to greet Mullo. From his tunic Mullo produced oatcakes and gave them to the soldiers who laughed with him and clapped him on the shoulders. Moving on, Mullo took Skarry down the corridor to an oak door carved with the features of the giant on the tapestry. Though Skarry could not compare the design with the animal carvings of the Olluden, the work was delicately cut and the face had a noble look to it.

'It is their Ymir,' Mullo said to Skarry. 'This is his temple.'

And so saying he swung open the door and they entered.

The room was long and high, the arch of its roof fading into darkness for there were few torches in the walls. Mullo laughed as Skarry gasped, for in the far shadows sat a huge figure, the features cast into a flickering life by the light of the flames. Mullo pulled Skarry forward and left him shaking in front of the seated giant while he ran behind. Looking up at the face Skarry saw the heavy lids rise and flames issue from the eye sockets. The jaw trembled and then dropped and a booming laugh echoed about the chamber. Skarry fell to his knees in sudden fear, unable to comprehend the sight.

Then the laugh became lesser and Mullo stepped back into sight clutching at his sides and bending double. When he had recovered enough to speak he came down and gave Skarry a shove that sent him sprawling.

'You simple savage!' he laughed. 'It is but a machine. The look on your face!'

There came the sound of footsteps and other doors opening

and Mullo stifled his mirth, ordering Skarry quickly to his feet. He bowed stiffly to the leading figure and when Skarry did not copy his action he hit him on the ear. Skarry winced at the sudden pain and then slowly made his bow.

There were two tall men in rich robes of purple velvet embroidered in gold and red that swept the floor at their feet. They held their hands folded before them and seemed to glide across the room. Behind them came a dozen or so women and men, girls and boys, all in plain tunics and flanked by soldiers.

'Hurry now!' one of those in purple velvet scolded and the chamber was suddenly busy. The guards took up positions at the corners and centres of each wall save the end one where the idol sat. The others began to prepare the chamber, some sweeping, others replacing the torches. The two in velvet hurried towards the seated giant making rapid gestures as they approached. Of Skarry and Mullo they took no notice and passed behind the giant's throne.

'This is your new life, simple Skarry,' Mullo said grimly and thrust a broom before Skarry's face. 'Believe it, for you shall never leave here.'

Skarry began to sweep for there seemed nothing else that he could do, yet with head lowered towards the floor he watched carefully all about. Some of the servants in the plain tunics were Monrolian, short and stocky with long noses that warmed the cold air before it reached their lungs. They had an ancient look to their faces not unlike the swarthy Hagarath and Skarry started when he first noticed that some of them wore stones at their necks, a dark soapstone lightly flecked with grey. Others of the servants had more familiar looks and Skarry guessed that many were prisoners taken at the fall of Midloth. There were more prefects among their number who gave sharp orders backed up by their sticks.

Mullo strolled easily back to Skarry.

'Look well,' he said to Skarry, 'for these are your life friends now. Those with the look of savages are from northern Monrolia, the wives and children of strong mountain chiefs. The Cunerdin holds them here so that their husbands will do his bidding. See there, the tall woman. She is the sister of Grimal Skoye himself. You'll find all of Monrolia and some of Taur present here in these women and children. Why, even the

Olluden!' And he laughed, tripping Skarry so that he fell, his broom clattering on the floor.

Some stopped and turned to the noise and one of those in velvet poked his head from behind the statue of Ymir, giving Skarry a hard look. Mullo dragged him to his feet, cuffing him about the head and pushing the broom once more within his grasp. As he rose up, Skarry caught sight of Ress. They had sat her upon a stool against the wall where she polished the ornaments that were brought to her from about the throne.

Before he could go to her there came a long drawn out note like the sounding of a mountain horn. The brooms were collected and placed within cupboards in the walls. The soldiers straightened themselves as the two priests in velvet arranged the servants. The women and girls were drawn up along one side wall and made to kneel, the men and boys, with Skarry and Mullo amongst them, kneeling opposite. Somewhere music began, its long deep notes rising up as though from the ground. Torches were kindled about the throne, the light passing through coloured silks, casting shadows of red and blue and orange. A mist arose from the feet of the huge figure and climbed in slow coils about it.

Then the main doors were thrown open and a group of Monrolian lords and commanders entered, laden with weighty badges of rank and medals telling of their heroic deeds. They bowed low and approached the seated Ymir with awe.

The huge eyelids opened ponderously, the flames dancing within and in a deep echoing voice the idol spoke.

'Hear the voice of Ymir,' it said. 'And know it to be truth. Mighty are the armies of Ymir and wisely does the Cunerdin carry out His word. The evil of Vidar manifest in Taur is thrown back and soon to be crushed utterly. Thus is the truth spoken by Ymir. Yet is the evil still powerful and taints those who are weak. So is Grimal Skoye tainted and his part is ended. Call him to council at Midloth and there take back his life for Ymir that Monrolia shall go on to victory. Take with you the blessing of Ymir in your noble purpose. Thus Ymir speaks.'

The flames roared up about the throne and then died as the eyelids closed. The Monrolian lords and commanders bowed low as the figure was cast once more into shadow. The priests came forward from the side of the throne and gestured to the servants on either hand, speaking to the lords.

'Choose of the servants of Ymir,' they said. 'And receive his blessing.

'They choose a bedmate,' Mullo whispered to Skarry, 'for there will be much wine and song before they return to the war. Such is the generosity of Ymir.' And he had to lower his head down to hide his grinning.

Skarry watched in growing fear as the lords and commanders debated their choice but Ress they overpassed, taking instead the tall woman who Mullo had pointed out as Grimal Skoye's own sister. She made no protest and held her head up proudly as she was led away.

With the departure of the lords and commanders light was returned to the chamber, more torches being kindled and placed in brackets upon the walls. The brooms were given out once again though Skarry could see nothing worth sweeping. Seizing the one Mullo handed him Skarry brushed his way to Ress's side without looking, seeming intent upon his work.

'Well met again, Skarry,' she said softly. 'Your necklace has a particular rattle.' Before he could say anything she went on, 'Of all the places I have been, this is the most godless. We must escape, for from what I have heard those held hostage here cannot count on too long a life.'

'But how Ress?' Skarry asked desperately, turning to her. 'There are guards everywhere.'

Ress seemed to look over her left shoulder.

'Where is your faith now, young forester?' she asked mockingly and looking at the statue of Ymir Skarry could only shake his head.

'Vidar is like this also,' she went on, her voice quiet but strong. 'They are but puppets set up to justify murder. Hold to the land, Skarry, your forest, for there lies your faith.'

Skarry stopped in his sweeping and raised one hand to the stones about his neck. Each one conjured a vision of Taur and the peoples he had met. The smooth blue of the Asgire and Crane of Mireside with his cloak of feathers, the Kirmire stretching flatly into the distance, its low tree-covered rises islands in the sea of mist. And here Sulla of the Ranneye stood before him with her black hair flying in the wind and the rolling plains of the Epona receding about her. Then Hook of the Hagarath, sad Hook, yet wise also and strong, standing as though rooted on the red stone of the Ridgeway. And last, the green stone of the Olluden and Skarry's own Gemel, seated cross-legged beneath the mighty boughs of the oak in the green of the forest. And it seemed to Skarry then that these were the people he loved and should wish to be with and that the lords and commanders were separate and different, as though having taken another way long ago.

'Not bad, eh?' Mullo whispered loudly in his ear and started him from his dream. 'she's not bad, eh?' and he gestured towards Ress.

Skarry flushed and pushed away Mullo's pointing arm.

'Do not touch her,' he said fiercely.

For an instant Skarry felt fear in Mullo, then the broad shoulders drew upwards, his head hunching forward and the cruel light came to his eyes once more.

'So, simple Skarry,' Mullo said and took the stick from within his tunic, 'you think she is yours, do you? Well indeed you are mistaken, for I am your master here and you will do as I say.'

Suddenly, from the open doors they heard loud shouts and crashings. The servants stopped in their work and turned to the doorway, some of the soldiers hurrying out to see what went on. Mullo also was drawn unwillingly from Skarry by this fresher disturbance. A soldier came running in.

'Quick!' he shouted, breathlessly. 'It is that bitch, Skoye's sister. She has stabbed the lord Magrat with his own knife and set fire to the Pleasure Room!'

A certain confusion broke out in the chamber as the soldiers made for the door, freeing their swords. The priests tried to herd the servants back to their own quarters, their sharp voices hardly penetrating the babble of excited chatter.

'We should use this moment,' Ress hissed at Skarry and gripped his arm. While Mullo's attention was still occupied, Skarry drew her to him and they moved into the shadows beside the throne of the idol. From without, the shouts grew louder together with sounds as of a door being battered. Behind the throne Skarry could make out the levers by which the priests had operated the idol and beyond, in the far wall, two doorways.

Leading Ress at his side he made for the one on the left. It was not locked and opened on to another long corridor. Turning to

178

close it behind them Skarry was in time to see a puzzled Mullo peering around the throne. In the instant before Skarry had the door shut their eyes met and Mullo's face took on its twisted grin as he came after them, his stick raised.

'Where do we go?' he asked Ress anxiously, looking quickly down and up the passage.

'Follow your heart, Skarry!' Ress said. 'I have not a clue.'

Skarry found himself running swiftly down the corridor with Ress holding to his arm. Before they had turned the corner at the end of the passage Skarry heard Mullo enter behind and his shout as he saw them.

'Steps, Ress,' Skarry gasped between breaths. 'Four, leading downward.'

They slowed to descend the steps, Mullo's footsteps closing loudly behind. Running on, Skarry found they were in another passage, a single black oak door at the far end. With sinking heart Skarry reached the door to find it locked and listening with his ear against the wood he could hear booted footsteps approaching from beyond. When he turned from the door he saw Mullo round the corner and stop as he in turn spied them.

'So Skarry,' Mullo called and cracked his stick into his palm. 'Simple Skarry, Skarry suck-a-stone. You have outdone yourself this time. Your foolishness will not go unpunished.'

Mullo began to come towards them slowly, taking wide steps and loosening his shoulders. His face twisted into a smirk as he coloured with the flush of blood. As he neared they heard the sounds of the soldiers beyond the door. The oak was shaken but not opened. Then came the sudden thud and shock of a blow against the wood and Skarry drew Ress away, having nowhere to go save towards Mullo.

'Skinny Skarry,' Mullo snarled. 'You shall not escape me now.'

Skarry had time to push Ress to the wall before Mullo fell upon him, the stick catching him on the shoulder, a fist following to land heavily on his right cheek. The blow spun him across the corridor and hard against the further wall. Behind he saw the top panel of the door begin to splinter from the flurry of blows that came from beyond.

Mullo hurled himself across the passage, pinning Skarry against the wall and crushing the breath from him. Dropping his stick Mullo put his square hands to the other's throat, his

179

lopsided grin and bulging eyes looming large before Skarry's face. He began to squeeze and though Skarry struggled he could not throw off the grip. With a sudden splintering Skarry saw a blade bite through the door panel and gnaw at the wood. The sword was of iron, stained blue as though from heat, notched towards the point.

Ress came to his aid, seeming to stare above him. She first felt Mullo's back then cracked him one on the ear. At the same moment Skarry brought up his knee hard and Mullo yelped in pain and sat suddenly down, rolling to one side and clutching at his crotch. The door panel at last gave way and fell inward to reveal Glimshpill's sweating face, Catskin beside him, both breathing heavily. Glimshpill took his dagger from his belt and tossed it through the hole. Skarry caught the weapon by the handle.

'Kill him!' Glimshpill commanded. 'Quickly, lest he raise the alarm.'

Skarry turned swiftly on Mullo as the two soldiers broke open the door. He stopped his writhings on the floor and, suddenly still, looked up towards the knife. Skarry leaned forward and held the point of the blade over Mullo's heart.

'Quickly!' Glimshpill called from the door. 'Kill him, lad!'

'The throat!' came the sound of Catskin. 'Then he shall not cry out.'

Skarry's arm wavered. He moved the blade to Mullo's neck then looked into his eyes. Tears filled them and ran down into his ears.

'Don't, Skarry,' Mullo said and he shook with fear. 'Don't, I beg you. We are of the same people, the same forest.'

And in Mullo's features, twisted now with fear, Skarry saw the boy he had played with, running beneath the canopy of green with the other children, in the high forest home of the Olluden and he could not kill him.

Mullo squirmed away from the knife and ran as the door at last burst open.

'Out of my way!' Catskin commanded and drew his bow but Mullo rounded the far corner and was lost from their sight though his cries of alarm echoed loudly back to them.

'Curse your dreaming!' Glimshpill snapped. 'You will be the death of us all.'

He turned and clambered back through the shattered door, his sword held before him. Skarry took Ress by her hand and led her after him, Catskin bringing up the rear. Beyond were steps leading upwards and a Monrolian soldier sprawled at the foot with Catskin's arrow protruding from his reddening chest. Skarry stooped to pull free the long cloak, taking it with him.

Glimshpill stamped his way up the steps. The sound of the wind came loud through the wall on their left and the thin arrow slits showered with snow. At the top a door took them out on to the walls into sudden cold. The roofs of the Fane spread away to their right, veiled in the first flurry of the coming blizzard. Smoke billowed blackly from one building to be caught by the wind and hurled away.

Between the battlements a grapple like a small anchor had lodged and a rope fell away to the snow covered ground outside the walls. The cold caught at them and Ress's teeth began to chatter. Glimshpill was first at the rope, squeezing his bulk between the battlements and lowering himself, cursing all the while. He had not gone far before he gave a last curse and let go, falling heavily into the snow below. Skarry threw the Monrolian's cloak after him and putting Ress's hands upon the rope he helped her up on to the parapet.

'Jump girl!' Glimshpill called up and caught her as she fell to him. Skarry and Catskin followed hurriedly. At the foot of the wall Skarry cut the cloak into two with the dagger and wrapped Ress in one half, keeping the other for himself.

They had come out on the northern side of the Fane. As they moved away from the walls, the bear's crag towered over them, rising beyond sight into the storm. Before they had gone far Skarry saw soldiers running on the walls. One found the grapple and called to his comrades. Looking out they began to point and shout and as more soldiers appeared the first began to climb down the rope. Turning again Skarry found Glimshpill looking back also. Their eyes met and Glimshpill shook his head, reaching out a hand for his dagger.

'Would that you had used it,' he said as Skarry returned the weapon, 'though I should expect no more from a young Dreamer.'

The noise of the storm grew and filled their ears. Glimshpill ploughed ahead and the others followed in his wake. Soon they were enclosed within the white and only by the rise of the land could they tell that at least they still moved upwards and away from the Fane. Yet looking back Skarry knew that even in such a blizzard the Monrolians could follow their easy trail.

After hard moments of toil in the deepening snow Glimshpill was at last brought up by a wall of rock that clambered icily from the drifts. In its little shelter they huddled together.

'Ah, what's the use!' Glimshpill shouted into the gale. 'I even took to a boat for you! And stole a sled from beneath the very nose of the enemy,' his bellow came to Skarry below the howl of the wind. 'Now all is wasted; not even a bard to sing of our exploits. I shall make an end here.'

He went beyond them and waited, swinging his sword from side to side, letting the blade turn in the wind. Catskin stared up at the rock as though seeking some secret way. Skarry put his arms about Ress and they clung to each other, shaking as one with the cold. He was taken back once more to his Angsoth and that bitter flight from the Ice Warriors across the snows of the Maen-hir. There the High Haven had been their saving and looking up at the crag Skarry thought that here too were mountains and that their people also would have shelters for times of storm. But he did not know where to look for the signs, or whether he could read them if he found them.

Almost he slumped in Ress's arms but her closeness gave him strength and he felt that if he should die now, out in the blizzard and far from the forest of his home, then at the least he should die together with one whom he loved and how few others could do likewise. He laid his head upon her shoulder and told her how he loved her, though the wind dragged his words away. And poised thus he saw beyond Ress the deep ruts in the snow where a heavy beast had passed, the prints dragged into each other, a bear's.

His heart began to pound loudly and releasing Ress he hurried to Catskin and showed him the track. Catskin in turn fetched Glimshpill and together they bowed over the trail. They looked at one another and Glimshpill shrugged his shoulders.

'Lead the way, young Dreamer,' he shouted above the gale. 'For your doom beckons you!'

And, taking Ress by the hand, Skarry began to follow the trail of the bear that led through the thick of the blizzard into the ice mountains of Monrolia, the Ulta-Zorn.

19

The Winter Palace

The howl of the storm enclosed Skarry, its cold hand gripped him, the shards of its windblown ice slashing at his bare face. He clutched the cloak tight about his throat, his other hand numbly fused in Ress's grasp. The danger of their plight was a weight about his shoulders and he clung to the tracks of the bear as his last hope for he felt that surely this creature of the mountains would know of a place of safety in such weather.

The trail led them first along the foot of the crag and then turned upwards into a ragged gully filled with snow-covered screes. This gave them a little shelter and with the work of the climb some warmth was driven through his body yet he knew that Ymir bit coldly at his fingers and would take them given but a chance.

The gully narrowed as they climbed, growing all the steeper until they were forced to scramble upon hands and knees, Skarry kicking holds in the frozen snow. Ress felt for a grip with her free hand and feet, hugging herself to the snow to escape the wind. At the summit they hauled themselves out between tall rocks, white to the windward side. Skarry took the time to look down and though he could see no sign of pursuit their trail was clear in the snow for any who chose to follow. Glimshpill looked up at him, the huge warrior panting heavily and though his mouth moved Skarry could hear nothing above the greater voice of the storm. He guessed the soldier was cursing.

Skarry would not let them rest long and helped Ress to her feet, brushing the clinging snow from her. Before them lay a wide plateau that sloped gently back towards the next uprising of rock. Once more they were exposed to the full force of the wind and bowed before its icy blast. Already the bear's prints were filling with snow and Skarry found it more difficult to pick out its passage. He began to wonder of their fate should the tracks become covered and with that thought he felt a growing fear within that tightened his stomach.

But the image of Gemel came to his mind, that old one of the Angsoth and it cheered him in his time of need. The wise face seemed to smile with the light of laughter in the eyes. He would have no fear of the storm. Almost Skarry could hear the creaking voice, 'Fear comes only from thought of the future. Look to the present and fear will not trouble you.'

So Skarry set aside the burden of his fear and drew Ress to him, putting his arm about her shoulder and she smiled. Looking upwards Skarry could see the far peaks of the ice mountains between flurries of snow, their summits reached by ridges as sharp as razors, flashing, icily reflecting the blues of the sky above the clouds.

Bringing his gaze down once again to their more immediate surroundings he saw a dark shape loom in the snow and hurriedly pulled Ress down. Yet it did not move and Glimshpill came floundering forward through the drifts.

'It is a cave!' he shouted into their ears as he passed them. 'Well done lad! Wait a while, I will evict its owner.' And he made to go on, holding his sword, Settler, pointing before him.

'Do not harm it!' Skarry called, gripping tightly to the warrior's sword arm.

Glimshpill turned and stared, then shrugged his shoulders. As he went forward the shadow of the entrance darkly absorbed his bulk. After moments shivering in the snow they heard the low growl of the beast and then Glimshpill's own throaty roar. The bear burst suddenly from the opening and stopped short when it saw them. Skarry raised a hand as though to salute it but it turned and lumbered off into the blizzard. With some sorrow that they had forced it to leave its place of shelter Skarry entered the haven leading Ress, Catskin behind.

Once within they fell to the ground, gasping for breath, relieved suddenly of the blast of wind. Snow blew in through the entrance in flurries and covered much of the surface, collecting in drifts in the shadows of the further walls. The smell of the bear was still strong in the air.

'Ah, I would not have thought I could be so grateful for a dark cave,' Glimshpill said from where he sprawled.

'I am grateful also,' said Ress. 'Though this is no cave, the floor is too level.'

Skarry looked more carefully about and saw that Ress was right for the line where walls met ceiling was as straight as a true spear. The snow piled about the opening lent it an irregular outline but even though no door remained the ancient frame could just be made out. Skarry began to examine the further walls, digging into the drifts with his boot. Though this shelter fulfilled their immediate need, still they shook with cold and he knew that only a fire could help that.

He stopped suddenly as his kicking boot returned a hollow thud. Digging more carefully he found a low door in the back wall, an ancient black door all bestudded with iron that peeled in rusty flakes as he brushed his hand across it. Calling to the others he cleared the snow from about this. Glimshpill took the door ring in his fist and gave a testing heave. The rusted hinges creaked and cracked and the ring tore from the old timber. Yet the door had budged a little and thrusting Settler through the narrow gap, Glimshpill levered it further. The opening beckoned blackly and the soldiers looked at one another.

'I'll tell you now, I'm not going in there,' Glimshpill stated. 'It's as black as the heart of Guise, no offence girl.'

'None taken,' said Ress, going close and sniffing at the air. She wrinkled her nose and pulled a face.

'It is old,' she said, 'and many years have passed since this was last opened. Let me through.'

Before Skarry could stop her she squeezed through the gap and the blackness swallowed her up. He called to her but Catskin tapped him on the arm.

'The darkness is her element,' he said simply. 'Let her be.'

For long moments Skarry waited, his heart pounding loudly in his ears, straining to hear the slightest noise within. He started when Ress came suddenly close out of the darkness. Her hair was filled with cobwebs and her hands grimed with ancient dirt.

'It is quite safe,' she said, 'a small inner chamber. But take care for there is much rubbish about and a trap door in the centre which may not take the weight of a true warrior.'

Glimshpill grunted and gripping the edge of the door he hauled it shrieking open. Then Catskin tore a strip of material from his cloak and Glimshpill carefully struck a spark from his

185

pipe-lighter and kindled the cloth. Ress stood back to let them enter, the light from the small flames striving to reach the corners of the inner room. Skarry saw the heavy oak trap door central in the floor and all about the walls broken casks and sacks and litter. Catskin hastily gathered what dry material he could find before the flames died and soon had a small fire burning to one side of the trap. Glimshpill heaved the door shut and hung his great cloak over it to lessen the draught. Then they all sat about the fire and held up their palms to the flames.

'We shall be warm at least when they come for us,' he growled and taking a pouch from his tunic he began to nibble at its contents. Catskin sat cross-legged beside him and rubbed his bow, warming the wood that it might draw well when the Monrolians found them.

'It is an ancient ruin, this,' Ress said, cocking her head to one side as though she heard faint whispers of age.

'We cannot stay here,' Skarry said. 'They are used to such weather. They will be here soon.'

'We must go down,'said Ress and she stamped on the trap door. It echoed hollowly.

Glimshpill started at the sound and shivered.

'Have a care!' he whispered fiercely. 'Vidar knows what may be lurking down there in the darkness.'

Ress laughed, turning towards the sound of his voice.

'The brave warrior!' she announced.

'This is all the bravery I need,' said Glimshpill holding the pouch to her as though she might see it. 'Ale, the green smoke and this.' And he ate more from the bag. Already his face was flushed and the light began to burn in his eyes.

'Then at least raise up the trap that we may escape,' said Ress.

Glimshpill was silent for a moment, his face twisting in the firelight as he stared at the dark square in the floor. He rose awkwardly and planting his feet astride the trap he grasped the ring and heaved. Slowly the door opened, releasing a thin billow of dust or mist and the smell of age. Glimshpill snorted and dropped the door. The flames danced in the draught as it banged heavily shut.

'Well I for one am not going down there,' he said.

Ress went to him and found his arm.

'It is our one hope,' she said. 'If we simply wait, then they will

186

surely find us and take us back, or kill us. It is only darkness, no more than that. Let me be your guide, for I know it well.'

In the light of the fire she clung to his arm, her red hair tumbling about her shoulders, he towering over her, dwarfing her.

'I am not going down there,' he said at last, 'for I have no liking for the dark. Yet I will open the way for you, if you choose such foolishness.'

So saying he strode once more to the trap and grunting, heaved it open. Catskin kindled a rag at the fire and dropped it into the black opening. It fluttered slowly downwards and they saw stone steps coiling away below before its flames failed.

'Ah, it goes to the very depths,' Glimshpill moaned. 'No doubt Ithunne is bound below and Ymir awaits whoever enters.'

From without came sudden shouts upon the wind. The two soldiers exchanged looks and took up their weapons. Glimshpill tipped the last of the contents from the pouch into his mouth and began to stamp, flailing his arms about to drive the drug through his bloodstream.

'We shall make a song of it!' he snarled, holding Settler in the light of the fire so that the notched blade shone blue. He turned suddenly on Skarry, his eyes glowing fiercely.

'Get thee below with thy woman!' he said. 'I shall make safe thy back.'

Skarry looked up at Glimshpill. The soldier's face was twitching and seemed old, the skin deeply seamed. Yet the eyes danced and he grinned widely. Skarry turned to Catskin but the other did not wait for his question.

'I cannot leave him,' he said simply. 'We have been together too long.'

'Descend!' Glimshpill roared and then laughed as they started. 'Into the darkness,' he went on. 'Into the depths.'

Skarry backed slowly towards the trap door, his gaze held by the two soldiers as they made ready to meet their doom. Ress already sat at the edge of the opening, feeling for the first steps with her feet. From without there came more shouts and the sound of heavy boots on stone. The cloak over the door shook as someone hit at the wood.

Skarry ran suddenly forward and clung to Glimshpill's great forearm.

187

'Come with us Glim!' he pleaded and the tears started in his eyes. 'We may yet all escape unharmed.'

The rage quieted in the soldier's eyes as he looked upon Skarry.

'Do you weep for me, young forester?' he asked quietly and put up his square fist to Skarry's cheek. 'No,' he said softly. 'I cannot change now. For me it is over. When you sit once more about the fire with your people in your forest home, tell them of Glimshpill, the mighty Glimshpill and loyal Catskin. Now begone.'

And he turned his broad back upon Skarry and strode towards the door, dragging aside the cloak. Skarry found Catskin leading him to the trap. The thin soldier smiled at him, the beak of his nose in the firelight lending him the grace of the sparrow hawk.

'Farewell Skarry,' he said thinly and thrust him towards the trap, standing ready to close it on them.

Ress was already a few steps down, calling up to him to make haste. As Skarry lowered himself, Catskin closed the trap and through the narrowing gap he made out Glimshpill's broad back as the warrior pulled open the outer door to greet the Monrolians with his roaring battle cry. Then he was enclosed in darkness, the sounds of the fight momentarily drowned as Catskin kicked rubbish on to the trap door in a bid to hide their way of escape.

Suddenly alone in the blackness with his own panting loud in his ears he froze.

'Ress!' he called, then louder, more fearful, 'Ress!'

'I am here,' came her voice, so close that he jumped. 'And here is my hand. Let me lead you now.'

Her clasp was warm and he breathed all the easier. Slowly she took him downwards, the stone steps cold through their boots. Above them came the sounds of metal striking metal, fierce shouts and sudden screams. Glimshpill was singing his cursing song, the words blurring together, becoming the raging shriek of the beast that is driven into a corner and, with no thought of escape, turns at last to fight. Skarry cried quietly as the sounds receded above them.

'It is their choice, Skarry,' Ress said to him. 'There is no blame in it.'

After a time no further sounds reached them. Enclosed in so complete a darkness Skarry strove to feel his whereabouts.

Visions arose before his inner eye, of mountains and his own high forest, glimmering in the light of the moon. Then caves and dark passages, the Firebolg waiting somewhere below, giving a low snarl of warning. And the faces of those he had known, rising like wraiths as though conjured from the stones about his neck. The visions only confused him and he stumbled and near fell. Ress steadied him.

'We are at the foot of the stair,' she said. 'Wait here for me.'

Her hand was suddenly gone and Skarry was alone. The air smelt of ancient dust and mould. He sat carefully on the lower step and stretched out his hands. He moved too fast, for the knuckles of his left hand caught against stone making him yelp. To his right he felt an open space then from before him came the sound of Ress returning.

'It is the ruin of the Winter Palace,' Ress said and to Skarry there was excitement in her voice. 'It can be nothing else. Much of it is long filled with frozen snow yet if we cross this room we can go down again.'

'For what, Ress?' Skarry asked in despair, 'What hope have we down here in the darkness? We have no food nor chance of a way out save back up, and the Monrolians will be waiting for us there.'

Ress took both his hands in hers and caressed his cold fingers.

'Don't be frightened, Skarry,' she said kindly. 'There is nothing evil in darkness. I have lived in it all my life and it is my home. It may be that there is a way below for it is said that the palace was built on more ancient ruins. You have led me far and bravely, let me now lead you.'

Skarry kissed her hands, shaking his head hopelessly, yet he rose with her for there seemed nothing else that he could do. As they moved away from the stairs he felt nakedly exposed but Ress drew him surely on by his left hand; his right he waved vainly about as though to ward off attack. She warned him of things on the floor and he brushed against them occasionally, feeling the worm-ridden wood of ancient furniture, chairs and tables. Within him grew a burning desire to see his surroundings, as though sight alone might banish fear.

The walls closed in again and he felt that they entered a narrow corridor. Then came the steps once more and they descended. This was a longer flight and in places one wall would pass beyond his reach such that he felt they were poised upon the very edge of some vast drop. At the foot of this flight they stopped and rested, sitting huddled close.

'It was a rich place,' she whispered to him. 'It has been looted at some time, yet a little of its finery lingers. These walls were painted, I can feel where it peels. And the furniture that remains is carved work. It is said that all those who were skilled in craftworks were called to make a piece for the palace. Then all was laid to waste when the blizzards came and the frozen mountain seas of the north flowed south. Many must have died here.'

Skarry's heart beat loudly and hearing it she laughed, the echoes flitting lightly above and below. He began to shiver and pulled the cloak tightly about him.

'We must go on,' Ress said firmly. 'It will be warmer below. Wait while I find the way.'

Her feet made hardly a sound as she moved away from him. Once more he was alone and he began to feel that it was always so, that his dreams of glory and honour were but bright illusions, summoned to disguise the empty void. There was no sense of time in this dark world, deeper than any night, and all thought of the past and hope for the future left him. Like the forest oaks giving up their leaves in winter, Skarry shed his own self and his mind came to a single point, focused in the black silence of that eternal moment. It seemed that he was at last truly alone, suspended, disembodied in the darkness.

Then sounds flowed back into this awareness, an excited voice and the warm grasp of a known hand and he felt a sudden surge of joy that there was another with him to share the present.

'There is a more ancient way below,' came Ress's voice and he felt that she was grinning. 'There are carvings on the walls. They tell a story.'

She pulled him to his feet and he was suddenly dizzy with this new movement. Then she led him on into the shadow.

20

The Womb of the World

Ress's voice sounded out of the darkness and Skarry could almost see her running her fingertips over the wall to read the carving.

'It has the feel of the work of the Olluden,' she said. 'There is a tree, an old oak, that rises from the stone globe, its boughs laden with life. A heron has just landed in the topmost branchings and feeds its noisy young. In the shade below, horses are drinking from a spring; they raise up their heads as though at a familiar sound and the water splashes from out their mouths.'

She moved along the wall and took up the tale again.

'There is a cave and within walks a bear, a huge bear leading two people, a woman and a man. The woman is dancing and he carries something, like a ball, a container with rays coming from it, as though of light.

'Here's a doorway,' Ress said after a moment. 'An ancient door that is bolted from this side and by it there's a niche set in the wall with a vessel in it.'

From the darkness within his own mind rose up the distant memory of the havens of the Olluden and the fire pots. Following her arm with his hand Skarry came to the recess within the wall. Its surface was thickly carpeted with dust and heavy cobwebs clung to the sides of the container. He put his hands about it and felt its weight, then carefully reached out, his fingers groping in the space. He was brought up by the touch of another object, a glass-stoppered bottle, by the smooth feel. He felt poised, delicately balanced as he drew forth the stopper and reached once more for the earthenware pot. The prayer came to his lips without thought and he called on Ithunne as he poured from the bottle into the container.

The cloud of steam, invisible in the blackness, stung his face and he drew back as the glow began within the pot. It was more light than warmth and he shielded his eyes before its growing glare. Ress was laughing quietly and when he turned to her they drew together and held each other close.

Lifting his head from her shoulder he could see now the carvings, the lines finely cut in the stone. The bear was not the brown one of the forest but much larger, the head broad, the shoulders rising like the peaks of mountains as it lowered its neck towards the human figures. The man wore stones on a necklace and Skarry's hands rose up to his own.

'It is the work of old peoples,' he said softly but Ress stood in silence before the door, her palms raised up to its ancient surface.

It was black oak, deep set within the rough hewn stone with a thick ring of rusted iron and heavy bolts that Ress found by feel and pulled upon. The metal creaked and tore from the worm eaten timber. Skarry's heart began to pound and going to Ress he gripped her wrists tightly.

'I know this door from my dreams,' he said urgently. 'Yet then I dared not open it, as though it hid something terrible.'

As if to strengthen his sudden fear there came a low moan from the depths and the floor trembled beneath their feet. Skarry's panic rose in his throat but it seemed only to increase Ress's excitement. She broke free from his grip and took hold of the ring.

'Don't Ress!' Skarry pleaded as his nightmares leaped to the forefront of his mind. 'Maybe there is another way, or the Monrolians have gone; we could go back up and find weapons.'

Ress released the ring and turned slowly, her arms outreaching until she found Skarry's shoulders. She held him gently.

'Skarry, Skarry,' she said softly, 'we have no need of warriors here. Have we been led so far only to turn back at the very last? This is our mystery and it is for us to resolve. Have no fear now, for I am at your side, as you are at mine.'

So saying she let slip her hands, sliding them down his arms to his own. She turned him and raised up their hands together to the ring. The iron flaked, pattering on the floor as they pulled upon it. Even though heart of oak the wood crumbled until almost in pieces the door opened. A draught greeted them yet though the air lost its stale stench it felt charged with energy.

'Can you feel it?' Ress whispered as vibrations moved through the rock.

'Glimshpill was right,' Skarry said desperately. 'We were fools to come down here.'

His fingers shook as he replaced the stopper in the glass bottle and tucked it within his tunic pocket. And then, with heart hammering, he raised up the container so that it cast its dim light about them, and looked through the doorway.

The guardian waited in the shadows before him, staring blindly down from bulbous, empty eye sockets, its broad flat horns first following the curve of the skull then sharply pointing forward. Skarry began to shake, the light-pot trembling in his upraised arms, casting the monstrous features into flickering movement. A groaning came up out of the dust between his feet, drowning his own moan of terror.

Yet Ress stepped forward, her arms swaying in front of her and as the tips of her fingers lightly brushed one horn of the beast, it toppled from its rocky shelf and fell to the floor, bursting noisily into several pieces.

Ress let out a short squeak of surprise and knelt to feel what she had done. She took up the shards and turning them in her hands, pieced some together.

'It's the skull of a musk ox,' she said as she felt the horns, 'that the Ice Warriors use to embellish their helms, seeking to strike fear into those that they fight.'

Skarry knelt beside her, setting the light-pot down. Shaking his head he held the empty skull, stroking the smooth bone. He began to laugh quietly at his own fear.

The feeling of the place had changed, the hand of humans less easily discerned, for the chamber they had entered was roughly hewn out of the stone and its rocky ceiling clambered unevenly above them. On the rough floor were dark shapes and when Skarry moved to look closer, holding the light-pot over them, he found that they were bodies, skeletons, skinned with webs and dust. They seemed so ancient to him that he felt no revulsion. In the grime beneath the necks, as though once held by a thong about the throat, were stones, to each body a stone, drilled carefully through the centre. When he wiped one free of dirt he saw that it was white and gleaming like quartz.

There were no signs of struggle. It was as though these people had simply lain down to sleep, some in each others arms, others cradling children.

'They are of the old races,' said Skarry as Ress stooped to touch the bones at her feet. 'And there are paintings upon the walls, as at Delgen, the Dream Haven.'

Going close to the stone he put up a hand to the designs. There was little colour, the black of charcoal mixed with a deep brown, perhaps the mineral umber after it is burnt in the fire. There were reindeer and still larger beasts with huge webbed antlers. An ancient woman with a bearskin upon her head led the people in a dance. Towards the end of the wall the work had a hasty feel to it, the lines less precise, more ragged. Here was the tribe going forward with their belongings and animals but their way was blocked by a gate or wall and within the barrier others looked out and threw spears and arrows.

'They will be the first city folk, enclosed within their new wall,' Ress said when he described the scene. 'The ones they fire down upon are travelling people, the Itheni. Those who died here were imprisoned, for the door was bolted from the other side.'

Rising, they went on and at the far end of the chamber found where another doorway had been walled up. Yet now the way was open once more, the stones thrown down as though beaten by a great fist. The passage beyond narrowed and became a crack delving downwards into the body of the earth. Thin streams of water had run from openings above and frozen into glistening pillars. Where the descent was steep, steps had been rudely cut in the rock. Skarry stopped to add liquid to the light-pot; in the brighter glow he went on after Ress who eagerly felt her way between the piled boulders.

The crack widened, the stones falling away on either hand and they came out into a cavern whose high roof arched upwards into blackness and its grandeur made Skarry move slower and more quietly. Here vast sheets of ice hung motionless, the frozen fall of water breaking the light into many colours that flashed brightly about the cave, the shadows dancing with life. Rock too, as though once molten and dripping, hung in thick spikes from above and similar forms rose up like spires from the rough floor, in places meeting, fusing into heavy columns. The stone was red like the mountains of the Ridgeway and glittered with crystals.

Ress stopped suddenly and knelt, putting her palms to the floor as though feeling for something. Skarry crouched low in awe as the sounds came. A rumble first, as of distant thunder. It

194

rolled towards them in bursting cracks and he near lost his footing as the shock passed through the cavern and away. Stones broke free from the walls and bounced about them before the silence returned. For long moments after came occasional roars as of the snow slides on the Angsoth at the dawn of spring.

Skarry went to Ress but she was unharmed and grinning with a wild light in her eye that warmed him.

'What is it Ress?' he asked. 'What is happening?'

'The earth is waking,' she said simply. 'It is Ithunne.'

Skarry shivered and looked about the cavern but the silence was once more complete.

'Let us go on,' Ress said and he agreed, feeling within the rise of an unknown or long forgotten hope. 'But softly,' she continued, 'for I smell a beast below.'

As though following a current in the air she went on, making her way between the pillars of stone. The water had flowed from the walls and roof and come together into a torrent that once carved its way into the mountains. Now frozen, motionless, its sleeping power was plain for Skarry to see in the convoluted shapes its passage had cut through the rock. Keeping to one side of the ice Ress felt forward with each footstep before moving her weight, her arms swaying as though to an ancient music such that she took on the grace of a dancer to Skarry who followed more awkwardly, his arms beginning to ache with weight of the light-pot.

A faint smell kindled dim memories yet it was the strangeness of his surroundings that kept him from recognising the scent. Only when it seemed all about him did he realise it was that of a bear. Ress stopped and knelt by large boulders long since fallen from the cave roof and Skarry joined her there.

'There is a bear close by,' he said.

'It will know the way out,' she whispered.

Skarry added more fluid to the light-pot from the bottle and then rising slowly he lifted it above his head on upstretched arms. Light issued forth from the dark vessel, reflecting from the icy sheets above them and dimly illuminating the cavern. Looking about he mistook it first for a great white boulder until he caught the slight movement of its low breathing. As if waking it raised up its wide head and its eyes opened and it looked directly at him.

Skarry lowered the light-pot as it rose ponderously and came towards him. He placed the vessel down upon the rocks and awaited its coming, his mind now quiet and untroubled by thoughts.

The bear's fur was thick and white as snow with a yellow tinge to her belly. Her claws were dark and sharp yet her eyes seemed so calm and peaceful as she sniffed at the air, the black nose wrinkling. Skarry felt her warm breath as she raised up her face to his, the head looming large and filling his vision, the nostrils widening. He felt the damp touch of her nose on his forehead and then on his chin when she lowered her head, as though smelling the stones about his neck. His eyes began to fill with tears and though he did not move he felt he could have reached out his hands to her and run his fingers through the soft fur.

'Ah, bear,' he said, 'I have met many of your kind on my way, yet none so beautiful, or so wise.'

The cave bear sat back slowly on her haunches and blinked her eyes, yawning widely, her huge red tongue curling. Then she padded the floor with her fore paws, cocking her head to one side as though listening. Ress felt along the stone for Skarry's hand and grasped it as the low rumblings began again, crashing suddenly loud in their ears as the shock came. The stone floor was suddenly fluid beneath their feet and they sprawled together. As the tremor passed the earth groaned about them in its wake as though stirring from sleep.

The light-pot rolled on the boulder, the cavern seeming to dance in its moving light and Skarry grabbed at it before it could fall.

When it was once more quiet, the bear looked down upon them and then with a shake rose up and padded off towards the shadows. Before she went from the light she paused and looked back over her shoulder.

'She waits for us,' Skarry whispered and he trembled.

Holding to each other's hands, Skarry clutching the warmth of the light-pot to his side, they scrambled over the piled boulders towards the bear. As they neared she moved away and entered a passage that led off from the cavern. Each time she reached the edge of their light she waited before going on.

The rocky walls were coated with ice that thickened until Skarry could no longer make out the red of the stone. Soon the

196

ceiling above fell away and the white of ice arched all about them, the flashings of colour like an ever changing rainbow that dazzled Skarry's sight. A frozen river ran below and the bear took this way, her claws clicking on the ice. Ress and Skarry followed, more slowly now, yet she matched her pace to theirs and seemed to hover at the shadows on the edge of their light.

Above them the ice lowered in glittering shards, at times like bars that they passed between, and gradually Skarry felt that the dim glow of the light-pot was aided by a fainter glimmer that struck the surface far above them, passing downward through the ice and illuminating it as though from within.

'I can smell the sea,' Ress said and looking at her he saw her face alive with excitement.

In the distance ahead, beyond the bear, Skarry found he could make out the tunnel glowing whitely as it arched its way over the frozen river. Soon he could see a brighter spot in the distance that grew as they neared, appearing first as the circle of the moon, white and full and hanging before them. Its light increased as they approached until its brilliance struck at his sight like the sun so that he shielded his eyes before it. Ress began to laugh and took on her dancing walk over the ice with Skarry trying to copy her. And if they slipped, they clung breathless to one another that they should not fall.

All about them now the ice shone with light and the distant opening came steadily nearer until the cave bear stood like a shadow against its brightness, looking back at them. Slowing their pace, Skarry and Ress came alongside the bear, their laughter stilled as though they approached an elder. The she-bear looked upon them long and Skarry thanked her for her guidance.

Peering out into the new brilliance of the daylight Skarry shaded his eyes and waited as they grew accustomed to the glare. Even then the light seemed too bright for the winter and he moved forward to see better and could not keep back a gasp.

'The sea is frozen,' he said in answer to Ress's question. 'We have come out on the western coast and the sea is frozen!'

Above them the sky was bright, clear blue, not a trace of cloud, the sun a small brilliant disc, low to the south. From here, looking over the icy sheet of the sea to the distant shores of Taur, Skarry could see the mountains of the Ridgeway peering over the horizon: there the rise of Stoneside and there the Angsoth that

197

had been his home. To their right the western coast of Monrolia receded into the north, the ice mountains of the Ulta-Zorn jutting upwards from the sea, climbing rapidly in sharp ridges and crags.

So the bear led them from out of the ice caves and turning, Skarry saw that they had gone beneath a finger of the glaciers that pushed in from the north, the ice creeping so slowly, flowing over long ages between the peaks of the mountains and bursting forth to meet the sea. Here, where the surface broke blackly into deep crevices, hills of ice would crack free to enter the sea and drift, slowly shrinking as they neared warmer climes. Not so now, for the frozen sea was piled with blocks of ice and groaned and creaked beneath their great weight.

The bear put back her head and gave a loud cry that echoed from the icy crags. As if in answer Skarry heard more human voices and on the ice below them small figures hurried, thickly furred and carrying spears. Almost he felt fear again, that these might be warriors, intent upon his death or capture, but it faded and he raised up his open hand towards them and once more the bear called. If anything he felt sadness as he descended to meet them, helping Ress with care across the shattered ice, sadness that they had left a place which seemed theirs alone and were once more thrown into a world that was torn by the desire of men.

The bear did not come with them and Skarry turned often to look back to where she sat, white as the ice about her. He waved to her and she called once more before moving off towards the north.

Those who came to meet them were swathed in sealskins with the fur of the white fox about the rim of their hoods. Though Skarry liked not to see the coats of animals taken by humans, still he knew that these peoples had little choice in the matter, for they were of the far north. Their long noses and snow-burned faces testified to their icy origin and they wore black stones at their throats.

As they neared, Skarry stopped and stood with his arm about Ress to wait for them. The snow people halted also and then came forward more slowly. When they were but a dozen paces distant they stopped again, laying down their spears and then they themselves went to their knees before Skarry and Ress, some pressing their foreheads against the ice while others raised up their arms to the sky and sang in a tongue that Skarry did not know, yet by the tone they seemed filled with joy.

21

Bethan of the Osilo

The snow people took Ress and Skarry down on to the frozen sea, passing between great blocks of ice. Singing and laughing they went, their excited chatter rising about the two as the noisy babble of young fledglings being fed. Those who came nearer quietened and walked with them in silence, casting shy sidelong looks, though their eyes twinkled and they could not keep from smiling.

Out on the vast and open expanse of white they came to the ice hole where they had been fishing. Others of their race were waiting here and rose to greet them as they approached. There were sleds also and the dog teams struck up a sharp barking, their breath steaming. The snow people took spare clothing from the packs on the sleds and dressed Skarry and Ress warmly in fur-lined cloaks, thick mittens and boots. Skarry placed the light-pot down and they sat about its gentle heat.

From her seat on a sled came an old one, shrouded in furs with only her eyes and the deep wrinkles around them showing. She was helped by two others and at her throat was a necklace of seals' teeth, whitely shining. She bowed low and offered them dried meat from a pouch but though he was hungry Skarry refused, for he liked not to eat of the flesh of animals. As though this was expected she nodded, unfastening the face flap of her hood and her sunken mouth was smiling.

'Be welcome, Heralds of Ithunne,' she said in a voice that creaked softly. Her accent was strange to Skarry with a lilt such that she seemed to sing.

'Please,' she went on, 'How may we serve your purpose?'

'Can you take us to Grimal Skoye?' Ress asked immediately and Skarry laughed at her haste.

The snow people also laughed.

'It is to our honour that you so ask for the Father,' the old one

199

said. 'For he is of our race and would be with us now was it not for war. Yet is that soon to change.' Her smile tightened and she shook herself a little, as though holding back an inner marvel.

'Ithunne has stirred,' she continued, 'she is waking. The walls of Cassan and Ramar are thrown down on the Isthmus and the way is open between the two lands. The time of Lords comes to its end.'

Skarry's heart began to beat rapidly with excitement. Ress sought for and found his hand and the old one stretched out her own to him. For a moment he was puzzled and then he drew back the cloak that she might touch the stones.

'Here are the voices of the old peoples,' she said quietly. 'There is space for another, yet it is not for me to give it. I am Bethan, of the Osilo. Though you have not met us on our own lands, this spell of cold has made us feel more at home.' She laughed, sweeping her arm outward, over the ice.

'Home,' Bethan repeated more slowly, savouring the sound. 'We are from the far north, from the plains of Osilo,' she went on and almost Skarry could see the flood of memory that swelled up within her and moistened her eyes as she spoke.

Ress reached out and clasped Bethan's wrinkled hands in hers.

'Ithunne shall not let this suffering last,' she said quietly, stroking softly the dry skin and Bethan returned to herself and looked at them.

'Yes,' she said, 'and we will take you to the Father, Grimal Skoye, if that be the purpose of Ithunne; while the sea ice is fresh and clear we will take you back to Taur. You can ride on Gudrun's sled.' And she bobbed her head, the smile returning widely to reveal ancient worn teeth.

'Then you shall have the light-pot with you, Bethan,' said Skarry and gave into her hands the earthenware vessel and the glass bottle.

'It will warm an old woman on her long journey,' she said, laughing and hugging its warmth to her body. 'Ithunne will be with you, ever.'

So saying, the Osilo gathered up their few possessions, their hunting spears and lines and quickly packed their sleds. Some moved off to the north, waving and calling back across the ice. Skarry raised up his open palm in farewell to these until but a half dozen sleds were left. Gudrun, a young man of the Osilo, gestured for the two to sit on his sled and gave them skins to wrap themelves in. Bethan waved across excitedly from her own sled, her eyes twinkling.

'Ho, Cufflum!' Gudrun shouted to his lead dog and it barked excitedly and strained in the traces.

The runners cracked free and the dogs sounded their call as they moved off. Gudrun first ran behind, holding to the rail, swinging the sled in a wide arc towards the south that sent the snow flying. The other sleds drew up behind, the drivers urging their dogs on. And there before them, across the plain of ice, lay the coast of Taur and the mountains of the Ridgeway.

Almost Skarry wept with the sight for he felt he need make no further effort; the distant peaks drew him back to them and he had no more concern with the how or the why, for he was alive now, in every tremor of the sled as it hurtled on over the white, in the cold sting of snow upon his face, kicked up by the dogs as they bunched their shoulders into the harness. Ress leaned into his shoulders and he put his arms about her and held her close. Soon she slept yet Skarry would not shut his eyes and savoured the world about him, the sky so clear with the small disc of the sun hanging low over the Angsoth on its westerly voyage.

Gudrun stood on the runners at the back of the sled and began to sing, at first shyly quiet but when Skarry turned smiling to him his voice grew in strength. He sang of the waking of Ithunne and the birth of the humans from her earthy womb. Around them, the others of the Osilo took up the song, passing the verses from sled to sled. The clear notes seemed to hang in the air behind them and resound from the gleaming ice.

Only the passage of the sun marked their time and as at last it dipped through thin clouds towards the ice, a halo formed about it and pale rainbows rose upwards to greet its descent. The frozen sea was lit with reds and purples that reflected in the sky above and there started films of light that hung, folding and unfolding upon themselves, like glowing veils in the air.

The Osilo stopped then to rest their dogs and waited, staring into the east where the lightening air heralded the rise of the moon. Bethan's sled drew up alongside Skarry. She gestured towards the ice about them and her voice came softly out of the silence.

'In the spring,' she said, 'when the melt came and the ways

opened in the sea ice, we would take our boats down to the water. Only small boats, made of bone and skin and very light. We would go down to the water, all together, all the young people of the tribe. We would take food and drink and go out between the ice floes on the blue water that we had not seen for many months. The sun was so bright and clear, the ice shining so that the air itself would seem to come alive with light. It was very beautiful, so beautiful.

'I remember that. One day, out on the water, all the young people together and we were laughing and singing. The next day the Cunerdin's soldiers came and spoke of the war and how we could end the evil of the enemy and live without fear in our homeland. Many of the young men went with them. When they did not return, the Father put out his own call across the land and left us also, to seek for them himself. The land became quiet, as with a held breath.'

The old woman's face lightened suddenly as the moon rose. Near full and huge she climbed the sky as though to balance the sun's sinking and the sharp ice took on a softer sheen beneath this more gentle gaze.

'Listen,' Bethan whispered to Skarry in the stillness. 'She speaks.'

A low note sounded, soon joined by others, like many far off voices singing. The song rose and fell as though on the wind and the Osilo joined their own voices to it. A sudden booming thundered distantly and they set their dogs once more running beneath the brightly shining moon. Into the long twilight they continued with the song of the ice in their ears and at last Skarry slept.

And when he dreamed, it was of the snow bear, leading them on across the frozen sea, her furry paws silent on the ice. Ever and again the black nose appeared as she turned to wait for them. Ress was dancing at his side but in the mountains before them an armoured warrior rose out of the snow like Ymir. Though Skarry's teeth rattled in fear and he hung back at the sight, the bear took no notice and continued her silent pacing. The image of the warrior faded and Skarry began to realise, with both joy and sadness, that the snow bear was leading him to her mistress.

Gudrun roused them only as they neared the coast of Taur.

The winter dawn woke the ice to light and once again the dark hand of man could be discerned upon the pale body of the land. In the west, towards Dunnerdale and far off Ringdove, palls of smoke blackly stained the air and armies swarmed together, fused into one mass and motionless from this distance. To the east, where the coast curved north into the Isthmus, the dividing walls of Cassan and Ramar could no longer be seen and long straggles of men led off, back into Monrolia.

The Osilo brought their sleds in at a small cove with snow-covered beach, east of Midloth. The walls of that city were buried beneath great drifts and the slope of land leading into Dunan and the foothills, where armies had passed, were near empty of men.

'We must leave you here,' Bethan called to them across the ice. 'I will return to Osilo now, for I am old and I would spread the word of Ithunne in my own home before I give myself back.'

Gudrun helped Ress and Skarry from the sled and gave them snow shoes of interwoven leather on bone frames.

'Will you go back to Osilo now also?' Skarry asked him but Gudrun shook his head.

'There are others of my people in these lands,' he said, 'and I will first take the news to them. Then shall we all return together.'

Ress was grinning as Skarry took her to Bethan's sled and they gave her their thanks.

'Farewell, Heralds of Ithunne!' the old woman called to them, hugging the light-pot to her belly as her sled turned and made off, clattering over the ice, back into the north.

'You will find him on the Pass!' Gudrun shouted over his shoulder as he headed into the west, following the coastline and was soon gone from their sight, leaving only the echoes of his song.

Skarry helped Ress put on her snow shoes and then tied his own as the sun crept above the eastern horizon and lit the crown of the Angsoth with its first rays. Joined by their clasped hands they crossed the beach and climbed the low rise on to the flats to the east of the Three Kings Basin.

'It seems an age since we last were here,' Ress said to him and Skarry agreed.

'And now I go to meet with Skoye,' he said, 'who is spoken of in Taur as the hardest and most evil of all the peoples of Monrolia.'

Ress began to laugh at this though when he questioned her she evaded an answer and he felt that she had a sad look to her face.

'Do not seek to rush into your future,' she said. 'It will come soon enough of its own accord.'

'This I have learned,' Skarry said and could not help but laugh with her.

On the flats he looked carefully about them. Monrolian soldiers were here though few in numbers and widely separated. In twos and threes they hurried east or west and there was a confused feel to their movements. If any met they would stand together for a moment, stamping in the cold, their arms waving wildly and then they would hurriedly continue or even go back the way they had come. Skarry and Ress were noticed but no one spared more than a single glance for they wore the cloaks and furs of the Osilo.

Skarry told her of what he saw as they crossed the flats and began the gentle climb up Dunan, keeping some distance from Illgill beck where the thick snows hung out over the deep ravine the river had cut into the land. The sound of its laughing journey to the sea rose up through its icy coat and Skarry was heartened to hear it in a valley that had known only the songs of battle for so long. Above Stoneside a pair of ravens wheeled high over the whitened crags and called to each other, their kronking resounding amongst the cliffs.

As the curve of Dunan brought them around to the south, the peaks of Ice Back and the Angsoth came into view. With the sun warming their backs they walked together over the crusted snow, Skarry delighting in the sight of the mountains so close and naming each crag and gill.

'Below the peak of the Angsoth lies the Dead Crags,' he said, 'named after an army that tried to pass along the curve of its ridge in winter and all were lost in the snow. There's a lake below that is the brightest green and filled with fish that we would catch when we came over the Pass for the shearing at Midloth. The western arm of the crags leads down to Stoneside which we crossed when the Ice Warriors took us.'

He broke off, for his words had brought back the memory of

Hook's death and suddenly he was ashamed at his gladness when so many had died. Ress sensed his sorrow.

'Don't, Skarry,' she said. 'You can't blame yourself for everything that comes from our small actions. Is it not rather that we carry out the purpose of Ithunne in all that we do? Trust in her hand to set things right, for men alone will surely never do it.'

Skarry fell silent and turned his mind to the climb. Though not yet steep it was a long haul up Dunan. They passed the snow-covered mounds that hid Fressingfield's men and strode on and up with their breath clouding before them. They rested twice, leaning against each other, before coming to the narrow way, where Dunan drew her sides in and Illgill's frozen torrent hung out from the steepening slope.

Here the snow had been blown into distorted waves by the blizzard, curling out over the crags, poised to break. Skarry stopped and they rested again before this last ascent that led up to the more level land about the Maen-hir.

Behind them, to the north, the flat white of the frozen sea folded and broke into shattered peaks as unseen currents moved below. The song of the ice had become a harsh shrieking with sudden thunderings that rose up to them thinly in the crisp air. The cry of the ravens came loud in their ears, as though a buzzard had disturbed them, flying too close to their crag. Snow pattered softly down upon Skarry's shoulders and he turned and looked up.

Above, where Illgill's icy fall arched downward, a drift of snow broke blackly open and he pulled Ress to him with the thought of an avalanche.

Yet the black shape within the snow took on form, rising out of the white like Ymir, the mighty war god of the north, the face painted in strident bands of colour, the horns of the helmet curving sharply forward. And when the mouth opened wide to give vent to a roar of attack, Skarry could see teeth, white against the red and filed to points.

Then the warrior raised up his fighting spear, leapt out into space, and fell upon them.

22

Grimal Skoye

Skarry pulled Ress away from the falling figure and they tumbled over backwards in the snow. The Ice Warrior's roaring battle cry became a hard grunt as he landed on his feet before them, the spear still raised, the steel point flashing sharply. His features twisted in rage, intensified by the bands of colour about the mouth and eyes, breath snorting in two plumes from out the flared nostrils. Distantly, the ravens could be heard calling to each other, high over the crags. And then the warrior spoke.

'Who so dares to come before Grimal Skoye?' snarled the Misery of Ice and his eyes burned into them.

Skarry's heart began to hammer loudly in his chest and his body shook. All the old stories came flooding back to wash reason away and leave only terror. The coldness of the snow beneath him was as nothing compared to that of the knot of fear in his belly as his wide-eyed stare took in the vision of violence standing mightily before him; the teeth like razors, the eyes grey and hard as iron, the helm with the horns curving down then stabbing forward. They were the horns of the musk ox he realised, somewhere in his fear, like the supposed guardian who had so shocked him before, beneath the Winter Palace.

Quite suddenly he saw the twisting grimace and harsh paint as though they were a mask, and he was no longer frightened.

Ress struggled to her feet and ran towards the sound of the voice, holding out her hands, laughing. Grimal Skoye caught her in his arms as she tripped over her snow shoes, Ress now crying, pressing her face against his chest. On a thong at his throat hung the dark soapstone of the Osilo and there were tears starting in his eyes.

'I thought it was you,' Skoye said to her and his tone had become kind and gentle. 'She always sees straight through me,' he went on to Skarry, speaking over Ress's bowed head, 'even though she makes no use of eyes.' And he shrugged his broad shoulders and laughed.

Skarry stood up to watch their meeting and it was as two old friends, long parted through trouble. Or a father and child, torn asunder by the evil of war, who at last by chance are drawn together once again.

'This is Grimal Skoye, Skarry,' Ress said after the long moments of their greeting. 'And this,' she said to Skoye, stepping back from him and raising up her arm, 'this is Skarry, of the Olluden, the Asgire, the Epona and the Hagarath, the old peoples.'

'Be welcome,' said Skoye, going to Skarry, taking his hands in both of his and smiling openly, 'though in truth I am your guest here on these mountains.'

When he smiled so close, Skarry could see the wrinkles beneath the paint and the sharpened teeth were age stained, one missing.

Abruptly Skoye sat down, taking bone snow shoes from his back. He made to put them on but then paused, holding them loosely, as though disliking the effort of straining forward. Without thinking Skarry took them and knelt at his feet.

'Made them myself,' Skoye said gruffly as Skarry fastened them to the Ice Warrior's boots. 'I well remember my first pair and the struggle I had in their making.' He laughed again and shook his head at the memory.

When Skarry had tied the shoes, Skoye hauled himself upright, leaning on his spear. Taking Ress by his left hand he gave the spear to Skarry to hold so that he could take his hand also. Then, rather than going on up the steep to the Maen-hir, he drew them both away westward.

Skarry did not speak, for he knew not what to say and he was amazed when Skoye started over the Dead Crags by way of Fox's Path, that he had thought only the guides of the Olluden knew of.

Skoye moved so easily across the snows, seeming to glide over the surface as though dancing to some music that he alone could hear, yet the rhythm flowed through his arms and reached the two also. Skarry could see Gemel in these fluid movements now that he could look beyond Skoye's horned helmet, his battle paint and sharpened teeth. The Ice Warrior saved his breath for the climb and shushed Ress into silence when she began to speak. She laughed at him as they went together across the steepening side of the Angsoth, under the mighty shoulder of rock to the west of the summit.

Here there were more Ice Warriors who rose up from concealment about the path and took up fighting postures with their spears levelled. These wore white hoods and cloaks that rendered them almost invisible against the snow. Their faces too were fiercely decorated with paint to heighten the appearance of a snarl. When they recognised Skoye they relaxed their stance and questioned him as he approached, casting bemused looks upon Ress and Skarry. But their leader said nothing as he passed smiling between them and they fell in behind and followed. Up close they were a mixed lot; one whose long, red stained beard showed white at the roots, others no older than Skarry.

As they climbed on, Skarry looked down at his snow shoes to save the coming sight and only when they stopped at the crest of the ridge did he raise up his head. The body of the land lay before them, vastly sprawling away from their high vantage, in ridges and valleys, the sharp rock of their peaks softened by the unfurled cloak of snow, the deep vales skinned with the dark web of trees. In the depths to the south, the hills faded to ripples and gently settled into the wide calm of marsh and plain. Nearer, below them, the steep slope of the Angsoth gentled as it lowered towards the Hanging Valley of the Olluden.

But the great longing Skarry felt rising within him, to look upon his people again and to share with them his story, was stilled. For smoke billowed upward from the forest and he could see where great rents had been torn in the tree canopy, where the ancient oaks had been felled to feed the many fires. In these new clearings, rows of tents had been set up and armed men went now beneath the knarled boughs, their shouts rising thinly on the wind. In the clearing of Havod the huts of the Olluden had been torn down to make space for the officer's camp and the Moot House flew a banner, of three ears of corn, yellow on green, of the Doth Auren of Wenlok.

Skarry sat down in the snow and raised up his hands to his face to shut out the sight. Skoye squatted on his heels beside him and laid a hand upon his shoulder.

'It's not so bad, lad,' he said quietly. 'Soldiers ever come and go. The trees will grow back, given time.' Yet he shook his head as he spoke as though he could not quite believe his own words.

'I used to think that I could end all this,' Skoye went on, 'when I first began to realise what was happening and feel the weight of suffering that burdens our world. I thought I could thrash all these little lords with their fine armies and halt the advance of their greed; give them an ice hole to sit and watch at, waiting for the seal to rise, or put an axe in their delicate palms and stand them up against one another that they themselves should feel what comes from their own designs. I summoned all the tribesmen together and we took violence for our own and armed ourselves in it; Fear and Panic rode before us into battle, glutted crows flocked above our heads and none could stand against us. Yet I have changed nothing.'

He finished and stared down into the valley where D'Auren's soldiers were setting up sharpened stakes across the mountain track. Ress knelt at his side and placed her arms about his thick neck.

After a moment the Misery of Ice stood and once more taking their hands in his he drew them on. Along the western ridge of the Angsoth they went, that first led downward before beginning the hard climb to the Dark Seat. Yet here he took them a little to the north, below the ridge and into the inner valleys that nestled between Stoneside and the Frozen Fells.

As they came down the snow-covered slopes Skarry was at first confused by deep drifts on the valley floor that seemed to have been blown into low mounds, spiralling outward from a centre. Only as they neared and he picked out the faces of the men on watch did he realise that it was the camp of the Ice Warriors, for the mounds were shelters builded of snow. No fires burned here nor even a single banner to declare the warriors' presence.

The watch greeted Skoye, calling him Father and more men came crawling out of their ice caves, pushing aside the blocks of hard snow that served as doors. They gathered in small groups, speaking quietly to each other, looking at the two. Behind the violent, painted masks Skarry could see the Osilo peoples now; they had human faces and suffered human hurts, of loneliness and sorrow and separation from those that they loved.

Skoye led them spiralling inward to his own shelter at the

centre. Like a small bird a single pennant fluttered there, showing a young seal, twisting as it dived through the water. They crawled through the entrance tunnel, one behind the other, Ress laughing at the scramble. Within, a low, rounded chamber had been dug out of the snow and a dim, even light filtered down through the icy curve of its roof. There were few possessions; a bag, a pair of skis and skins upon which they sat. The fur was coarse like hair, yet matted thickly almost as wool and Skarry guessed that it was of the musk ox.

Skoye took food from his bag and gave them berries and some nuts which they ate hungrily. He placed a lamp before them, of the soft soapstone, the edges gently rounded, the centre a shallow hollow filled with fat. A thin wick of twisted hair was set in this and Skoye lit it carefully with a pipe lighter. The single flame brought a glow of gold to their faces as they turned towards its flicker of warmth.

Then Grimel Skoye began to speak.

'They are saying that Ithunne is waking,' he said, sweeping his arm about as though to indicate the camp. 'And that the Two who were One have come forth from the earth to bring peace to the land.' He looked long upon them both.

'Many of my people died in snowslides when the earth shook,' he continued. 'They fear for the safety of their families for we have had no news from Osilo. I climbed Stoneside to see what went on and found the walls thrown down on the Isthmus. Juss took it to be the wrath of Ymir and has set off with his army to sack Ringdove. The Cunerdin's men are more humanly panicked and have fled, back to Monrolia. Now I don't know what course to take.'

'The Cunerdin plots your death,' Ress said with concern. 'They were to draw you to Midloth and kill you there.'

'I am not amazed by this,' said Skoye. 'The Cunerdin knows that we of the Osilo have no liking for his ambition. He has used us and his work has done damage to the land and brought much suffering to its peoples.'

'Go home, Grimal,' Ress said softly, putting out her arm, feeling for and finding Skoye's hand. 'You have the choice to end this waste.'

'Home is not something I have yet found,' he replied. 'I have been bred for war. When I was but a child, Rimon, who was then

210

a captain of the guards in Darlak, took me to the walls on the Isthmus and slashed my arms with his own knife that I should never forget where the lands of the enemy began. My home was an armed camp and I dared not have a family, for the Cunerdin would only have taken them as hostage. Now is my life drawing towards an end and I cannot speak, nor even think of the things that I have done.'

'You may yet find a home, and a family,' Ress said to him, holding his broad hand in both of hers. 'Take your people back to Osilo, Grimal. I will come with you, for you were like a father unto me when first we met.'

Skoye smiled and bowed his head and when next he spoke it was to Skarry.

'And what would you do, Skarry of the old peoples, if you were I?' he asked and Skarry shook his head slowly, looking at Ress.

'I would do anything for her,' he said quietly.

'Then if you will come with me,' said Grimal Skoye to Ress, 'I shall return to Osilo with my people and we shall serve the Cunerdin no more.'

Ress leaned her head upon his knees and began to cry as he softly stroked her red hair. And Skarry felt his own sorrow well up, for he knew now that they were to part. But Grimal Skoye's wrinkled and painted face was smiling as he looked up at Skarry and his eyes were bright.

'I am sorry, Skarry,' he said, 'if I have upturned your hopes. She is as my own child and as such will I care for her. Yet you are welcome in Osilo also, should you so choose.'

Skarry shook his head for he could find no words to speak.

'Then I will tell my people that we shall go home in the morning,' Skoye went on and he kissed Ress's hair then rose. 'I would wish you to wear this,' he said to Skarry, giving him the stone from about his neck, 'that my people will know you as a friend.'

He left, crawling through the tunnel and soon the camp was alive with shouts and songs as the Osilo learned they were to return to their homeland. Skarry could not look upon Ress and bowed his head within his hands, the stone of the Misery of Ice clutched between his fingers. Yet he found he could not cry. Ress came over to him and he felt her lightly touch his arms, shoulder and head as she read his posture.

'I am sorry also, Skarry,' she said quietly. 'But this man has been as a father to me, for a short time. Now his life comes to its close and all the violence he put on that thrust him ever onward is turned to nought. I shall not leave him now.'

'How did you come to meet him?' Skarry asked, raising up his head.

'When I was to marry the Doth Auren,' said Ress, 'to heal the rifts in Taur, I made my father's counsellor, Malik, take me to Wenlok by way of the High Pass, so that I might stand upon the mountains and feel their presence. I was filled with the stories of my childhood and thought that here surely Ithunne could not fail to hear my prayer.

'Perhaps she did, for the Ice Warriors had come over the Isthmus in secret and they captured us. Grimal himself took me in and cared for me and spent what time he had with me. Much joy grew from our company; it was not something I was used to, coming from Ringdove. Later, Malkah's jealousy overcame her and she took me for her own purposes.'

'And what did you pray for?' asked Skarry.

'Many things,' she said. 'That Ithunne might wake to save our world, that I could see, that I should find love amongst humans.'

'The last at least has come true,' Skarry said quietly. 'I had hoped that you would wish to come with me to my people's home.'

'We are of all peoples, Skarry,' she said and she touched the necklace at his throat. 'I go to your home in Osilo which you have yet to see and it may be that Ithunne shall draw us once more together. Such is my hope.'

Skarry looked upon her face and her eyes so blue seemed to stare over his left shoulder. He could think of no words to say.

'Say nothing then,' Ress said, raising up her fingers to feel his lips and she kissed him once and he laid his hand upon the softness of her hair and felt that always this would remind him of his sorrow.

Skoye came back noisily through the entrance tunnel and they turned to meet him. The old man was breathing heavily yet his eyes shone and he grinned largely at Skarry. He had wiped the paint from his face to reveal a double spiral, faded blue, upon his wrinkled forehead. He took off his horned helmet and balanced it idly upon his palms.

'When I set out to win these horns,' he said, 'I followed the wolves and after many days they led me to the herd. While they took out only the sick and weak, the white bull stood his ground and the earth shook with his stamp of rage. How could I kill him, so fine a beast? Later, I found an old corpse and took the horns from that instead. No one was any the wiser.' He looked almost shyly at Skarry and Ress laughed and hugged him.

As the long winter twilight drew upon them they sat about the single flame and Skoye went on to tell of Osilo in the spring, when the tundra blossomed and the snowdeer came back out of the south. Later, Ress spoke of Ringdove as a prison that bound its inhabitants to a single will. Skarry only listened at first though soon he was drawn to speak of his own forest and the life within it. When he came to tell of the Doth's army, encamped in the sheltered fold of the Hanging Valley, he could not go on and fell silent.

'He will not stay there long,' Skoye said, 'not when he learns that I am gone.'

'He will go home also,' Ress said surely.

Yet Skarry was thinking of the trees and as he made up his bed on the skins, the image of lopped oaks seemed to hang before him, their scars a lasting witness to man's violence.

In his dreams the oak took on human form, first as Guise of Ringdove with his rage rising from within and bursting forth as though it would rip him open. Then Hook, the fit rigidly withheld yet always there, to be summoned at will. The features behind the red beard merged into those of Glimshpill, struggling to finish a last flagon of wine, to drown the madness.

Then the Doth appeared, a long cloak held tightly against his bony frame. He carried a thin sword that he turned this way then that with light flicks of his wrist. His face was expressionless; no emotion escaped his imprisoning will and when the wind blew his cloak aside, his arm was without flesh.

As though a blizzard lifted Skarry up, all became white until a single figure appeared, seated at an ice hole on a frozen sea. Going closer he first thought it to be Glimshpill, the large frame poised in the act of looking into the black water. But it was Grimal Skoye. His mask of violence was set behind him on the ice, together with his weapons of war, as though the part he had learned and played so well was at last over and forgotten.

213

At his side was Ress, her red hair blowing out in the wind. She motioned Skarry to come closer and look. He crept forward to join them and in the very moment of leaning to peer into the dark hole, the thin ice covering its surface was shattered upward from within. A young seal leapt out and up, on to the snow and drew in one long, deep breath.

The start woke him to find Skoye crawling into the chamber and daylight brightly shining through the walls and roof.

'Well, wherever you are off to,' Skoye said, 'at least we shall not be leaving you on your own.' And he drew him to the tunnel.

Outside, Skarry was struck at first by the blue of the robes. The Dreamer smiled at him and the stocky, bracken-red pony at his side called a shrill greeting.

23

The Dream of Ithunne

The Ice Warriors of Osilo went north by way of Stoneside into Dunan, their white cloaks blending with the snow and concealing their numbers. They went singing and at their head was he whom they called the Father, Grimal Skoye, and with him Ress whom they spoke of now as the Herald of Ithunne. Long after they had at last passed from his sight, Skarry remained as though frozen at Felder's side, looking up over his broad back to Stoneside's sharp skyline. The Dreamer made no move to hurry him and stood motionless in the snow.

When he had done looking, Skarry felt empty. Felder turned his head and strongly nudged him with his nose so that Skarry scrambled to keep his footing and laughed. He spoke softly to the pony, gently scolding and they turned together away from the north. The Dreamer's quiet smile greeted them and he motioned for Skarry to lead the way as they set out into the deepening snows of the Inner Vales.

Skarry took them first across the valley floor where the camp had been and some way up the southern side below the Dark Seat until they came to a narrow level strip, no more than a pace wide, that followed the contour of the mountain. The tread of a thousand feet over as many years had worn this way through the inner valleys and Skarry knew of its northern end through the knowledge of the guides of the Olluden, yet its south-eastern passage lay in the mountains of the Hagarath.

Here he leapt up on to Fell's back and swung his leg over to sit upright, feeling the pony's warmth through his clothing. He had put a halter about his head and taking up the lead rope he set him walking along the path, trusting to the pony's own sure feet. The Dreamer came silently behind on foot in their wake.

Soon they came to trees, the tall pines with their sparse branchings laden with snow and graceful birches, empty of leaves, the delicate lace of twigs at their crowns faintly red and purple like a thin mist. The level way curved in wide sweeps along the shoulders of the mountains, dipping into their bulk to turn sharply over deep ravines whose frozen streams hung out in icy veins. Above them the sky was still a clear blue and the sun low, shining from the south, casting long, sharp shadows on the white. And though Skarry felt empty there was no sorrow or pain in that moment. From below his navel came low stirrings, as of the surge of the tide, and seeing, feeling the world about him, he felt only a great gladness to be alive in so rich and varied a land.

'Where are you going?' came the Dreamer's voice from behind and Skarry turned a little towards the blue-robed one.

'I don't know,' Skarry said and he had to laugh. 'I had not really thought about it. To the Goleth, I would suppose, the winter home of the Olluden. What do you think?'

'I can't speak for you, Skarry,' the Dreamer said. 'Your own way shall come upon you soon enough. Myself I go to Ringdove, for the walls of the city are thrown down and it may be that my presence there will help to ease the suffering in this time of change.'

'How is this so?' Skarry asked in surprise. 'Surely Juss has not sacked the city?'

The Dreamer laughed loudly.

'Of course not!' he said grinning. 'He is only a man. No. The earth has trembled, as though irritated by the weighty boot of warriors, and the armies of both lands are thrown into disarray. I have heard said that the travelling peoples, the Itheni, are returning from the south, singing of the waking of Ithunne. This is their way that we tread, though long have they been absent from it and their stories have not been heard in the land for many years. I too have a tale to tell the people of Ringdove.'

'I should like to hear it,' Skarry said.

'You know it already,' the Dreamer replied, 'for it concerns a son of the old peoples, a stone bearer who would not raise his fist in anger and a daughter of the new who, even though needful herself, turned her back upon the city. Many will be the tales of their trials and hardships before the Two who were One at last came together again and descended into the body of the earth, sharing their senses. And deep within the womb of the world

216

they found and woke Ithunne from her long sleep and she sent them forth into the two lands as Heralds, to speak her message and bring peace to the world.'

Skarry turned forwards in silence, Felder's head bobbing before him, the ears alertly twitching to catch the slightest sound.

'It will make a fair story,' he said after a moment. 'But what do you think will happen?' and he turned so that he might look directly into the blue eyes of the Dreamer.

'I don't know,' the Dreamer said simply. 'To put on the blue robe is to shed all belief. Yet I cannot know pain while I am part of this.' And he swept his arm up and about to take in the whole of their vision, the narrow vale lined with the bare crowns of trees, the snow softened summits of the Ridgeway, the arch of sky so blue above.

'But now,' he went on, 'it is winter in aphelion, the darkest and coldest hour as our world swings furthest from her star. Yet is it also the time of the birth of hope, for soon we will journey back, towards the sun.'

Felder stopped where the level way widened a little and Skarry slid down from his back. The thick green of a holly, long since planted to mark the way, cast the slight hollow into shade and the air was chill. Skarry wrapped his cloak about him and walked forward into the space, stopping only when he felt the Dreamer's hand touch lightly upon his left shoulder. Turning he seemed to fall into the black pits of the other's eyes, bounded by the brilliant blue of the iris.

'It is time for us to part,' came gently the Dreamer's voice, rising and falling as though with the wind or the waves. 'You should sleep,' he said softly. 'It is time for you to dream.'

And raising heavy arms as though to cling to the blue-robed figure who now seemed to float before him, Skarry slid backwards, fell slowly over backwards, the sun wheeling through the sky to his right and as if he lowered his eyelids, though he could not feel his body, all became dark as the darkest, moonless night.

It seemed at first that he was once more beneath the Winter Palace, hanging within an immeasurable space without light, enclosed by a darkness that had no direction, neither up nor down, north or south. He felt fear in his empty isolation and it seemed that fear was all there was, fear that grew as he felt it and threatened to consume his very being. There was no Ress to

217

come to him now, no kind voice or warm hand to lead him and he would have wept and wailed the pain of his loneliness had he a body to do so. The swell of the feeling washed away all trace of fear and left him drained, so that he simply looked, for there was nothing else that he could do.

Before him, a swirl of darkness took on form and as though from a vast and alien height he looked down upon his world. Here the white of the ice caps curved into the bright forest greens and the blue of sea, partially veiled by the lace of cloud. The rhythm of night and day was like the steady pulse of a heart, or the deep and regular breathing of one who sleeps.

As though with the eyes of the hawk he stared downwards, his gaze piercing the haze of cloud. Within the forest, people made their way, passing beneath the boughs of the oaks, singing and laughing as they went. Yet as he watched, the trees were felled, the land ploughed, the stony gleam of cities appeared. And now the people moved across the face of their world in vast armies and where they met, a great confusion and fighting arose. They built huge machines of war that they dragged behind them, sweating and stumbling over the bodies of women and children and in their footsteps was left only dust.

The brilliant green of the forest began to mottle and fade as Skarry watched, sweeping fires broke out and palls of smoke stained the sky. The land was turned to desert and the moon swung dark and low across the body of the planet, like a vast cinder, wrenching earth and trees up towards it. Then did he howl his grief out into the blackness, for he saw what Man had wrought and no part of it did he want and he strove to turn away from the baleful vision.

It seemed that he did so, for he found lights hanging in the blackness about him, many lights like stars, coloured and shining; some pale blue with sparks of green, others deep red or yellow. Like his own stones they seemed to speak with the voices of ancient peoples, united in grieving for their world, that it need not be so.

And as they turned their loving gaze upon the planet it became like a blue, misted jewel, a radiant sphere whose inner colours ever swirled together and drew apart, as though dancing. Within the veil of blue he could see green become irridescent and spread across the surface like a skin, climbing the gentle folds and ridges. The green was bright with flashings and streaks of coloured light, veins or nerves that pulsed and rippled and sounded notes like distant voices. The song rose up and echoed about him.

The strands spread throughout the sphere and showered upwards from its surface, filling the space, meeting with the distant lights and Skarry also. Its web flowed through him and drew him down and as he neared, the green became the great forest, alive below him with the moving points of light that were the creatures who lived within it. And the wide curve of the planet seemed to welcome him back to the fold of her body.

'Ithunne! Ithunne!' he was crying as he woke wild eyed.

The blue of the sky was darkening above him and a red glow came out of the west. The Dreamer had gone; Skarry could see his track in the snow, leading off along the level way into the setting sun. Nearer, by the holly, Felder nibbled at the bark of a hazel, his ears turned towards Skarry.

As Skarry stood and brushed the snow from his clothing, Felder came to him and when they met they were both laughing in their own ways, Skarry with tears into the pony's neck. There was no desire nor need to follow the Dreamer. From higher up he would see more before night came. They turned together from the path and began to climb.

Entering the deeper snow, Skarry took off his glove to feel the coldness. It melted on the warmth of his skin and putting some within his mouth he savoured its icy sharpness. Then he turned to the climb and Felder came beside him, at times up to his belly in the drifts. Soon Skarry was panting with the effort yet half laughing with each breath for he was alive in every footstep, in each raised arm as he crawled upwards. At his side the pony snorted with excitement, sweat glistening upon his neck and he began to rear forwards, clearing a wide swath that Skarry might follow, clinging to his tail.

At the summit Felder halted, blowing hard and shaking himself, a darker shadow against the sky beyond. Skarry came up beside him, lifting his gaze from the snow and turning with his arms outstretched for balance. The world lay spread about them, the mountains of the Ridgeway clambering off on either hand, the foothills lowering to the plains in the south, to marsh and sea. And north, the vast sheet of the icy sea rose unbroken to become the towering heights of the Ulta-Zorn.

Looking up at the clear night sky, almost he could see into the space beyond and further still, other stars shining brightly down on other worlds, other peoples. And poised thus he was Ithunne and Felder was Ithunne also and they lived and moved and had their being within her body, and that humans should fight and make suffering seemed so foolish that tears began to flow down his cheeks.

Then he felt the weight of his stones as though for the first time and it drew his gaze once more downwards, to the icy flats of the Kirmire and the rolling downs of the Epona and his own great forest. And the thought that he was not alone, that there were others who would share in the healing, as though removing a final obstacle, allowed his joy at last to come forth and it flowed from his centre throughout his body and shook his limbs so that his teeth rattled.

He thought of the suffering of people, of the creatures of the world, of the land itself beneath the weighty tread of men yet in that moment the joy surpassed all this and blew it tumbling away and he could only laugh and then roar with Felder rearing and whinneying beside him and of itself the sound took on form.

'Ithunne!' he cried, echoing within the hills and out over the land, 'Ithunne!'

And later, as the moon rose full to greet them with her soft light, Skarry would throw off Felder's halter and together they would come laughing down from the high places and return to the people.

Also available from Unwin Paperbacks:

CRYSTAL AND STEEL
Book 1 of The Eye of Time
Lyndan Darby

The tale of Eider, Prince of Rhye, dispossessed of his throne by Zarratt the Usurper. He must win back his kingdom, but he cannot do so without the mystic Triad: the gauntlet, the cloak, the sword.

And he must find it before the Dark Lords seize it as their own: for when Moon and Mercury align, the occult force ignites, unleashing the power of the Triad for good . . . or for ill.

BLOODSEED
Book 2 of The Eye of Time
Lyndan Darby

With Eider as its King, Rhye basks once more in a summer of joy and celebration. The gates of the palace are thrown open; yet among the guests is a masked actor and his troupe, whose dumbshow brings the first bite of autumn frost.

Mystics or tricksters? Truth or illusion? A shadow falls across the halls of Rhye, but the eye of the Crystal is blind to its progress.

The Dark Lords have regrouped: vengeance has spawned a vile alliance, and from the bloodseed comes the instrument for the Triad's destruction.

PHOENIX FIRE
Book 3 of The Eye of Time
Lyndan Darby

These are strangely troubled days of rumour and omen, of failing light and dark winter.

Now is the time for Rhye's elders to perform their ancient rite atop the barrow-grave of Kings. Here the destiny of the Triad's wielder is revealed, and when the Dearth Hand rises Eider is condemned to the Shadow-Land and to his Fate.

Yet can he find Phoenix Fire and bring about his final redemption?

THE DARWATH TRILOGY
Barbara Hambly

Book 1

The Time of the Dark

For several nights Gil had found herself dreaming of an impossible city where alien horrors swarmed from underground lairs of darkness. She had dreamed also of the wizard Ingold Inglorion. Then the same wizard crossed the Void to seek sanctuary for the last Prince of Dar and revealed himself to a young drifter, Rudy. But one of the monstrous, evil Dark followed in his wake and in attempting to help Ingold, Gil and Rudy were drawn back into the nightmare world of the Dark. There they had to remain – unless they could solve the mystery of the Dark. Then, before they could realise their fate, the Dark struck!

Book 2

The Walls of Air

In the shelter of the great Keep of Renwath eight thousand people shelter from the Dark. The only hope for the besieged is to seek help from the hidden city of Quo. Ingold and Rudy set out to cross two thousand miles of desert. Beyond it they have to penetrate the walls of illusion that separate Quo from the world.

Book 3

The Armies of Daylight

The survivors of the once-great Realm of Darwath shelter, squabble and struggle for power. Meanwhile the monstrous Dark threaten their great Keep. Is there a reason for the re-awakening of the Dark? The final volume of *The Darwath Trilogy* builds to a shattering and unexpected climax.

MIRAGE
Louise Cooper

Raised by a sorceress from the depths of Limbo he came into the world without a past or a name.

They called him Kyre – Sun Hound – avatar of an ancient hero; summoned as the last chance to save the dying city of Haven from the ravages of the evil witch-queen Calthar and the sea-dwellers.

But Kyre sensed that he was more than a cipher: he felt a power within him, and a post existence which lurked in his dreams and hazy memories. He had to solve the mystery of his true identity before the hour of the final confrontation.

In the sky, the Hag cast down its baleful light: the Great Conjunction was close at hand. Soon the followers of Calthar would rise from the sea and obliterate the city of Haven and its people, forever.

THE INITIATE
Book 1 of the Time Master Trilogy
Louise Cooper

The Seven Gods of Order have ruled unchallenged for an aeon, served
by the Adepts of the Circle in their bleak Northern stronghold. But for
Tarod – the most enigmatic and formidable sorcerer in the Circle's ranks
– a darker affinity had begun to call. Threatening his beliefs, even his
sanity, it rose unbidden from beyond Time; an ancient and deadly
adversary that could plunge the world into madness and chaos – and
whose power rivalled that even of the Gods themselves. But though
Tarod's mind and heart were pledged to order, his soul was another
matter . . .

THE OUTCAST
Book 2 of the Time Master Trilogy
Louise Cooper

Denounced by his fellow Adepts as a demon, betrayed even by those he
loved, Tarod had unleashed a power that twisted the fabric of time. It
seemed that nothing could break thorugh the barrier he had created
until Cyllan and Drachea – victims of the Warp – stumbled unwittingly
into his castle. The terrible choice Tarod has to make as a result has
far-reaching consequences . . .

THE MASTER
Book 3 of the Time Master Trilogy
Louise Cooper

Tarod had won his freedom – and lost the soul stone, key to his
sorcerous power. Cyllan, the woman he loved, had been taken from him
in a supernatural storm. With a price on both their heads, Tarod had to
find her before the Circle did. Only then could he hope to fulfil his
self-imposed pledge to confront the gods themselves – for they alone
could destroy the stone and the evil that dwelt in it. If touched by the evil
in the stone, Tarod would be forced to face the truth of his own heritage,
triggering a titanic conflict of occult forces, and setting him on the
ultimate quest for vengeance . . .

Welcome to the nightmare world of Paradys!

BOOK OF THE DAMNED
Secret Books of Paradys 1
Tanith Lee

Jehanine: demon or saint?

Her days spent at the Nunnery of the Angel; her nights in the vicious backstreets of Paradys, wreaking revenge on men for the wrongs she had suffered at their hands.

'How fast does a man run when the Devil is after him?' Andre St Jean is about to find out, as a young man collapses at his feet and presses into his hand a strange scarab ring, containing the secret of life . . .

The stranger pushed a note across the table: 'In a week or less I shall be dead.' In a week, he was, and most unnaturally. She found herself drawn to the house where he died, to unravel the web of mystery and horror that had been spun about him . . .

BOOK OF THE BEAST
Secret Books of Paradys 2
Tanith Lee

It was created on the fifth day of the Earth; scaled not feathered – the Beast.

From the most ancient of days, passed through the seed of generations, still it preys on the unlucky, the unwary and the unchaste. Its appetite is ravenous and eternal.

Tanith Lee weaves a chilling tale of horror through the streets of Paradys: from the times when the Legions ruled the Empire, and Centurion Retullus Vusca hoped to change his luck . . .

To the wedding of an innocent maid who hoped to win the affection of a cold, but handsome lord, unaware of the consequences of her seduction . . .

To a scholar, wise in the ways of magic, who was determined to end the terror . . .

And all the while there were cries in the night, and blood on the stones in the morning.

REINDEER PEOPLE
Megan Lindholm

Tillu was a healer, her magic bright and pure, working always for the good of others. No man had owned her since the one who left her heavy with Kerlew, her strange, slow, dreamy child.

Living on the outskirts of the tribe Tillu was happy enough communing with the spirits to heal the sick and bring blessing on new births.

But now there was Carp: Carp the Shaman, a wizened old man whose magic smelled fetid, stinging and foul to Tillu, Carp had no woman, and no apprentice. Tillu was attractive and still young, and Kerlew – Kerlew was gifted with a strangeness that allowed him to enter the spirit world. Carp wanted both of them, and he would use his dark powers to bind them to him.

Tillu knew Carp's magic would steal her son and her soul. Death waited in the snows of the tundra. Tillu knew which she would prefer . . .

Forthcoming in September...

A stunning new fantasy series by a rising American star:

NEW MOON
Book 1 of The Queen's Quarter
Midori Snyder

Two hundred years ago the Fire Queen destroyed her rival queens of Earth, Air and Water in the fateful Burning and took power over the land. Every child that carried the ancient elemental magic was murdered.

Now the country of Oran trembles under her oppression and the dangerous imbalance of power. There is unrest in the city, and rumous of hope. They say that four bearing the ancient magic escaped the harrowing, and in the hills the rebel New Moon are gathering their forces to lead an insurrection.

Meanwhile, in the underworld of the city, Jobber and the other street children steal a living and elude the authorities. But under the cover of darkness someone is stealing the children. In the morning their withered bodies float down the river . . .